Mills & B...
sparkling...
whe...

Meet…

Fall in love…

And marry…

*All in
a Day*

Could it happen to you…?

Carole Mortimer was born in England, the youngest of three children. She began writing in 1978, and has now written over one hundred books for Harlequin Mills & Boon. Carole has four sons, Matthew, Joshua, Timothy and Peter, and a bearded collie called Merlyn. She says, 'I'm happily married to Peter senior; we're best friends as well as lovers, which is probably the best recipe for a successful relationship. We live on the Isle of Man.'

**Look out for Carol's latest novel,
THE VENGEANCE AFFAIR, out this month
in Modern Romance™!**

Rebecca Winters, an American writer and mother of four, is excited about the new millennium because it means another new beginning. Having said goodbye to the classroom where she taught French and Spanish, she is now free to spend more time with her family, to travel and to write the Harlequin Mills & Boon novels she loves so dearly. Readers are invited to visit the author's website at www.rebeccawinters-author.com

**TO MARRY FOR DUTY is out this month, in
Tender Romance™. Let Rebecca Winters take you
on an emotional rollercoaster...**

Jessica Hart had a haphazard career before she began writing to finance a degree in history. Her experience ranged from waitress, theatre production assistant and outback cook to newsdesk secretary, expedition PA and English teacher, and she has worked in countries as different as France and Indonesia, Australia and Cameroon. She now lives in the north of England, where her hobbies are limited to eating and drinking and travelling when she can, preferably to places where she'll find good food or desert or tropical rain.

**Jessica Hart is a rising star of Tender Romance™ –
don't miss her next romance, later this year.**

All in a Day

CAROLE MORTIMER

REBECCA WINTERS

JESSICA HART

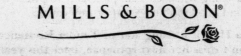

MILLS & BOON®

*First published in Great Britain 2005
Harlequin Mills & Boon Limited,
Eton House, 18-24 Paradise Road, Richmond, Surrey, TW9 1SR*

ALL IN A DAY © by Harlequin Enterprises II B.V,. 2005

The publisher acknowledges the copyright holders of the
individual works as follows:

His Darling Valentine © Carole Mortimer 2005
The Bridesmaid's Proposal © Rebecca Winters 2005
The Billionaire's Blind Date © Jessica Hart 2005

ISBN 0 263 84526 5

024-0205

*Printed and bound in Spain
by Litografia Rosés S.A., Barcelona*

CONTENTS

His Darling Valentine

by

Carole Mortimer

CHAPTER ONE

WHAT the—!

In the process of stepping out of her own front doorway, Tazzy came to an abrupt halt, instead staring down wide-eyed at the tiny kitten that sat in a basket on the doorstep.

Where on earth had it come from? More to the point, what was it doing here?

Well, one thing was for certain, it hadn't arrived here of its own volition; a stray kitten did not come complete with basket, bowl, and sachets of food. Or with a red ribbon tied in a neat bow about its tiny neck!

Tazzy bent down to look at the ball of grey fluff, suddenly finding herself the focus of startled blue eyes as it became aware of her presence.

'Hey, it's okay,' she soothed as the tiny thing leapt to its feet in surprise, holding out her hand—for it to either lick or scratch, depending on whether it saw her as friend or foe.

While it made up its mind, Tazzy took the opportunity to glance up and down the street. As expected, at seven-thirty in the morning, it was totally deserted. The lights were on in several of the houses, but all the cars were still in the driveways. Only Tazzy, it seemed, with her innate sense of responsibility, left the house at seven-thirty in the morning in order to be at her desk by eight-fifteen. There was certainly no one visible who could possibly have delivered the kitten to her doorstep.

She gave a start of surprise herself as she felt the moist rasp of a minute tongue on the back of her hand, the kitten jumping back too at this sudden movement.

'We could go on like this all morning.' She laughed, reaching out to pick the kitten up, absolutely enchanted by the way the little ball of fur, its face looking at her so trustingly, fitted neatly into the palm of her hand.

But even as Tazzy acknowledged that she noticed the small white card attached to the red ribbon. 'To Anastasia. With love', the card read.

How very peculiar. No one ever called her by her full name of Anastasia, in fact most people weren't even aware that was her actual name. And why on earth would someone give her a kitten, with or without love? Christmas had been and gone, and her birthday wasn't until August.

Not that it mattered why someone had thought she would appreciate having a pet, she simply couldn't keep the kitten. She was Personal Assistant to Ross Valentine, a computer software troubleshooter of unparalleled skill. His business took him all over the world, and Tazzy usually accompanied Ross on those trips, which didn't allow for attachments of any kind.

Talking of which, what was she going to do with the kitten today while she was at work?

The frown deepened between clear green eyes. She might not be able to keep it, but she couldn't just leave the poor little thing out here in the cold, either; it might wander off and get itself lost, or worse—run over. And she certainly couldn't take it with her—she could already imagine the look of surprise on Ross's face if she were to arrive at his house, their place of work as well as Ross's home, with the kitten in tow!

She really didn't have any choice; she would just have to make it comfortable in the kitchen until she returned later, when she could turn her mind to finding somewhere—or someone—who would take the kitten off her hands.

'I'm sorry, but that's just the way it is,' she told the kitten ruefully as it continued to look up at her with those trusting blue eyes.

It took her a few minutes to take off the bow, to make the kitchen safe and put out food for the tiny creature, by which time, she realized agitatedly, she was going to be late into work this morning.

The traffic, usually minimal at that early hour, was

already starting to build up by the time she finally got on the road, Tazzy's tension building along with it.

Consequently, she was not her usual calm, collected self when she finally made it into her office at eight-thirty. Her agitation deepened as she found Ross Valentine already standing beside her desk, a pile of her carefully logged files in his hand, files Tazzy knew from experience would no longer be in any sort of order. Served her right for being late, she inwardly remonstrated with herself.

Being a computer expert, Ross had pooh-poohed the fact that she kept everything on paper as well as on disk, but as her system had saved him work on several occasions when his computer had crashed, he had stopped mentioning how antiquated her own system was.

Ross raised dark brows now over eyes the colour of sherry. 'Dare I say that you're looking less than your usual unflustered self this morning, Miss Darling?' he mocked, those brows shooting up even further as Tazzy, her cheeks flushed, scowled at him in reply. 'Perhaps not,' he muttered under his breath.

Tazzy wordlessly took down the hanger from behind the door, carefully hanging her outer coat on it before replacing it neatly back on the hook. She smoothed back the neat chignon of her copper-coloured hair before moving to switch on the coffee percolator that stood on top of one of the filing cabinets, using the normality of her usual morning routine to try to bring some calm to her day, totally thrown by the fact that Ross had appeared in her office before her.

The day had not started well, with the mysterious arrival of that kitten on her doorstep—and being late for work certainly didn't improve matters!

Ross Valentine watched her as she moved efficiently about the room, preparing a coffee tray for him and a separate cup for herself. 'Tell me, Miss Darling, how long have you worked for me now?' he asked, arms folded across the muscled width of his chest.

Tazzy turned to give him a puzzled frown. 'I don't understand—'

'Just answer the question, hmm?' he encouraged lightly.

'I believe it's eighteen months, Mr Valentine,' she said smartly.

Eighteen months, one week, and half an hour, to be exact. And she had been in love with this man, it seemed, for every minute of that time!

She loved the way his dark hair was inclined to curl slightly if he forgot to get it cut—which was often!—the deep sherry-brown of his eyes, eyes that became incredibly warm when he smiled. His high cheekbones gave him a slightly foreign appearance, his nose was long and aristocratic, and his sensual mouth was wide above the squareness of his jaw. His body was athletically slim, and as for his hands—! More than once she had sat and daydreamed about what it would feel like to have those long, slender hands move caressingly over her body...

She loved his sense of humour too, the closeness he had maintained with his parents, despite having lived in this house on his own, apart from the housekeeper, the last ten years. Sylvia and Nigel Valentine were frequent visitors to the house Ross used to work in as well as live in, two rooms that overlooked the back garden having been converted into offices for both Ross and Tazzy.

Having been orphaned at five years old herself, and brought up by an elderly maiden aunt who had died five years ago when Tazzy was twenty, she rather envied Ross his warm family life.

But none of her thoughts or love for this man showed in her expression now as she continued to look at him enquiringly.

Ross nodded. 'And in all of that time how many times have you failed to be seated at your desk by eight-fifteen in the morning?'

She eyed him warily. 'Just this morning,' she finally replied, still uncertain as to what point he was trying to make; either he was about to sack her for

being late, or congratulate her for never having been
so before!

'Exactly,' he acknowledged dryly. 'So why are
you skulking around the room as if you expect me
to fire you at any moment?'

Because by arriving at eight-fifteen every morning
she gave herself enough time to tidy her appearance,
check e-mails, and be her normal efficient self by the
time Ross usually came in at eight forty-five. The
arrival of that kitten on her doorstep had completely
thrown her normal routine into disarray—and Tazzy
along with it! She simply wasn't her usual calm, controlled self this morning, which made her feel
slightly defensive.

'I—something happened to delay me this morning. Someone left me—left a present on the doorstep
for me,' she explained.

'It's the day for it, isn't it?' Ross shrugged.

Tazzy frowned. 'Day for what—? Oh.' She broke
off abruptly as she suddenly realized exactly what
day it was.

The fourteenth of February. Valentine's Day. And
the kitten had had a red bow tied about its tiny neck,
the gift card that accompanied it unsigned...

Ross nodded. 'So what did you get?' he prompted
interestedly, making himself comfortable on the side
of her desk. 'Red roses? A cuddly teddy bear? A box
of chocolates? Or perhaps some sexy underwear—'

'It was a kitten,' she cut in sharply, embarrassed colour in her cheeks at his last suggestion.

The only way she had been able to cope with loving Ross in the way that she did was to maintain a certain formality in their relationship, insisting on calling him Mr Valentine, and having him always refer to her as Miss Darling. Having him talk about 'sexy underwear' was not conducive to that formality!

'A kitten?' Ross repeated incredulously. 'I had no idea you liked cats.'

'I'm not sure that I do,' she answered slowly, at the same time aware that the defenceless ball of fur left on her doorstep earlier had already made a dent in her heart. 'I told you, it was a present,' she added.

A Valentine present...

But who from? Oh, she had dated often before coming to work for Ross Valentine eighteen months ago, occasionally accepted invitations even now, if only to stop other people from drawing their own conclusions concerning her single status when her boss was so obviously an extremely eligible bachelor of thirty-seven. But the fact that she rarely dated the same person twice meant that she now had no idea who could have placed the kitten outside her front door!

'What are you going to do with it?' Ross looked amused.

Good question. The truth was, she had no idea, very much aware that her job as Ross Valentine's Personal Assistant, travelling around the world with him, did not even allow for the luxury of owning a goldfish.

But, at the same time, she couldn't shake off the vision of that endearing little face, the tiny black nose, those beautiful blue eyes that had gazed up at her so appealingly earlier as she'd left the kitten in the warm snugness of her kitchen.

But, tempted as she might be, there was no way she could keep it!

'I have no idea,' she answered honestly. 'Try to find someone who will take it in, I suppose.'

'I'll take it if you don't want it,' Ross offered.

Tazzy stared at him in surprise. Admittedly, he had the luxury of a housekeeper who could look after the kitten any time he had to be away on business. But even so...

'I haven't definitely decided what I'm going to do with him yet,' she resisted.

'Or her,' Ross pointed out.

Tazzy frowned. 'Or her,' she acknowledged slowly, having no idea whether it was a she or a he! 'But its name is Shadow,' she added without thinking.

Now exactly where had that come from? She

hadn't even been aware until the word had come out of her mouth that she had actually named the kitten!

When she had finally left the house this morning, the kitten safely ensconced in the kitchen, she had had every intention of delivering it to a cat sanctuary when she returned home later on this evening. Ross's offer to take the kitten off her hands seemed to have brought out a possessive streak in her.

Ross smiled, brown eyes warm. 'You named it already.'

Tazzy once again felt flustered. 'Not really. I— Shadow would do for a boy or a girl, though.'

'So it would,' he agreed, standing up.

Allowing Tazzy to breathe normally once again. Outwardly, she managed to remain efficient and professional in front of this man, but inwardly, whenever Ross was close, she felt a constriction in her throat, a fluttering in her chest. It didn't exactly make for calm working conditions—but the thought of not working for Ross was completely unacceptable to her.

'I'll bring your coffee through in a moment,' she told him with cool dismissal.

'Thanks.' He nodded. 'Could you bring the e-mails through when you're ready, too?'

'Of course, Mr Valentine,' she answered briskly, finding her usual confidence in adopting her role as his PA.

'Oh, and Tazzy...?' He paused before moving away.

She looked up at him with calm enquiry, deciding to ignore his slip of addressing her by her Christian name in preference to hastening his departure.

'Happy Valentine's Day,' he murmured huskily, bending his head and briefly brushing his lips against hers. 'Mmm, nice,' he said appreciatively, hands lightly cupping each side of her face. 'In fact, it was so nice, I think I'll do it again,' he added softly before his lips claimed hers a second time, a lingering kiss this time as he tasted and sipped the softness of her lips.

Tazzy was too stunned to do any more than kiss him back, her lips tingling from the touch of Ross's, her body trembling with rising desire, breasts up-tilted as they pressed against the hardness of his chest.

Finally, when Tazzy felt as if her knees were about to give way completely, Ross raised his head to look down at her. 'Happy Valentine's Day, Tazzy,' he murmured again before moving away to leave the room, softly closing the connecting door behind him.

Leaving Tazzy in a state of total shock!

CHAPTER TWO

WELL—!

For the second time that morning Tazzy found herself at a complete loss for words. And it wasn't even nine o'clock yet!

She moved to sit down abruptly in her chair behind the desk, moving a hand up to tentatively touch lips that still tingled from contact with Ross's.

Not by word or deed had he ever before stepped over that line between employer/employee. Leaving Tazzy to wonder why he should have done so now... She didn't—

'Tazzy, could I have the file on the Hanson hotel chain?' Ross stood in the open doorway between their two offices, his manner completely businesslike now.

Just as if those kisses, that melting touch of his lips on Tazzy's, had never happened!

He raised dark brows at her silence. 'Today, if possible?' he teased.

She stood up abruptly, inwardly urging herself to pull herself together; Ross Valentine was far from the first man to kiss her, for goodness' sake. But at the same time, he was the first man she had ever been in love with who had kissed her!

'Yes, of course, Mr Valentine.' She moved to one of the filing cabinets that stood along one wall of her office.

At least, that was what she intended doing—until she sensed that Ross still stood in the doorway, leaning nonchalantly against the frame as he made no effort to hide the fact he was watching her every move.

Making Tazzy feel extremely self-conscious! 'I'll bring it through once I've found it,' she assured him sharply.

'Fine,' he accepted, making no effort to move. 'You know, Tazzy—'

'I thought we had agreed that it was much more suitable, during our hours of working together, if we stick to Mr Valentine and Miss Darling?' she reminded him coolly. Goodness knew it was strange enough actually working in this man's house, without being any more familiar with each other.

She had thought it an unconventional arrangement when she'd first come for her job interview eighteen months ago, but once she had met Ross Valentine she would have agreed to work out in the garden shed!

'As I remember it, you were the one to come up

with that particular rule,' Ross drawled. 'Personally, I've always thought it sounded very unfriendly.'

'Unfamiliar,' Tazzy corrected briskly, at the same time whipping the appropriate file from the drawer and holding it out to him. 'I really do think that it's best during office hours.'

He took the file, his expression one of reproach. 'Well, as we don't seem to have any ''out of office hours,'' when do I get to call you Tazzy?'

Her eyes widened with impatience. 'You don't.' That was the whole idea, for goodness' sake!

She wasn't sure, spending as much time as she did in his company, often travelling abroad together for several days at a time, if she would be able to cope with working for him at all if she hadn't put up some sort of barrier of formality between them from the first.

'I'm not sure I particularly care for that,' he pondered.

She looked at him in exasperation. 'Mr Valentine—'

'Tazzy Darling?' he came back blandly, dark brows raised in innocent query.

Her exasperation deepened. Not that she wasn't used to her surname being the butt of jokes, had been teased about it unmercilessly ever since she'd first started school; it was just that she wasn't used to her employer resorting to such inanity.

'Miss Darling will do,' she said impatiently. 'I—'
She broke off as a knock sounded on her office door,
Ross's housekeeper opening the door seconds later
to admit the man who accompanied her.

At least, Tazzy presumed it was a man. It was a
little hard to tell when he—she?—was carrying the
hugest bouquet of red roses Tazzy had ever seen in
her life!

'The gentleman has instructions to deliver the
roses personally,' Mrs Brown, the housekeeper, explained apologetically.

Tazzy turned accusing eyes on Ross Valentine;
she knew that he dated occasionally, but none of
those women seemed to last very long—which
begged the question, which one of them had sent him
this huge bouquet of red roses for Valentine's Day?
Honestly, it was totally out of—

'Miss Darling?' the delivery man prompted as he
looked at her hopefully.

Tazzy turned slowly to look at the man, her tone
wary as she answered him. 'Yes…?'

The man nodded his satisfaction with her answer.
'Then these are for you.' He placed the bouquet into
her unresisting arms. 'Whoever he is, he must have
it real bad!' he added, giving a knowing wink in
Tazzy's direction before departing the room, Mrs
Brown following behind him.

Tazzy didn't move. Couldn't move. Could only

stare at what had to be dozens of deep red roses in her arms.

There had to have been some sort of mistake. These flowers couldn't possibly be for her. She never received roses, on Valentine's Day, or any other day.

But thinking of Valentine…

She glanced across at her employer, a blush warming her cheeks as she saw he was looking straight back at her, dark brows raised in a question.

That look was enough to shake Tazzy out of the daze she had lapsed into on being presented with the red roses. 'I think there must have been some mistake, and these were meant for you.' She grimaced as she held out the flowers to him.

Ross shook his head, making no effort to take the blood-red blooms from her. 'He distinctly said they were for Miss Darling, and as we both know that's you…' He strolled over to pluck out the white card that nestled amongst the roses. '"To Anastasia. Much love,"' he read out. 'No, they're definitely for you, Tazzy.' He grinned teasingly. 'As the man said, someone's got it bad,' he added with an appreciative glance at the dozens of roses.

To Anastasia. Much love…

The card attached to the kitten earlier this morning had read, 'To Anastasia. With love.' The messages were so similar that it was impossible not to wonder if the kitten and the roses hadn't been sent to her by the same person. But if so, who could that person be?

She had no idea!

She really didn't. Oh, several of the men she had met while travelling with Ross had flirted with her or paid her compliments, but she was certain that none of them knew her name was Anastasia.

The postman occasionally paid her a compliment when she went to the door to collect the mail from him, as did the young man from the courier service they habitually used, but as there had to be at least fifty red roses here, delivered on Valentine's Day too, Tazzy would hazard a guess at such an extravagant gesture of love being out of either of their financial leagues. No, she really had no idea who could have sent them to her.

Neither did she appreciate their being delivered here at her place of work, in front of Ross, of all people; on today's evidence he was going to believe there was someone serious in her life!

'Have you been holding out on me, Miss Darling?' Ross's next words seemed to confirm that particular worry. 'You aren't thinking of leaving me in order to get married, by any chance?' he asked.

'Certainly not!' Tazzy dropped the roses down onto her desktop as if she had been pricked by one of their thorns. 'I think someone must be playing a practical joke on me,' she excused lamely.

'An expensive practical joke,' Ross disagreed with a shake of his head. 'No, Tazzy—Miss Darling,' he corrected himself as she gave him a pointed look, 'I think you should look at the distinct possibility that you have a secret admirer.' He lightly touched one of the velvety soft flowers.

Then whoever it was had kept it such a secret that she didn't have a clue as to who it could possibly be!

'Don't be ridiculous,' she snapped, deciding that office protocol had been broken enough for one day. 'I have some work to do,' she added pointedly when Ross still made no effort to leave but continued to look at her speculatively.

'I think, Miss Darling,' he finally murmured consideringly, 'that you and I ought to have lunch together today in order to discuss the possibility of someone stealing you away from me, don't you?'

She glared at him. 'I told you, there is nothing to discuss!'

Ross shook his head. 'I disagree.'

Oh, great, not only did she not know who was indulging in these ridiculous Valentine pranks, but now she had to try and explain it to her employer!

She gave a heavy sigh. 'I'll ask Mrs Brown to make us both some sandwiches.' It would be far from the first time Tazzy had worked through her lunch-hour.

'No, I don't think so.'

Tazzy gave a puzzled frown. 'You would prefer me to ask her to prepare something else?' A cooked lunch would save her the problem of cooking for herself this evening when she got home. In view of the fact that she had to do something about the kitten, that arrangement could work out quite well.

Ross smiled as he shook his head. 'I would *prefer* it if we went out somewhere to eat. What's the name of that little place you occasionally go to with that friend of yours—Anne, isn't it?—that sometimes calls for you here?'

'Luigi's?' Tazzy supplied with a frown.

'That's the place!' His smile deepened. 'We'll go there for lunch.'

For one thing, Luigi's was a small Italian bistro, hardly the sort of place Ross usually frequented, with his accumulated wealth and preference for French cuisine. For another, she did not relish the idea of going there with Ross only to bump into her friend Anne—who did go to Luigi's often. Knowing Anne, she would demand to know all the details the next time the two of them met! What was wrong with Mrs Brown's cooking anyway? It had always been good enough before!

Then she remembered...

'Have you forgotten what day it is today?' she reminded Ross.

'That would be a little difficult, wouldn't it, when your office is full of red roses?' He gave the long-stemmed blooms a pointed look.

Tazzy felt the warmth in her cheeks. 'Hardly full,' she said, shifting the bouquet to one side of her desk. 'I was actually trying to point out to you that there is no way we will get a table at Luigi's for lunch today. He was fully booked weeks ago.'

'He was?' Ross looked startled by this information.

Tazzy found it quite endearing that it obviously hadn't even occurred to him that almost all restaurants would be fully booked today, both at lunch-time and this evening; apparently he had never tried to take anyone out to lunch on Valentine's Day before!

'Okay, forget Luigi's,' Ross dismissed impatiently.

Tazzy nodded. 'Shall I ask Mrs Brown to get us both a sandwich, after all?'

'Certainly not!' he said firmly. 'I invited you out to lunch, and out we will most definitely go.'

'But—'

'Leave it to me,' Ross interrupted. 'I'll book us a table somewhere for lunch.'

Her eyes widened. 'You will?'

'I will.' He nodded, his expression becoming mocking at her obvious surprise. 'Tazzy, believe it or not, before the advent of your undoubtedly efficient self into my life, I was quite capable of telephoning a restaurant myself and booking my own table!'

She knew that he still did that if he was taking a woman out to dinner. Something, in view of her own feelings towards him, she had always been grateful for.

But that wasn't the point she had been about to make; it was the fact that this didn't sound like a business lunch to her, and the two of them having lunch together under any other circumstances was not a good idea...

'I'm sure you were,' she soothed. 'It's just that—'

'I said leave it to me, Tazzy,' Ross insisted, moving towards the connecting door.

'Use the intercom the next time you need something,' Tazzy was stung into advising him sharply as he was closing the door, inwardly wondering when the strangeness of today was going to end!

The door opened again, Ross grimacing across at her. 'I loathe that damned intercom,' he muttered. 'I rue the day I ever let you persuade me into having it installed.'

She was well aware of Ross's feelings concerning the intercom system between their two offices. But, for her part, it was yet another move to keep their relationship on a businesslike footing; before the intercom had been installed Ross had been altogether too fond of just wandering into her office whenever he felt like it, sitting on the side of her desk to discuss whatever problem was bothering him at the time. And in the process usually managing to upset Tazzy's equilibrium for at least half an hour after he had left—by which time he had usually wandered back in again! The intercom system had stopped all of that. At least…until today, it had…

'Nevertheless, it's there to be used,' she insisted primly.

'So was the guillotine!' Ross pointed out. 'And we all know what use that was put to! Not all machines are progress, you know, Tazzy.'

This sounded more than slightly ridiculous coming from a man who specialized in clearing any glitch or bug that might attack a computer or its software!

He had also called her by her first name yet again! It was way past time this familiarity was put to an end!

'I'm afraid I really can't have lunch with you today,' she told him determinedly. 'I have to go and check on the kitten,' she explained as he gave her a frowning look.

His brow cleared. 'We'll both go,' he offered. 'We can go on to the restaurant from there.'

Tazzy stared at him. Never once during the eighteen months she'd worked for him had there been a need for him to go to her home. 'I don't think—'

'Oh, come on, Tazzy,' he encouraged. 'After all, I might end up taking the kitten off your hands.'

'I told you, I haven't decided yet whether or not I'm going to keep it myself!' she came back defensively.

'Going to wait and see who gave him to you first, is that it?' Ross teased, brown eyes definitely laughing at her.

'Certainly not,' she denied crossly. 'Oh, very well, you can come with me at lunch-time,' she capitulated. 'You'll just have to excuse the mess,' she added ungraciously, knowing there was no mess, that she kept her home as tidy as she kept her office.

But the thought of Ross in her home, the one place she never had to remember him having been, was not a pleasant one. Her little terraced house was her sanctuary. A sanctuary that was about to be invaded!

'I'll do that.' Ross grinned knowingly. 'While we're there, you could also change into something a little less...businesslike,' he added before continuing on his way to his own office.

Tazzy glared at the now closed door between the two rooms. She had no intention of changing into something less businesslike! Businesslike was how she liked to be whenever she was around Ross, and she had no intention of ever changing that.

Whoever the practical joker was who had sent her first the kitten, and then these roses, had a lot to answer for. Because she had no doubts that it was the anonymous gifts she had received today that had prompted Ross into inviting her out to lunch, if only to try and find out from Tazzy exactly how serious the relationship was.

When there was no relationship!

CHAPTER THREE

'PIERRE will be more than pleased to see us both at about one-thirty,' Ross told Tazzy with satisfaction as he strolled back into her office a couple of hours later.

Pierre Gaston owned one of the most select restaurants in London, with extortionate prices to go along with that prestige; no doubt he would be pleased to see another two customers in his restaurant at lunch-time!

But, Tazzy noted with a certain inner smugness, it had taken Ross almost two hours to come up with a restaurant that had availability.

Although the fact that it was Pierre's meant she might just have to rethink her decision not to change out of the grey suit and white blouse she had worn for work today. The women that frequented such a restaurant had a totally different idea of 'power dressing' from the one she had: designer suits and diamonds, probably!

'You were right about everywhere being full,' Ross admitted with a grimace as he came over to sit on the side of her desk. 'I tried Pierre's as a last resort.'

That was one of the endearing qualities about Ross that so made her love him; he hadn't needed to admit to her that he had found difficulty, after all, but he had done so anyway.

'Not that you aren't worth it,' he hastened to add with a boyish smile. 'I just had somewhere a little more—well, less formal, let's say—in mind.'

'There really is no need to take me out at all,' she assured him, calmer now than she had been a couple of hours ago. Everything was back under control, even the red roses were out of the way on top of a filing cabinet in a couple of vases she had borrowed from Mrs Brown; she simply hadn't the heart to throw such beautiful flowers in the bin—whoever they might have come from! 'I can promise you, I'm not involved in a relationship, and have no intention of letting anyone ''steal me away'' from your employment,' she added impatiently.

He shrugged. 'The roses say differently.'

Admittedly, the roses, five dozen of them in all— Tazzy had counted them as she'd put them in the vases!—must have cost someone a small fortune, especially today of all days, but, as she couldn't even take a wild guess at who might have sent them, the gesture was totally wasted on her!

She shook her head. 'Couldn't you just take my word for it that they don't? It would save you having to go to the expense of taking me out to lunch.'

'No, I said I was taking you out, and that's what I'm going to do,' Ross insisted. 'So we had better leave here—' He broke off as the second knock of the morning sounded on Tazzy's office door, a rather bemused Mrs Brown once again the perpetrator, another man trailing in her wake.

Tazzy had tensed the moment the knock had sounded on the door, and as she saw the enormous box of chocolates the man carried in his hands—a red heart-shaped box of chocolates, tied up with a red ribbon—she knew she was right to feel that way!

She closed her eyes, hoping—and praying!—that the chocolates hadn't come from her mystery admirer too, that they weren't even for her. Although perhaps, in the circumstances, that would be hoping for too much!

Mrs Brown looked even more bemused than she had earlier. 'This gentleman has instructions to deliver the chocolates personally, too,' she told them.

'Miss Darling?' The man looked at Tazzy enquiringly.

'Yes,' she confirmed abruptly, unable to even look at Ross this time as the delivery man crossed the room to place the box of chocolates into her hands—goodness knew what Ross was making of all this! 'Thank you,' she said stiffly.

The man grinned. 'Eleven o'clock the man said, and eleven o'clock it is,' he said with satisfaction.

Tazzy's gaze narrowed. 'What man?'

'Oh, the office didn't tell me that, love,' the man replied jovially, shaking his head. 'I'm just the delivery man, you see.'

No help there, then, with the identity of this mystery admirer. Pity. For a moment there—

'Here.' Ross moved forward to tip the man.

'Oh, no, guv'nor, that was already taken care of when the chocolates were given to us for delivery,' the man explained.

Tazzy was so stunned by this second Valentine delivery to her place of work that she hadn't even thought about tipping the man. The fact that he refused Ross's attempt to do so, because he had already received a tip, was doubly odd. The mystery admirer was taking no chances on having his identity discovered, was he?

Which was strange in itself. Surely the whole point of gifts on Valentine's Day was that the person receiving them should eventually realize who they had come from? After all, there wasn't a lot of point to the exercise otherwise.

But it wasn't even lunch-time yet, Tazzy reminded herself; plenty of time left yet today for the man to somehow show himself as the giver of these gifts.

'Thank you,' she told the delivery man once again before he left with Mrs Brown, still unable to actually look at Ross as he stood silently across the room, wishing that he hadn't been in the room when this second delivery had been made.

At least then she might have stood some chance of hiding these chocolates from him—although quite where she would be able to hide such a huge box, she had no idea!

This was all so ridiculous. *She* felt ridiculous. And she couldn't even begin to guess at Ross's feelings!

'Aren't you going to open them?' he encouraged hopefully. 'They're my favourites. And we aren't going to be having lunch for at least another couple of hours.'

Tazzy didn't answer him immediately, staring down at the white card that had been tucked beneath the red ribbon. 'To Anastasia. With affection and love.' Affection as well as love now!

Strangely, she found the claim of affection more confusing than the love; surely to feel affection for someone they had to know that person rather well? Which begged the question, how could some man feel this way about her and she not even know about it?

Well, she knew about it now—and she wished that she didn't.

'You open them.' She thrust the box across the desk towards Ross. 'I'm starting to think that whoever this man is he must be some sort of a crackpot!'

A kitten, red roses, and now a heart-shaped box of chocolates; where was it all going to end?

Ross chuckled as he began to undo the ribbon that secured the box. 'I'm sure most women don't think that when they receive gifts from a man.'

She wasn't 'most women,' and it was the fact that she had no idea who the man was that made her feel so confused. Besides, if this continued, Ross was never going to believe her when she kept insisting there was no one serious in her life!

She might stand absolutely no chance of ever having her love for him returned, but at least she could work with him, see him almost every day, and that was better than nothing.

'You keep the chocolates, as they're your favourite brand,' she told him stiltedly.

'Oh, I couldn't do that, Tazzy,' he refused. 'After all, how would you explain not having them?'

She frowned. 'To whom?'

'Your admirer, of course,' Ross reproved teasingly.

'I don't have an admirer!' she bit out through gritted teeth.

'Of course you do,' Ross contradicted, sitting on the edge of the desk to lift the lid of the box of chocolates. 'Ah.' He paused. 'Tazzy…?'

'What is it now?' she sighed, so weary from all of this that she just wanted to put her head on her arms on the desktop and go to sleep—or weep! 'Don't tell me, there aren't any chocolates in the box, just empty papers!' In truth, she really would prefer that this was a practical joke rather than someone seriously secretly in love with her.

Because she was never going to be in love with any man but Ross...

'Oh, no, there's chocolates,' he assured her. 'But there's also this.'

'This,' Tazzy found out seconds later as Ross lifted it up for her to see, turned out to be a gold chain with a gold heart suspended on it!

'Certainly not one of the usual fillings to these particular chocolates,' he murmured with amusement. 'Let's put it on and see how it looks—'

'No!' Tazzy protested sharply as Ross would have stood up to fasten the chain about the slenderness of her neck. 'Let's not.' She stared at the necklace as if it were a snake about to strike her.

Ross frowned. 'But you never wear jewellery. And this is rather a beautiful necklace, even if I do say so myself.' Once again he made a move to stand up.

'I said no, Ross.' Tazzy raised a protesting hand.

She never wore jewellery because she couldn't afford jewellery. It was all she could do to feed herself, pay her mortgage, and maintain and run her car, let alone spend her money on frivolous things like jewellery!

She stood up abruptly. 'I don't want it,' she told him flatly. 'If I want a necklace, I'll buy it myself,' she added at his puzzled look, 'not accept it from a complete stranger.'

Ross relaxed back on the desk, the gold chain still dangling from his fingers as he looked up at her. 'Obviously this man doesn't want the two of you to remain strangers,' he said slowly.

Her eyes flashed deeply green as she glared at him. 'Then he can behave like any other man would have done, in the circumstances, and introduce himself—not use the excuse of Valentine's Day to send me an assortment of expensive and impractical gifts!

Ross looked at her quizzically for several long seconds, finally giving a shake of his head. 'You know, Tazzy, I don't think I'll ever understand women. The man has done everything to show you how he feels but propose—and you still don't want to know!'

'Of course I want to know,' she snapped. 'I want to know who on earth he is—if only so I can give back his expensive presents.'

Ross shrugged. 'Maybe he doesn't want them back.'

'Don't you understand? I don't care what he wants!' Her voice rose in her agitation.

'No, Tazzy, I really *don't* understand…' he said.

'Then that makes two of us!' She breathed out heavily.

He shook his head. 'Most women that I know would be at least flattered by this—attention. And if not flattered, then amused. You just seem angry.'

Maybe that was because she *was* angry! Because this was sending out all the wrong messages to Ross. The man she was in love with.

'After all,' Ross continued, 'you seem to like the kitten well enough. And the roses are beautiful. Is it that you don't like this particular brand of chocolates?'

Tazzy looked at him in astonishment. Could he really not see—? No, she acknowledged wryly, of course he couldn't see why it was that she was so angry. Because, despite those kisses earlier this morning, he didn't see her as anything other than his efficient PA!

And she would do well to remember that... 'I like them fine,' she answered in a calmer voice. 'And perhaps you're right,' she added ruefully. 'Perhaps I should find all of this amusing.'

'Hmm.' He nodded consideringly. 'But perhaps not too amusing. After all, the man must have his feelings too,' he reasoned.

He might have, but those feelings were causing her severe embarrassment!

'Never mind, let's just forget about it for now.'

She glanced at her watch. 'Do you think we should leave now? After all, I have to check on the kitten before we go to lunch.'

Ross nodded, standing up. 'What do you intend doing with this?' He held the necklace up pointedly.

Tazzy took it from him, carefully placing it back inside the box before replacing the lid. 'When—if,' she corrected heavily, 'I ever get to meet the man who sent me these, I shall make sure it is safely returned to him.'

He raised an eyebrow. 'If that's the way you feel about it.'

'It is,' she said with finality, moving to collect her coat from the back of the door. 'Are we going in your car or mine?' She stood ready to leave.

'Mine. But give me five minutes, will you?' He turned to go back to his own office. 'Perhaps you could use the time to go and explain things to Mrs Brown?' he suggested teasingly. 'The poor woman was looking completely befuddled earlier!' he added before going through to his office.

Mrs Brown was befuddled? How did he think Tazzy felt?

She gave one last lingering glance at the box of chocolates, easily able to envisage the beautiful necklace that nestled inside it. No one had ever given her jewellery before. And it was such a beautiful necklace, with an old-fashioned style that appealed to her, the heart a solid piece of gold.

Oh, well…

It would have to go back, and that was the end of the matter.

Pity…

CHAPTER FOUR

'THIS is nice,' Ross commented admiringly as he looked around the comfort of Tazzy's kitchen.

Being an end-of-terrace house, it obviously wasn't very big, but Tazzy had tried to make the most of the space, having had the dining-room and kitchen knocked into one room, a small table at one end at which two people could sit to eat, the rest of the room taken up with the green kitchen cabinets and the Aga she had allowed herself as her only indulgence.

Growing up with her aged aunt in an old, draughty house in Norfolk, Tazzy had come to loathe the idea of ever being cold again. And the Aga burning away all day certainly ensured that the kitchen, at least, was always warm and welcoming.

In fact, the kitten had been curled up fast asleep in her basket beside it when Tazzy and Ross had arrived at the house a few minutes ago.

Tazzy had tried to get Ross to wait outside in the car, still not comfortable with this intrusion into her home, but his request to be allowed to see the kitten made her suggestion seem churlish.

He looked so big in the confines of her kitchen, his head almost brushing the low ceiling, and he had to take great care not to hit the range of copper saucepans that hung from a rack from the ceiling.

'She's gorgeous, isn't she?' Ross murmured now as he squatted down beside her next to the kitten's basket.

Yes, the kitten was certainly a lovely little thing, had actually seemed to recognize Tazzy when she'd come in. At least, she had stretched languorously in her basket and given an almost soundless miaow of greeting!

'Won't you find it a little difficult giving her back?' Ross prompted gruffly.

Tazzy had already thought of that, and knew that she was going to find it incredibly difficult, but if the gold heart-shaped necklace had to go back to its giver—and it did!—then, unfortunately, so did the kitten. She couldn't just pick and choose what gifts she was willing to accept!

'Of course,' she replied. 'But I'm sure you'll agree, travelling as we often do, that it's totally impractical for me to have any sort of pet.'

Ross gave her a considering look. 'Have you always based your decisions on practicality?'

Tazzy felt the warm colour in her cheeks. 'You find something—wrong, in that?' she challenged.

'No, not wrong, exactly.' He shrugged. 'But what about spontaneity?'

What about it? It must be difficult for Ross to understand the lack of it in her own life, being the only child of fairly wealthy parents, and then having been so successful himself as a freelance trouble-shooter for any company that needed his assistance with their software—and plenty of them did. But the most recent spontaneity for Tazzy had been whether or not to buy a new winter coat this year or make do with the old one; she had finally decided to make do with the old one!

'Forget I asked.' Ross apologized, seeming to have read at least some of her thoughts. 'That was insensitive of me. It is a pity you can't keep the kitten, though.'

Yes, it was, especially as the kitten had now climbed out of its basket and was padding Tazzy's ankles with velvet paws in an effort to persuade her into picking it up.

Tazzy bent down and scooped the furry bundle into her arms, nuzzling into its fur as it began to purr softly, knowing as she did so that she had already lost her heart to it. Probably because she sensed that the kitten was as much in need of love as she was…

She blinked as sudden tears blurred her vision. This was silly; what on earth was she crying about?

'Don't make any hasty decision about it, hmm?' Ross encouraged as he moved to stand beside her, the kitten's neck arched in ecstasy as he moved a caressing finger against her fur.

Tazzy's breath once again felt constricted—and she knew it had everything to do with Ross's close proximity. Even if it was only so that he could stroke the kitten!

'No,' she agreed huskily. 'I—er—I think I'll just go upstairs and change, after all, if you don't mind?' She thrust the kitten into his arms, moving away abruptly.

'Go ahead.' Ross sat down in one of the kitchen chairs, the kitten on his knee. 'We'll be fine down here. Won't we, Shadow?' He spoke softly to the kitten as it settled itself more comfortably on his knee.

Tazzy nodded tersely in acknowledgement before hurrying from the room, her breathing returning to normal as she walked slowly up the stairs to her bedroom.

It wasn't only the kitten that was throwing her into confusion—Tazzy knew without a doubt that after today she would never be able to walk into her kitchen again without sensing Ross's presence there.

Which was precisely why she had tried to prevent her private life and her business one from ever crossing over each other; it was sweet torture to spend every day with Ross and know how much she loved him, but her home had always been the one place she could go to lick the wounds of unrequited love.

But not anymore…

Deciding what to wear to go out to lunch was a little harder than she had thought it would be. On the one hand she wanted to keep her working relationship with Ross as comfortable as it had always been, but, on the other hand, she was conscious of the fact that this was not a business lunch.

Quite what it was, she had no idea, but, on the positive side of things, at least while she was out of the office there couldn't be any more deliveries from her mystery admirer!

Tazzy finally settled on a black sheath of a dress, teamed with the red jacket from a suit she rarely wore to work, on the basis that it was a little too— too vibrant, to wear to the office, especially with her copper-coloured hair.

She looked smart, but still elegantly businesslike, Tazzy decided after one last glance in the mirror before she hurried back down the stairs to rejoin Ross.

'Very nice,' he complimented as she entered the kitchen. 'Smart, but elegant.'

Tazzy felt an inner glow as his words echoed her own thoughts about her change of clothes. Not that she should read too much meaning into Ross's approval of her appearance, but nevertheless—

'Except for your hair, of course,' he added softly.

She gave him a sharp look before moving to stand in front of the mirror hooked on the end kitchen cupboard; she had tidied her hair while upstairs, could find nothing wrong now with its neatness.

'You never wear it down anymore,' Ross murmured as his reflection came to stand next to hers in the mirror. 'I've never forgotten how it looked that day you came for your interview.'

Tazzy couldn't move, barely breathed, could feel the warmth of his body as he stood directly behind her, aware of him with every fibre of her being.

'Such a beautiful copper colour,' Ross continued gruffly. 'With blonde highlights. And please don't tell me those highlights come from a bottle,' he added ruefully. 'I don't think I could stand the disappointment!'

She swallowed hard, trembling slightly at his closeness. 'They don't,' she assured him huskily, her gaze riveted on his reflection in the mirror beside her own.

'Good,' he murmured with satisfaction, one of his hands moving up to start deftly removing the pins that held her hair in place. 'Don't, Tazzy,' he instructed as she would have put up a hand to stop him.

Her hand dropped back to her side, and she was totally aware now of the touch of his fingers against her nape and down her neck, tiny ripples of pleasure moving down the length of her spine as she continued to watch his reflection.

'Better.' He nodded approvingly as her hair fell down in rippling waves onto her shoulders, his hands—those hands Tazzy so loved!—threading through the fiery strands to loosen them out even more onto the collar of the red jacket.

The effect was startling even to Tazzy, her hair long and silky, emphasizing the deep green of her eyes, her slightly flushed cheeks giving her a beauty that wasn't always apparent.

'Much better.' Ross admired her reflection, his hands resting caressingly on her shoulders. 'How old are you, Tazzy?'

She was way past the stage today of trying to get him to stick to the rules of formality she was usually so insistent on, knew that she was just wasting her time, anyway; Ross was a man who always did exactly what he wanted.

Although quite what he wanted at the moment Tazzy wasn't sure!

'How old am I?' She repeated his question, frowning slightly.

'Mmm.' He nodded, his reflection smiling at her, his thumbs lightly caressing the silkiness of her throat now.

Was it the fact that they seemed to be talking to each other in a mirror that made their conversation take on an intimate note? Tazzy had no idea; she only knew that after this she was going to have a problem maintaining her own side of their business-like relationship.

'Twenty-five,' she answered him slowly, wondering what her age had to do with anything; unless he was going to point out that at that age she was well on her way to being an old maid, and should perhaps consider her mystery admirer's attention with a little more seriousness!

'That's what I thought. Then why do you do everything you can in order to make yourself appear older? Like wearing this glorious hair confined,' he continued determinedly as she would have protested. 'Very little make-up. And those nondescript coloured suits teamed with white blouses that you always wear to come to work.' He held her gaze in the mirror, those hands caressing the lobes of her ears now.

For exactly that reason! She was all too aware that Ross was twelve years older than she was, that his taste ran to more mature women, usually aged in their thirties, women who knew exactly where the relationship was going—absolutely nowhere!—and were quite happy with that arrangement.

Not that she wanted Ross to think she was at all like those women in that way, she had just thought that if she were to look a little more mature, more confident, he might one day at least notice she was female!

She deliberately broke their gaze in the mirror, moving away from those caressing hands at the same time. 'I had no idea you so disapproved of my appearance,' she said. 'Maybe if you had said something earlier—'

'I don't disapprove of your appearance, Tazzy.' He sighed deeply as he turned to look at her.

'Really?' she snapped. 'It certainly sounded that way to me!'

'If it did, then I apologize,' he told her quietly, his gaze searching.

'I just wondered as to the reason for—for— Well, for looking so prim and proper.' He grimaced. 'When you can actually look like this.'

'Like this' meaning slightly tousled, her cheeks naturally flushed from the touch of his hands against her sensitized skin, her eyes glittering emerald-green, the dress and jacket giving her a look of slim sophistication!

She gave him a scathing glance, more hurt by his criticism than she would ever let him see. 'I'm your assistant, Ross,' she bit out tartly. 'An efficient one, I hope?'

'Efficiency could be your middle name.' He nodded ruefully. 'By the way, what is—?'

'Never mind what my middle name is, Ross,' She cut him off, having no intention of ever revealing to him that her middle name had been chosen in deference to her mother's aunt Mabel, the maiden aunt who had brought Tazzy up after her parents were killed in a car crash. Anastasia Mabel Darling; what had her parents been thinking of? 'The point is that I'm your assistant, and as such I dress the part.'

'Yes, but if you just— Never mind.' He obviously thought better of what he had been going to say as he saw the deepening gleam in her eyes. 'I fed Shadow while you were upstairs, by the way.' He indicated the plate of food and saucer of milk. 'So if you're ready, I think we should be on our way to the restaurant?'

'I'm ready,' Tazzy answered him stiffly before picking up her handbag, still smarting from those comments he had made concerning her usual— drab?—appearance.

Surely he didn't want her to look like some over-made-up underdressed vamp when people came to his office, or they went away on business together? If he did, he would have to continue to live with that particular disappointment!

'See you later, Shadow,' Ross murmured as they went out the door.

Tazzy wondered exactly when 'later' he thought he was going to see the kitten again. This was the first time Ross had ever been to her home, and, after his recent comments, she thought it would probably be his last!

CHAPTER FIVE

PIERRE'S was exactly what it sounded like—a very exclusive French restaurant in the most fashionable part of the city. And the proprietor greeted Ross as if he were an old family friend.

As, indeed, it turned out he was!

'Your parents are both well?' Pierre beamed down at Ross once he had personally seen them seated at a table near the window that overlooked the river.

'Very well,' Ross confirmed warmly. 'They're away on a Caribbean cruise at the moment,' he added enviously. 'Can I introduce you to my friend Anastasia?' he continued, at the same time giving her a reassuring smile. 'Anastasia, Pierre.'

To Tazzy's embarrassment she found her hand being taken in the dashing Pierre's before he raised it to brush his lips lightly against her skin.

'*Enchanté, mademoiselle,*' he murmured admiringly.

Tazzy resisted the temptation to pull her hand sharply away as the handsome Frenchman continued to hold it in his grasp long after etiquette dictated he should have released it. Instead she settled for looking around the busy restaurant. 'You're very busy today.' She smiled.

'But of course.' Pierre finally released her hand as he straightened. 'It is the day for love, is it not?' he added huskily, dark brows raised suggestively over sleepy come-to-bed blue eyes.

Tazzy shifted uncomfortably, feeling slightly flustered by such open flirtation. Really! She wondered how this man ever found the time to run a restaurant at all when he possessed such a lethal brand of Gallic charm.

'Not for you it isn't, Pierre.' Ross laughed. 'Get back to your kitchen and give me some space to charm my own girl!'

The Frenchman gave a throaty chuckle of enjoyment. 'As long as you do that, my friend.' He nodded. 'Ozerwise…'

'"Ozerwise," nothing!' Ross continued to smile. 'First things first—could you bring us a bottle of your very best pink champagne?'

Tazzy's eyes widened at the request; she had never drunk champagne in her life, let alone the very best!

'This young lady, she is worth the very best, no?' Pierre said approvingly.

'Yes.' Ross nodded, shooting Tazzy a mischievous grin.

He was enjoying himself! She had found the last

five minutes embarrassing, to say the least, the request for champagne completely surprising her, and Ross was enjoying himself!

'You needn't have bothered with a good champagne on my account,' she told him awkwardly once they were alone, the flamboyant Pierre having gone off in search of his very best champagne. 'I wouldn't know the best from the mediocre!' she admitted ruefully.

'Then it's time you did,' Ross told her.

'But—'

'Tazzy, you've had a very unsettling morning, the least I can do is buy you a decent lunch,' Ross cut in firmly.

In truth, she had briefly completely forgotten the events of that morning; being out to lunch with Ross, the owner of the restaurant having obviously assumed she was his lady-love, was much more unsettling than anything else that had happened to her already today!

'Very well,' she conceded. 'But, really, any old champagne will do,' she added quickly, having taken a glance at the menu by now, nearly falling off her chair as she saw the prices quoted next to the champagnes.

Ross began to chuckle, shaking his head as Tazzy looked at him reproachfully. 'Pierre doesn't stock "any old champagne,"' he teased.

'Oh.' She grimaced, once again turning her attention to the menu.

Obviously it was primarily written in French, with English translations underneath—translations that didn't make much more sense to Tazzy than the original! What on earth was—?

'I can recommend the onion soup and the Steak Diane,' Ross told her softly.

Tazzy glanced up at him beneath lowered lashes; had it been so obvious how nonplussed she was by the menu?

Ross grinned at her, his eyes dancing with amusement. 'If it makes you feel any better, his name is really Peter Garstang.'

'Sorry?' She frowned her puzzlement.

Ross leant slightly across the table, lowering his voice even more. 'Pierre,' he enlightened her. 'His name is actually Peter Garstang, and he was born in the east end of London.'

Tazzy turned to look at the owner of the restaurant as he continued to move effortlessly around the room, charming the patrons as he went, that roguish look in his eyes every time he spoke to the women seated at the tables.

She turned back to Ross. 'He isn't French?'

'Not in the least.' He smiled. 'He and I were at school together, that's how I know of his real origins. But what the hell, if it's good for business?'

Indeed. Except… 'That's rather deceitful, though, isn't it?' she said slowly.

Ross gave her a considering look. 'You're very hot on appropriate behaviour, aren't you, Tazzy?'

Was he criticizing her, or complimenting her? She couldn't tell. 'My aunt was,' she answered quietly.

'That will be the aunt that brought you up?' Ross nodded to the wine waiter as he arrived with the champagne.

'Mmm,' Tazzy replied distractedly, her attention on the wine waiter as he deftly dealt with the removal of the cork from the champagne bottle without spilling a drop, pouring a small amount into Ross's glass before standing back.

Ross sipped the pink bubbly wine before signalling his approval, the waiter then filling Tazzy's glass before topping up the first one and then moving discreetly away.

The whole process had only taken a minute or so, and yet Tazzy found herself enchanted by the whole ritual. It certainly beat the carafe of house red that she and Anne usually ordered!

'Aren't you going to try it?' Ross tempted when the two of them had given their order for food, and Tazzy still hadn't attempted to drink any of the sparkling wine.

She picked up the fluted glass, tipping it up so that

she could drink some of the light pink wine, instantly starting to sneeze as something tickled her nose.

'Sorry—I think it was the bubbles!' She gasped, her eyes watering slightly.

Ross smiled affectionately. 'Try again,' he encouraged indulgently.

She did—finding the champagne delicious: light and bubbly, with a wonderful flavour. 'Mmm,' she told Ross appreciatively. 'Why pink champagne, though?'

He eyed her teasingly. 'I could say it was out of deference to the day!'

'You could,' Tazzy agreed dryly—after the morning she had just had she was well aware of what day it was!

'But that wouldn't be the real reason?' He gave an acknowledging inclination of his head at her astuteness. 'Tazzy, I may work with machines all day, but I do have some romance in my soul, you know,' he rebuked gently.

Her cheeks felt warm, whether from what seemed to be his light flirtation, or the effects of the champagne, she wasn't sure. And at this moment, in these exclusive surroundings, with the attentive but unobtrusive service, seated opposite Ross at the dining table, bathed in the glow of his undistracted attention, she didn't particularly care!

'I'm sure you do,' she said warmly.

'The pink champagnes tend to be a little sweeter than the white, too,' he explained. 'I thought if you hadn't tried it before you might prefer that to the drier white champagnes.'

But she hadn't told him she had never drunk champagne before until after he had ordered the pink!

Not that it would be too difficult for him to guess that she hadn't; after all, she made no secret of the fact that her social life usually consisted of a trip to the cinema or a meal in a bistro...

'It's lovely,' she assured him.

'Good.' He nodded. 'You were telling me about the aunt who brought you up...?' he prompted softly.

'I was?' She frowned across at him, her brow clearing as she remembered their previous conversation. 'So I was.'

'Don't get me wrong, she was a lovely lady, and I'm very grateful to her for taking me in the way she did—she certainly didn't have to take the responsibility of a five-year-old into her life! But she was already in her fifties when I went to live with her, with rather set ideas about acceptable behaviour. I suppose—well, I suppose some of those ideas were passed on to me,' she accepted heavily.

'Hey, I wasn't criticizing you or your aunt.' Ross reached across the table to rest his hand briefly on hers. 'I find your—code of behaviour, I suppose you would call it...' he smiled '...well, I find it very refreshing.'

'How can such an old-fashioned viewpoint possibly be refreshing?' Tazzy protested, sure that Ross was just being nice to her.

'Oh, believe me, it can,' he assured her with feeling. 'You—' He broke off as their soup arrived. 'Try it,' he tempted as Tazzy looked down at the cheese-encrusted bowl. 'But take care, it will be very hot, and I wouldn't like you to burn your mouth!'

Tazzy suddenly found herself unable to break her gaze away from Ross as his own gaze rested on the softness of her lips, sure this time that she wasn't mistaken, that Ross was flirting with her.

Because it was Valentine's Day?

Because Pierre/Peter had seemed to expect it?

Or could it possibly be because of the obvious attentions of another man, namely her mystery admirer? If it was, if it had finally prompted Ross into seeing her as a woman rather than just his assistant, then maybe all these strange gifts weren't such a bad thing, after all...

There was absolutely no elegant way, Tazzy quickly discovered, to eat the French onion soup; the cheese seemed to have a mind of its own, the onions behaving likewise, and while she was busy trying to tackle the two of them all the liquid ran off her spoon! If it weren't for the fact that the combination of the three was absolutely delicious, she would have given up even trying to eat it after the first few mouthfuls.

'Good fun, isn't it?' Ross chuckled sympatheti-cally as she twirled the melted cheese around her spoon, obviously having the same problem, but com-pletely unconcerned by it.

It was fun, she acknowledged privately. In fact, today was the most fun she had ever had in her life. Made more so, she knew, because she was spending it exclusively with Ross.

'Are your parents enjoying their cruise?' she asked interestedly.

'As I haven't heard a word from either of them since they left ten days ago, I have no idea,' he said. 'But as this month's cruise is by way of being a second honeymoon—to celebrate their fortieth wed-ding anniversary—perhaps that's understandable. After all, I wasn't even around for their first hon-eymoon! They were very disappointed you didn't make it to their party, by the way,' he added softly.

The Valentines had celebrated their wedding an-niversary two weeks ago by throwing a large party, inviting all their family and friends. And Tazzy.

She had been very touched by her inclusion in their guest list, but at the same time, there had been no way she'd been going to attend. She worked for their son, as a paid employee, and therefore did not belong in their social circle of family and friends. The only person she would really have known, apart from the Valentines themselves, had been Ross, and she certainly couldn't expect him to dance attendance on her when there would be so many other people present that he knew. Or, even worse than that, Ross might have taken his own partner and she would have been forced to watch them together all evening…

She drew in a deep breath. 'It was very kind of them both to invite me—'

'But?' Ross prompted.

She shook her head, not quite able to meet his gaze. 'I did write and tell them that I wouldn't be able to attend because I was busy that evening,' she evaded, knowing that doing her weekly wash, before drying and ironing it, wasn't really a viable excuse.

'Pity.' He shrugged. 'My mother seems convinced it was just an excuse, that the real reason you didn't come was because I'm unkind to you.'

'What?' Tazzy was shocked that Sylvia should ever think such a thing. Especially if the other woman could see just how 'unkind' Ross was being to her right now!

'You don't think I'm unkind to you?' Ross queried huskily.

'Of course not.' She frowned at the very thought.

He raised an eyebrow. 'My mother says I treat you like part of the furniture.'

'But that's ridiculous.' Tazzy gasped her consternation.

'I thought so too—until I sat and thought about what she had said.' Ross spoke consideringly. 'You run my business life so efficiently, Tazzy, that I often forget how disorganized things were before you came to work with me eighteen months ago.' He shook his head. 'Given time, I can fix any problem a computer or its software chooses to throw at me, but my records were in such a mess I often didn't know where I was supposed to go in order to fix the problem. That certainly doesn't happen anymore, now that you put everything on disk and back it up with hard copy.'

'I should hope not.' Tazzy sounded scandalized at the thought.

He looked amused at her indignation. 'My home life wasn't much better,' he admitted with a grimace. 'In fact, I very often had trouble finding a pair of shoes to go out in that matched!'

Ah. Now that was something different...

Tazzy had been absolutely horrified by Ross's complete disorganization when she'd first gone to work for him, but had determinedly concentrated on putting his office in order rather than interfering into his equally chaotic home life. After all, it wasn't in her job description to interfere in the way he ran his personal life.

But the day Ross had been unable to find a pair of socks that had been clean enough for him to go away in had been the day she'd known all that had had to change; it simply didn't give the right impression, computer whiz or not, for Ross to go away on business looking as if he had taken his clothes out of the laundry bag—before they had been washed!

Her first suggestion had been that he get himself a live-in cook/housekeeper; at least then his laundry would be dealt with, and he would be fed on a regular basis—something else he didn't bother with if he was busy.

Unfortunately, when it had finally come to the day of interviewing the three women who had applied for the job, Ross had been called away to deal with a problem that had needed his urgent attention, leaving Tazzy to see the three women instead. Or... perhaps not so unfortunately.

The first woman had been a widow of thirty, with two young children she would have wanted to bring with her. The second had been even younger than the first, single, a tall beautiful blonde, who had been basically looking for somewhere to live in London, and hadn't minded doing 'a little light work' to secure that privilege. Thankfully, the third applicant had been Elvira Brown, a widow of sixty, with excellent references from her last post. Tazzy hadn't hesitated in offering the job to the older lady.

The fact that the first two women had both been young and attractive had had nothing to do with her decision, Tazzy had told herself!

'In fact,' Ross continued, 'Dad seems to be of the opinion that I have all the comforts of a married man without actually being married.'

'I beg your pardon!' Tazzy almost choked on her mouthful of champagne.

Ross looked a little bewildered for several seconds, and then his brow cleared, a grin spreading across his face. 'Anastasia Darling!' he reproved teasingly. 'I'm sure my father didn't mean it in that way at all!'

The warm colour in her cheeks seemed to have become a permanent fixture—although that didn't stop her blushing all over again. Well, in her defence, it had certainly sounded that way to her!

'Sorry,' she finally managed gruffly.

'No need. Perhaps I could have put that all a little more—delicately,' he conceded. 'Dad was really having a go at me because I haven't provided the two of them with any grandchildren that he can "bounce on his knee," was the way he put it, I believe. He seemed to be of the opinion that by the time I get round to it his knees will be too arthritic to support him, let alone any grandchildren!'

Considering that any grandchildren of Sylvia and Nigel Valentine would have to be provided by Ross, their only child, Tazzy found she wasn't too eager for the event herself. If—when, Ross married, she was very much afraid she would no longer be able to work for him; she just couldn't bear to see him with another woman day after day...

'I—' She broke off as a mobile phone began to ring, quickly turning to search through her bag in case it was hers, very doubtful that the charming Pierre/Peter would welcome this noisy interruption to the calm of his elegant restaurant.

'I think that's me,' Ross said as he took his phone out of his jacket pocket, the ringing immediately becoming louder before he hastily pressed the button to take the call. 'Yes, it is. Yes. Just hold on a minute, will you?' he instructed the caller abruptly, putting his hand over the mouthpiece to speak to Tazzy. 'I'll just go over there and take this call.' He nodded in the direction of a little alcove near the rest rooms. 'I won't be a minute,' he promised as he stood up and moved quickly away.

As far as Tazzy was concerned, he could take his time; she was still recovering from the comment he had just made about him supposedly having all the comforts of a married man. Not all the comforts—

there was certainly one 'comfort' of a married man that was missing from their particular relationship!

She was sure that Nigel Valentine had just been teasing his son; his next comment about grandchildren certainly seemed to imply that he had been.

'Why haven't you?' Ross's voice rose agitatedly as he spoke to his caller. 'But you said— He is? Yes. No, I won't be able to do that. Yes, I appreciate that it isn't your fault, but—' He sighed his impatience. 'Okay. Thanks.' He ended the call. 'For nothing!' he muttered as he rejoined Tazzy.

She looked across at him enquiringly. 'Trouble?'

'You could say that,' he said, his expression having taken on a slightly hunted look.

'Anything I should know about?' she pressed; after all, if it was to do with work—

'Definitely not,' Ross stated, sitting back slightly to allow the waiter to remove their used soup bowls, waiting until they were alone again before speaking. 'Tazzy, I—' He broke off, frowning at something over her shoulder.

Tazzy turned to see what Ross was looking at, her eyes widening as she saw a tall, dark-haired man approaching their table in what looked like a very determined way, the man looking extremely handsome in a black dinner suit and snowy white shirt.

He came to a halt next to their table. 'Anastasia

Darling?' He smiled down at her warmly, totally ignoring Ross.

Tazzy stared back at the man, feeling very much like a rabbit must do caught in the headlights of an oncoming car—because she had a feeling, a terrible sinking feeling in the pit of her stomach, that something was about to happen that she had no more control over than the poor rabbit did!

Was this him? Was this the man who had been sending her Valentine gifts all morning?

There was no doubting that he was good-looking; probably aged in his late twenties, dark-haired and blue-eyed, athletically fit in the fitted dinner suit.

But the only problem was, Tazzy just knew that she had never set eyes on him before!

CHAPTER SIX

'YOU are Miss Anastasia Darling?' The man looked slightly uncertain now, leading Tazzy to the conclusion that he didn't know her, either. Which meant he couldn't be her mystery admirer. But if not, who was he? And what did he want with her?

'Yes,' she confirmed warily.

'Oh, good.' The man grinned, reaching into the breast pocket of his jacket to pull out a rolled-up piece of paper tied with a red ribbon.

And suddenly Tazzy knew exactly who—what—he was! 'Oh, please, not a kissogram!' She groaned disbelievingly; she had thought she would be safe from her mystery admirer by going out of the office to lunch with Ross at a restaurant—she had obviously thought wrong!

'Certainly not,' the young man said with a smile. 'I am under strict instruction not to kiss you,' he assured her regretfully. 'I am, however, going to serenade you with a love-o-gram.' He untied the piece of red ribbon and unrolled the piece of parchment.

Serenade her—? Before Tazzy could even begin to guess what he had meant by that remark the man had launched into song!

'I love you, Anastasia, with hair of fire and gold, and lips so warm and tender—'

Tazzy couldn't bear it anymore; she buried her face in her arms as they rested on the tabletop, her shoulders moving emotionally.

The man carried on singing. 'Your legs are long and fine, your waist so curved and shapely, your breasts are so div—'

'Stop right there! Enough!' Ross interrupted loudly, effectively silencing the other man.

Tazzy still didn't look up. She couldn't. And as the other diners in the restaurant began to applaud she knew that for the moment she didn't want to, either!

'More than enough,' Ross stated firmly. 'Thank you,' he added belatedly. 'Now kindly go away,' he ordered.

The applause increased for a few seconds, leading Tazzy to assume that the 'love-o-gram,' having delivered his message, was taking Ross's advice and departing the restaurant.

'Tazzy?' Ross prompted gently. 'Tazzy, are you okay? What a damned stupid thing—' He broke off as Tazzy at last raised her head, frowning as he saw the expression on her face. 'Are you—laughing?' he said disbelievingly, the two of them once more alone at the table.

Of course she was laughing, so much so that the tears were running down her cheeks!

It might be the effects of the unaccustomed champagne, or the craziness of the day, but that—that love-o-gram had to be the funniest thing she had ever heard in her life.

Ross looked astounded. 'But I thought—I thought you were crying.'

'What on earth for?' She still chuckled, taking a tissue from her bag to mop up the tears of laughter. 'Didn't you think it was funny?' She began to laugh again as she thought of the complete absurdity of what had just happened.

'Not that funny, no,' Ross muttered as she couldn't seem to stop the laughter.

'Oh, Ross!' She grinned as she shook her head, once again mopping up the tears. 'It was hilarious! The words were so—so ham, as to render them farcical!'

He still scowled. 'I'm sorry.' He shook his head. 'I just can't see anything funny about it.'

Obviously he couldn't, leading Tazzy to the conclusion that she had better stop laughing too. Perhaps it was the champagne, after all. Whatever the reason, it had certainly changed her mind as to the significance of her mystery admirer; any man that could come up with the words to a song like the one she had just heard couldn't possibly be taken seriously.

'Sorry.' She bit her bottom lip to stop herself smiling, aware that her response to the love-o-gram was just increasing Ross's disapproval. 'Still feel sympathetic to the man's feelings?' she teased lightly.

He sat forward. 'I—'

'Well, zat was certainly different.' Pierre/Peter chuckled as he came over to their table. 'I was not aware that you were a poet, my friend.' He slapped Ross playfully on the back.

That was the reason Ross was so annoyed, Tazzy realized with a wince; he was frightened the other diners would think he, as her dining companion, had also composed that awful song to her! Why hadn't that occurred to her earlier?

'Oh, it wasn't Ross,' she hastened to correct the other man—and save Ross's blushes!

'It wasn't?' The other man was so startled by this disclosure that for a moment he forgot his assumed accent. 'I mean, you allow ozer men to seduce your woman?' He frowned at Ross.

A Ross who was obviously squirming with embarrassment!

'But I'm not,' Tazzy said quickly. 'I'm not Ross's woman,' she enlarged as the restaurateur raised dark brows. 'I'm his Personal Assistant,' she explained—and instantly wished she hadn't as the speculation in Pierre/Peter's eyes increased.

Ross gave a low groan. 'Stop while you're not

ahead, Tazzy,' he advised. 'As for you, Pierre—go away, will you?' he told his friend irritably.

Pierre/Peter grinned unabashedly as he bent down to speak softly in his old schoolfriend's ear. 'Just one more word of advice, old boy; I don't have a licence for live music, so next time could you—? Okay, okay.' He straightened, holding up his hands defensively, his eyes dancing with merriment at the outraged look on Ross's face.

'It wasn't you,' he drawled. 'But it certainly livened the place up for a few minutes; no doubt the other diners will be talking about it for weeks!' he added wickedly before moving on to the next table.

Tazzy shot Ross a rueful look, wincing as she saw the stony expression on his face. It really hadn't occurred to her until the last few minutes that anyone would assume he had sent her that love-o-gram. No wonder he was so annoyed!

She leant across the table, lightly touching his hand with her own to attract his attention. 'Don't worry about it, Ross,' she soothed. 'We don't actually know any of these people—apart from Pierre, of course,' she said wryly, pretty sure the other man wouldn't forget the incident in a hurry. Or let Ross forget it either, if she had read the other man correctly! 'I know you didn't write that song,' she added consolingly.

Ross focused on her with slightly dazed brown

eyes. 'That was, without a doubt, the most awful thing I've ever heard in my life!' he declared disgustedly.

Tazzy straightened, bristling slightly. 'It wasn't that bad! Obviously someone went to considerable trouble—' She broke off, frowning. 'How on earth did he know I would be here…?'

Ross blinked, the same thought obviously occurring to him for the first time too.

'Oh,' Tazzy gasped, biting her lip uncomfortably. 'I told Mrs Brown where we were having lunch,' she explained guiltily at Ross's questioning look.

At least, she thought it was a questioning look; it was difficult to tell when Ross still seemed slightly dazed by the event of the love-o-gram!

Which wasn't so surprising. It really had been the most extraordinary thing she had ever witnessed in her own life, let alone in Ross's. No doubt he was wishing he hadn't invited her out to lunch in the first place!

'That would explain it.' Ross nodded curtly.

Tazzy gave him a considering look. He really did look shaken by what had just happened, more so than she was, actually. 'Would you like to leave, Ross?' she asked. 'I realize this has been—embarrassing, for you.' She grimaced. 'I really don't mind, if you would like to go instead of finishing our meal.'

He straightened, smiling as he obviously made a

concerted effort to shake off the events of the last few minutes. 'Don't be silly, Tazzy. We haven't even had our main course yet. Watching Pierre prepare our Steak Diane is an experience not to be missed!' he assured her even as the other man arrived beside their table to do just that.

Ross's prediction proved correct as Tazzy watched in fascination as the other man cooked the ingredients for their meal right there beside their table. Not only did it look wonderful when Pierre placed their laden plates in front of them with a flourish a few minutes later, but it smelt delicious too.

'He may not be French,' Tazzy leant forward to murmur to Ross, 'but he certainly knows how to cook!'

Ross nodded, his good humour seeming to have been restored during the last few minutes. 'Oh, he's the genuine thing when it comes to cooking,' he assured her. 'He trained under a cordon bleu chef in Paris.'

'It shows.' Tazzy nodded before enjoying her first mouth-watering taste of the tender steak. 'Mmm,' she breathed, closing her eyes briefly in ecstasy. 'This is gorgeous!'

Ross watched her indulgently. 'You know, Tazzy, your complete enjoyment of everything is— Well, you're very nice to be around. That didn't come over too well, did it?' He frowned self-derisively.

She laughed softly, shaking her head. 'Don't worry about it. I think I've had more than enough gushing compliments for one day!'

'But— Never mind,' he muttered, turning his attention to his own meal.

Tazzy looked at him beneath lowered lashes. There was definitely something different about Ross today—and she didn't just mean his embarrassment of earlier. Maybe the Valentine gifts, the obvious attentions of another man, really had made him see her as a woman at last; if they had, then even her own embarrassment at the love-o-gram was worth it!

'Is everything all right for you both?' Pierre appeared beside their table once again.

'Wonderful!' Tazzy looked up to glow warmly at him.

Pierre looked at her with admiration. 'Your Personal Assistant, I believe you said...' he murmured to Ross without even looking at him.

'I didn't say at all,' Ross denied. 'Tazzy did.'

'Tazzy...?' Pierre repeated huskily, blue eyes frankly appraising as he continued to look at her. 'How unusual.'

'She's an unusual woman,' Ross bit out curtly. 'Now for the third time today, Peter, will you go away?' he snapped.

His friend turned to give him an amused glance.

'My, my, you are rattled today, aren't you?' he teased softly.

'I'm not in the least rattled,' Ross rasped, glaring up at the other man. 'I'm just asking you to remove your charming presence somewhere else—preferably Outer Mongolia!'

His friend laughed before turning his attention back to Tazzy—a Tazzy who was more than a little puzzled by the exchange between the two men. If she hadn't known better, she would have said Ross was jealous of the other man's marked attention towards her. Which was ridiculous.

For one thing it was obvious that Pierre was charming to all his female customers. For another, for Ross to feel jealous of his friend would imply that he was interested in her himself. And she knew that certainly wasn't true. If his reaction to her mystery admirer was anything to go by, he just didn't want some other man coming along and stealing his Personal Assistant from under his nose!

'It appears that Ross wishes to be selfish and keep you to himself,' Pierre murmured as he lifted her hand to his lips once again. 'I bow to the adage that the customer knows best,' he added with a mischievous twinkle in his laughing blue eyes. 'Might I suggest that the next time we meet it is without the presence of my jealous friend?' he added, giving a mocking bow in Ross's direction before once again taking his leave.

It might all be part of the charming patter that Pierre/Peter indulged in with all his female customers, but even if it was he was certainly doing Tazzy's morale a lot of good. Or maybe it was the champagne that was doing that; whatever, she had enjoyed having such a handsome man flirt with her!

Ross didn't agree, she discovered as she turned back to him, finding herself the focus of his dark scowl.

'What?' She frowned her puzzlement at his behaviour.

'The man's nothing but an accomplished charmer!' he growled.

Very firmly bringing Tazzy back down to earth! 'You're right, he is very accomplished,' she snapped, the colour back in her cheeks.

'But, then, some people might benefit from learning a little charm themselves!' She glared across at him.

Ross frowned. 'Meaning me?'

She shrugged. 'I didn't say that.'

His mouth twisted scathingly. 'You didn't need to! You surely aren't taking any of that rubbish seriously?'

'Of course I'm not taking it seriously!' she returned impatiently. 'Honestly, Ross, what do you take me for?' Her eyes glittered angrily at his obvious criticism; he surely wasn't implying that she had actually *encouraged* Pierre?

If Ross were seriously looking for someone to blame for the other man's flirtatious behaviour, then he should look no further than himself; Pierre was simply responding to what he believed was his friend's display of possession. Which might not be strictly accurate, but Ross was certainly displaying something!

He gave a deep sigh, shaking his head in self-disgust. 'I'm sorry if you think I'm coming on a little heavy, I just—well, I wouldn't want you to take Pierre too seriously, that's all,' he finished lamely.

'I don't think I'm the one that's doing that,' she returned stiffly, his apology, quickly followed by what seemed like yet another insult to her intelligence, doing little to mollify her ruffled feelings.

Ross grimaced. 'Probably not. Let's just forget about it, shall we?'

Tazzy looked at him wordlessly for several long seconds, and then she gave a slow nod of her head. 'Fine,' she said, turning her attention back to her half-eaten meal.

But she was very aware as she struggled to regain some of her previous enjoyment of the food—and failed!—that something had subtly changed between Ross and herself during this lunch-time, that there was a strain between them that hadn't previously been there.

It was a strain she had always feared might happen if they should ever step over that line between employer/employee—and having lunch together in this way was certainly stepping over that line.

She should never have agreed to come out to lunch with him, should never have accepted his invitation. Except…Ross hadn't really made it an invitation, more something that he'd considered was a good idea, and that she'd been expected to go along with.

Well, it certainly hadn't been a good idea—and she didn't know where that left the two of them now!

CHAPTER SEVEN

THEIR departure from the restaurant half an hour later certainly wasn't made any easier by Pierre's parting comment. 'Remember what I said about the live music licence, Ross!' Or the fact that he deftly pulled a single red rose from the vase on the reception desk and handed it to Tazzy as she preceded Ross out the door.

'For goodness' sake, don't take it all so seriously, Ross,' Tazzy finally sighed impatiently. The two of them had driven the two miles back to the house in complete silence, Ross scowling darkly at her side as he parked the car in the driveway.

He turned to give her a rueful glance. 'Lunch didn't turn out quite the way I expected it to.'

She shrugged, inwardly wondering exactly how he had expected it to turn out... 'So let's move on, hmm?'

He gave an appreciative chuckle. 'As easily as that?'

She gave another shrug. 'What's the point of dwelling on something you obviously didn't enjoy?'

'I wasn't the one who was supposed to enjoy it,' Ross protested. 'I wanted to take you out for a

Valentine lunch. The love-o-gram, or whatever the man called it—' he grimaced disgustedly '—was a bit of a shock, let's say. And I had forgotten what an affected pain in the butt Peter can be!'

'Don't be mean!' She laughed.

He glanced disparagingly at the red rose she still held in her hand.

'Another one to add to your collection.'

Tazzy looked down at the single red rose, newly in bud, its deep red colour symbolic of the day. She had never received one red rose in her life before today, let alone dozens of them.

'You have this one.' She held it out to him.

And just as quickly wished she hadn't! What on earth was she doing? A single red rose, when given to the right person, was just as significant as the dozens of them she had received this morning. More so, in this case!

Ross looked at the red rose she held out to him, and then up into her face.

A face rapidly suffusing with embarrassment. What had possessed her? What was Ross going to think—?

'Thank you.' He reached out to take the rose gently from her grasp before leaning forward and kissing her lightly on the lips.

Tazzy's lips tingled from his touch, her own gaze

completely mesmerized by the gold flecks in the brown of his eyes. Had Ross really just kissed her...?

'I think we can do better than that, don't you?' he murmured huskily, bending his head to claim her lips once more, his arms moving about her as he moulded her softness against him.

She had to be dreaming! Ross couldn't really be kissing her!

But he was. And not just kissing her. But touching her too, his hands moving caressingly across her back.

If she had been standing her knees would have buckled. As it was she just melted against him, melted into him, her arms moving up about his neck as her hands became enmeshed in the darkness of his hair, the red rose crushed between them, forgotten.

His mouth moved searchingly against hers, seeking a response—and receiving it as Tazzy's lips parted beneath his to welcome the kiss.

She had dreamed for months of having Ross kiss her like this, of being able to kiss him; she never wanted this moment to end!

Her spine arched as his caressing hand moved lightly over the firmness of her waist and up to her pouting breast, the nipple hardening against the palm of his hand as he cupped her there, Tazzy groaning low in her throat at the sheer pleasure of having Ross make love to her.

Ross deepened the kiss, his tongue seeking, and finding, the warmth of her mouth, and all the time his hand caressed the pertness of her breast.

Tazzy felt as if she were on fire, the heat pulsing through her body until she hungered for something more, something that was as yet elusive, but that Ross's kisses and caresses promised to fulfil.

He felt so good, so hard and muscular as he crushed her against his chest, only the two of them existing at that moment, no one else—

'Hey, guv'nor!' The call was accompanied by a sharp rap on the car window.

The two of them sprang apart as if they had been struck by lightning, Ross giving Tazzy's blazing face a quick look of apology before he turned sharply in the direction of that intrusive voice, opening the car door to get out to talk to the man who stood there.

Giving Tazzy time to gather her scattered wits together!

What on earth had they been doing? What did she think *she* had been doing?

She should never have allowed their kisses to deepen into such passion, should have called a halt after that first brief touch of their lips. Instead of which, she had given in to the sheer need she had to experience Ross's kisses and caresses.

She had never felt so—so awkwardly uncomfortable in her life!

Not only had they been interrupted by a third person, but how could she and Ross possibly expect to carry on working together after what had just happened between them?

She wasn't sure they could...

Tazzy took a deep breath, tidying the tangles from her hair, giving a regretful glance at the crushed rose, before climbing out of her side of the car to look across at the two men as they talked together.

'Sorry about that, love.' It was the same delivery man who had brought her the box of chocolates earlier this morning. 'I have instructions to deliver this—' he held up a Cellophane-wrapped teddy bear '—at four o'clock today.'

Not another one! was Tazzy's first thought. She would like to tell her mystery admirer to take his teddy bear and—

'Thanks.' Ross impatiently took the bear from the other man. 'I trust you won't be delivering anything else here today?' he added icily.

The man eyed him warily. 'Not here, guv, no.'

'Good,' Ross said with obvious satisfaction.

'Er—I was told to give that—' he pointed to the bear in Ross's arms '—to the young lady.'

Ross moved around to Tazzy's side of the car in two strides, thrusting the bear into her arms. 'There,' he told the other man irritably, his expression grim. 'Satisfied?'

'Er—yes. It's only—' The delivery man looked undecided for a moment. 'Never mind.' He shook his head, his smile more of a grimace as he turned away.

'Thanks,' Tazzy called after him lamely as he climbed back into his van.

'You're welcome,' he told her ruefully before hastily slamming the door and driving away.

Leaving Ross and Tazzy—still clutching the Cellophane-wrapped bear against her breasts!—standing on the driveway...

Ross drew in a harsh breath. 'I shall be glad when today is over!' he snarled before striding across the gravel to let himself in by the front door.

Tazzy slowly followed him into the house, totally miserable now, unsure even what to say to Ross. What could she say to him after what had just happened in the car? *It was a mistake. Let's just forget it.* It had been a mistake. But she doubted that either of them would just be able to forget it had ever happened!

Ross was standing in her office when she entered a few seconds later, and it was difficult, with the irritation still evident on his face, to relate him to the man who had just kissed her with such passion.

'Aren't you going to open that?' he growled, nod-

ding in the direction of the bear she still clasped
protectively against her.

'I can already see what it is,' she replied, placing
the unwrapped bear on her desktop.

A beautiful honey-coloured bear, at least two feet
in height, clasping a bright red heart, with the words
'I love you' emblazoned across it in gold letters.
There was also a white card attached to the red ribbon that secured the Cellophane at the top of the
bear's head, but at the moment Tazzy was loath to
read it. For obvious reasons!

Ross eyed the bear frowningly. 'Someone seems
intent on wearing down your defences,' he muttered
at last.

Couldn't he see? She didn't care about the bear,
or the roses, the chocolates, or the necklace—the
jury was still out on Shadow! But at the moment all
she really cared about was what had happened between the two of them outside in the car.

'Someone who's too cowardly to even identify
themselves,' she dismissed without interest.

Ross looked at her, dark brows raised. 'It seems
like a deliberate, and sustained, plan of action to me,'
he said.

'It seems like a nuisance to me!' she returned heatedly. 'Ross, about what happened just now—'

'What does it say on the card this time?' He
moved to turn the white card over. '"With great af-

fection, and much love,''' he read evenly before turning back to look at her. 'You have to give him marks for consistency, surely?' he drawled.

'After the fiasco earlier in the restaurant, I think he wants shooting!' she muttered impatiently.

Ross shrugged, sitting on the side of her desk. 'Like you, I'm starting to see the funny side of that now.' He grinned.

Tazzy's heart seemed to stop beating at the charm of that grin, her breath catching in her throat as she found herself once again mesmerized just looking at him.

Ross shook his head. 'I'm sure that whoever he is he can't have known how ridiculous that supposed declaration of love was going to be!'

It had been ridiculous, she had said as much herself at the time. And yet a part of her now bristled resentfully at Ross's mockery.

Did he find it funny that another man found her attractive, to the point where he believed himself in love with her? Was that the reason he had kissed her himself, to see what all the fuss was about?

One thing she knew for certain: it was perfectly obvious from Ross's behaviour, since they had entered the house, that he was not about to discuss what had happened between the two of them in the car a few short minutes ago. In fact, he had done everything he could to avoid the subject!

She gave a weary sigh, knowing she needed some time to herself to decide what she was going to do about the situation. It didn't matter how much Ross might try to pretend those kisses they had shared had never happened. They had happened, and Tazzy needed time to think. Alone. In peace and quiet.

'Ross, I have a bit of a headache,' she told him with a frown. 'It's probably the champagne,' she attempted to fib—when in reality the relaxing effects of the champagne had worn off the moment Ross had begun to kiss her. 'Would you mind if I went home early?'

'Not at all.' He stood up, his expression one of concern as he looked at her. 'Would you like me to get you something to take for it before you go?'

'No, thanks.' She turned away to pick up her handbag.

'Sure?' Ross probed worriedly. 'It isn't like you to have a headache, Tazzy.'

It wasn't like her to make a complete idiot of herself by so obviously falling into his arms, either—but she seemed to have done that today too!

'It won't last for long,' she assured him hopefully—in fact, her temples had begun to throb in earnest now.

'Lie down in a dark room for half an hour or so,' Ross advised.

She wanted to bury herself completely in a dark

room—for the rest of her life! Anything to avoid having to come into the office in the morning and face Ross as if nothing had happened.

'I'll bring these out to the car for you,' Ross said, beginning to collect up the gifts she had received throughout the day.

Tazzy opened her mouth to tell him to leave them, and then changed her mind. It might have been these gifts that had sparked off this awkwardness she now felt between herself and Ross, but having them sitting here waiting for her when she came back to work tomorrow would not help the situation.

'Thanks. I—I'll work later tomorrow evening to make up for it,' she offered.

'No need,' Ross refused lightly, the chocolates and teddy bear held firmly in his arms. 'What do you want to do about the roses?' He looked pointedly at the huge vaseful of dark red blooms.

Throw them away! Destroy them! Crush them, like the one they had left abandoned in the car!

'Just leave them,' she told him wearily, sure that she must have had worse days than this—she just couldn't think of any for the moment! 'I—I'll see to them tomorrow.'

She just wanted to leave now, to run away and lick her wounds—to build back her defences so that she could face Ross in the morning!

Ross walked out to her car with her, putting her

gifts in the boot before walking round to where she already sat in the driver's seat. 'I'll give you a ring later to see how you are,' he suggested, smiling his sympathy at her.

She didn't want his sympathy! She wanted— wanted—

'There's no need,' she assured him dully.

'I'll call anyway,' he insisted, reaching out to gently touch one of her cheeks. 'You are looking a little pale.'

Tazzy flinched away from his touch; she was feeling too vulnerable, her emotions too exposed, to be able to cope with Ross's gentle concern.

'I'll take your advice and lie down,' she bit out abruptly, firmly closing the car door before he could say anything else, not even glancing his way again as she drove away from the house.

She could breathe easier once she was well away from Ross, her head already starting to clear, her thoughts taking on a semblance of order now that she could look back on the situation logically.

A consequence of Valentine's Day, was what she told herself about the kisses she and Ross had shared. They had been surrounded by love tokens and love messages all day, and Pierre/Peter hadn't helped, with his flirtatious behaviour and his constant hints that she was Ross's lady-love.

No, by tomorrow, with the madness of today firmly behind them, everything would look normal again.

Whatever normal was!

CHAPTER EIGHT

TAZZY stared at the man as he stood on her doorstep, sure that she must have fallen asleep as she lay on her bed, and was now caught up in some sort of nightmare.

The delivery man gave a sheepish smile. 'I only said I wasn't delivering anything to you at that particular house anymore today,' he pointed out. 'I didn't say anything about *this* house!' He held out a large flat package to her, a red ribbon tied decoratively about it.

A package Tazzy made no effort to relieve him of. This simply could not be happening! She would wake up in a minute. And when she did maybe she would find that the whole day had been some sort of horrible dream!

'Go on, love, take it,' the delivery man encouraged. 'It's my last delivery of the day. And I have a wife of my own who expects me to take her out tonight and wine and dine her!' he added with a roguish chuckle.

Tazzy blinked in confusion, at the same time coming to the sorrowful conclusion that she was awake after all. 'Who—?' She cleared her throat, moistening her lips before attempting to speak again. 'Who's been sending me these things all day?' she asked hopefully.

He gave her a knowing wink. 'You should know that better than me, love.'

'But I don't.' She shook her head dazedly.

'Give it a little thought, love,' he advised in a brotherly way. 'I'm sure it will come to you.'

And she was equally sure that it wouldn't!

When she'd arrived home a couple of hours ago she had gone over and over in her head all the men she had even come into brief contact with during the last year, finally coming to the conclusion that it certainly wasn't any of them who were showering her with these gifts.

She frowned at the package the delivery man held. 'This definitely is the last thing you're going to deliver to me today?' She wanted confirmation of that, at least, before she took the ribbon-wrapped package from him.

'Definitely the last, love.' He nodded happily. 'But with any luck, the man himself will turn up before the evening is over!'

Her eyes widened. 'Do you think so?' It was a thought that had never even occurred to her.

'I would have thought it was a pretty safe bet.' The man grinned. 'So, if I were you, I would change into my prettiest outfit and just wait and see.' He pointedly eyed the faded denims and baggy green jumper she had changed into when she'd come in from work.

'Right,' she murmured distractedly, taking the package from him.

Oh, she would be waiting for the man, all right, she might even let him explain himself too—before she hit him over the head with the box she now held in her hands!

Whoever he was, he had caused her more than enough trouble today, to the point where she wasn't even sure her working relationship with Ross—let alone anything else!—was salvageable.

'Thanks,' she added belatedly.

'You're more than welcome,' he told her warmly. 'I hope you have a good evening.'

'You too.' She smiled, returning his cheerful wave a few seconds later as he drove away.

Well, it wasn't his fault, for goodness' sake, he was just the middleman!

Tazzy slowly closed the door before carrying the package through to the kitchen, placing it on top of the table. 'What do you think, Shadow?' She looked down at the kitten as it rubbed against her denim-clad legs. 'Shall I open it first, or just hit him with it if he does dare to turn up on my doorstep? Hmm—' she nodded '—that's what I think too.' She didn't hesitate anymore but began to untie the red ribbon, standing back with a gasp seconds later as the contents of the box were revealed to her.

Unbelievable!

Unacceptable!

Beautiful…!

Tazzy had lifted the lid of the box to find pink tissue paper, had carefully folded back the tissue paper, to reveal the most beautiful white silk and lace nightgown she had ever seen in her life!

How dared he? had come her immediate thought. Quickly followed by a totally feminine response to something so beautiful: a need to just touch the gown!

She reached into the box now with shaking hands, lifting up the white silk to let it fall down in all its glory.

It really was the most beautiful thing Tazzy had ever seen, let alone touched, the straps and cups made of pure white lace, the knee-length gown shaped in white silk.

A white card had fallen from between its delicate folds, and Tazzy gently replaced the frothy silk in the box before bending to pick it up. 'Eight o'clock this evening?' the card read.

Tazzy glanced at the silk nightgown, and then back at the card, a deep frown furrowing her brow. If he meant what she thought he meant—!

Who did this man think he was? More to the point,

what did he think *she* was? If the implication of the silk gown, and its accompanying message, was anything to go by—!

'Right,' she snapped, folding the tissue firmly back over the nightgown before slamming the lid back on the box. 'Eight o'clock, is it?' she muttered angrily. 'We'll see about that!'

Her headache was certainly forgotten as she sat down at the kitchen table to wait for her so-called mystery admirer, but her head was buzzing with indignation as she constantly glanced at the array of presents she had placed on the table before her: the box of chocolates, the beautiful gold-heart necklace, the still-Cellophane-wrapped teddy bear, the box containing the silk and lace nightgown. And of course there had been the dozens of red roses and that dreadful love-o-gram.

Tazzy's frown deepened as something—she wasn't quite sure what—kept niggling away at the edge of her brain, something that had been said to her today that for some reason she knew was significant. But what was it? And who had said it?

No matter how hard she tried—and she tried very hard!—she just couldn't bring the memory back into focus. Which wasn't surprising, after the day she had just had!

But it was important. She was sure that it was. Was sure that—

Her head went up sharply as the front doorbell rang, a quick glance at her wrist-watch showing her it was still only seven forty-five. He was early! Whoever *he* was.

No doubt his eagerness had something to do with the silk nightgown!

She could see someone standing on the other side of her frosted-glass front door now, someone tall, dressed in dark clothing, but other than that his form was indistinguishable.

Tazzy moved quietly down the hallway, ducking into her sitting-room—almost like a fugitive in her own home, for goodness' sake! But she intended trying to get a look at the man from behind the drawn curtains in her sitting-room before she actually confronted him on the doorstep—knowing who he was would be of some help!

She drew back with a gasp as she saw it was Ross standing there.

He hadn't telephoned earlier to see how she was, as he had said he would; instead he seemed to have come over personally to make sure she was okay, and, from the dinner suit and snowy white shirt he was wearing, he was going out himself this evening.

He couldn't have arrived at a worse moment!

With her mystery admirer due to arrive any minute, she would have to get rid of Ross as quickly as possible; after reassuring him all day that there really wasn't a man in her life, all she needed was for him to be here when her secret admirer actually arrived!

'Ross!' she greeted him brightly as she opened the door. 'How kind of you to call in this way. As you can see, I'm feeling much better,' she assured him with a smile, at the same time admiring how handsome he looked in his black evening wear—infinitely more distinguished than the young man who had sung her the love-o-gram earlier today!

'As I can see,' he repeated with a perplexed frown.

Tazzy waited for him to say something else—preferably along the lines of 'I'll be on my way, then'—feeling perplexed herself when he didn't.

'You're obviously on your way out somewhere, so don't let me keep you,' she added with casual dismissal, desperately trying not to appear too obvious in her anxious glances past him in anticipation of the other man's arrival.

Ross gave her a quizzical look. 'I'm in no hurry,' he said slowly.

Pity. Or…perhaps not. Perhaps it would be better if Ross was here when this her secret admirer arrived; after all, going on the man's behaviour today, he was slightly deranged, if showering gifts and words of love on a complete stranger was anything to go by!

'Come in and have a coffee, then. Or perhaps you would prefer a glass of white wine?' she offered as he closed the front door behind him before following her down the hallway to the warmth of the kitchen.

'Er—white wine would be fine. Thanks,' he added. 'You certainly seem to have made a full recovery.' He looked across at her, frowning slightly as he sat down at the kitchen table.

'I think it must have been the champagne, after all,' she dismissed laughingly, opening the bottle of wine to place a poured glass down on the table in front of him before going back for her own. 'A hair of the dog,' she explained ruefully.

More like Dutch courage in order to get through the confrontation that was undoubtedly ahead of her!

She glanced across at Ross, but he seemed rather preoccupied as he stared down into his wineglass. 'Are you going anywhere nice?' she prompted politely, inwardly doing an inventory of the choice of women he could be taking out to dinner this evening. She thoroughly disliked the thought of his spending the evening with any of them!

'I'm not sure yet,' he answered. 'Tazzy—' He broke off abruptly, staring at the array of presents she had placed on the table earlier.

'Impressive, aren't they?' Tazzy nodded in their direction. 'Oh, I forgot, you haven't seen the last one I received.' She moved to pick up the box. 'It is, without doubt, the most insulting thing I have ever been given!' She took the lid off the box.

'Insulting?' Ross repeated with another frown. 'But—'

'There!' Tazzy shook the white nightgown out so that Ross could see it. 'The message with this one read, "Eight o'clock this evening?" Can you believe the nerve of the man?' Her eyes sparkled angrily as she dropped the silk and lace back into the box. 'I think he expects me to be wearing that when he arrives!' she added disgustedly.

Ross's eyes widened. 'No—'

'Oh, yes, I think so,' Tazzy continued furiously. 'Needless to say, he's going to be out of luck! How dare he?' She warmed to her subject now, giving vent to the outrage she had been feeling since receiving this last gift. 'He's obviously the sort of man who sends a woman expensive presents but expects something back in return!' She stood up impatiently. 'But he's picked on the wrong woman this time.' Her cheeks were hot with anger. 'And the sooner I tell him that I have absolutely *no* intention—'

'Tazzy, it was me,' Ross cut in softly.

'—of being seduced by expensive presents— *What* did you just say?' She stopped dead, staring down at Ross in disbelief.

He couldn't really have just said—!

Ross drew in a sharp breath, his eyes dark as he looked up at her. 'I said, it was me, Tazzy. I sent the roses and all the other gifts,' he expanded heavily, obviously determined there should be no further confusion.

Tazzy stared at him.

And stared at him.

And stared at him...

CHAPTER NINE

'IT WAS *you?*' Tazzy finally managed to blurt out accusingly, still staring at him disbelievingly.

Ross winced at her obvious incredulity. 'Yes,' he sighed. 'I'm a little early, that's all. So if you're waiting for someone else to arrive at eight o'clock, you're going to be disappointed!' He stood up to move restlessly about the room, his face slightly pale.

Disappointed? *Disappointed!* At this precise moment, disappointment was the least of her emotions!

She was shocked, confused, but most of all hurt. To think that Ross thought so little of her that he had believed she would be seduced by expensive gifts and meaningless words...

'But—but why?' she finally managed to gasp. 'Why would you do such a thing?'

'I— You— Why do you think I did it?' he asked finally.

Tazzy gave a pained wince. 'You don't want to hear what I think!' she assured him forcefully, something else having occurred to her. 'Ross, if this was your idea of a joke, then—'

'It isn't a joke, Tazzy,' he cut in protestingly. 'I—'

He swallowed hard, shaking his head. 'I'm sure it's not supposed to be like this!'

Like what? The two of them had worked together for a year and a half now, and, although they had always got on well together, not once during that time had Ross so much as attempted to step over the line of their working relationship. His behaviour today—she still found it hard to believe he was the one who had sent her all those presents and messages!—said he not only wanted to step over it, he actually wanted to obliterate it by making her his mistress, to claim that one 'comfort of a married man' that was so far missing from their relationship!

It certainly made a complete mockery of the love she felt towards him.

'How was it supposed to be, then, Ross?' she asked bitterly. 'Was I supposed to be so over-whelmed by the roses, the chocolates, the teddy bear—? *You* said that earlier today!' The phrase that had been eluding her all evening had suddenly come to her, leaving her more stunned than ever.

Ross had been the one to tease her about the Valentine gift she had received at home this morning. He'd asked her whether the gift had been red roses, a cuddly teddy bear, a box of chocolates, or sexy underwear…!

He had said that because he had known he would

be sending her all of those things before the day was over!

As he had delivered the kitten to her doorstep first thing this morning…

'What if Shadow had wandered off this morning before I came out of the house?' She rounded on him furiously, relieved to have something else to vent her anger on; she was still so bitterly hurt that she didn't even want to think about Ross's calculated motivation behind all of this anymore. 'What if he had been run over? What if he—'

'I was parked round the corner the whole time, Tazzy,' Ross assured her wearily. 'I didn't leave until you had taken her safely into the house. It is a her, by the way,' he added ruefully.

He had been there when she'd found the kitten, when she'd looked up and down the street for the person who could have left it, when she'd picked the basket up and carried it into her house…!

She looked at him stonily. 'I want you to leave, Ross.'

'I—'

'Now!' she insisted forcefully, feeling as if her whole world were falling in on top of her. 'And take all your presents with you,' she snapped.

He gave a pained wince at her vehemence. 'Tazzy, if you would just let me explain—'

'But not Shadow. I'm keeping her,' she told him

defensively. 'She, at least, is an innocent in all of this.'

'Tazzy, you've misunderstood—'

'I don't think so, Ross,' she said scathingly. 'You certainly aren't the man I thought you were.'

His mouth tightened. 'I'm not the man you think I am now, either,' he grated. 'You're taking all of this the wrong way,' he tried to cajole. 'We've worked together for eighteen months now, and—'

'Not anymore,' she told him coldly, knowing there was no way she could go on working for him under the circumstances. 'I don't know how you came by the impression that I—what signs you could have possibly thought you saw, from me, to encourage today's behaviour—but you were wrong, Ross if you thought any of those *things*—' she made a dismissive gesture towards the presents on the table '—would impress me, would sweep me off my feet to the point where I would listen to any proposal you might care to make!'

He drew in a harsh breath, straightening his shoulders, his expression remote. 'I was—?'

'You most certainly were!' Her eyes flashed angrily.

He swallowed hard. 'In that case, I'm sorry.'

Tears stung her eyes. 'So am I,' she said gruffly. 'I—I really think you had better go now, Ross.' And give her the privacy to let her heart break into a thousand pieces, as it longed to do.

'Yes,' he accepted distantly. 'I— Keep the gifts. Or throw them away. Although I would unwrap the bear before you throw that out,' he added enigmatically before quietly letting himself out by the back door.

Tazzy dropped down heavily into one of the kitchen chairs, feeling totally numb, unable to think, unable to feel, totally lost in the black misery that threatened to engulf her.

And then she reached out an arm and swept all the gifts from the table, crashing them onto the floor, Shadow giving a nervous leap to one side as the chocolates cascaded around her.

'I'm sorry, so sorry,' Tazzy murmured brokenly as she lifted the kitten up into her arms. 'Oh, Shadow,' she groaned before burying her face in the silky fur. 'What am I going to do?' she cried emotionally, the pain she felt inside almost too much for her to bear.

What *was* she going to do? As she had said, she certainly couldn't go on working for Ross, seeing him day after day, knowing that he had thought he could buy her with expensive gifts.

Although even he had looked dismayed by the love-o-gram, she remembered with tearful satisfaction. And no wonder; he surely couldn't have guessed how embarrassing that particular *gift* was going to be!

But the delivery man's enigmatic comment and knowing wink when she had asked for the identity of the giver of the gifts now made perfect sense; he must have known all the time that it was a Ross Valentine, of the same address, who had asked for the deliveries to be made to her. He had probably thought it all extremely romantic!

What could she do? There was no way she could ever pretend today hadn't happened. After this evening's fiasco, she doubted that Ross would want to, either…

What had he thought he was doing? If he had asked her out in the normal fashion, if they had seen each other for a few months out of work, loving him as she did she might have been seduced into a relationship with him. But this—!

She shook her head. Had her love for Ross been so obvious to him? Was that the reason he had thought he could dispense with even the briefest of courtships? It was worse than she had initially thought if that were the case; she had lost her pride as well as Ross and her job.

'But I still have you, don't I?' she told the kitten emotionally as it nestled against her.

A day-to-day reminder of Ross during the long years ahead without him…

*   *   *

The ringing of the telephone woke her early the next morning. Tazzy turned over with a groan to look at the clock on her bedside table, frowning as she saw it was only six-thirty.

No one telephoned at that time of morning unless it was an emergency.

Unless it was Ross, checking to see if she would be going in to work today!

Which she wasn't. How could she, after yesterday?

She had lain awake for hours the previous evening, going over and over each embarrassing event of the day, finally falling into a fitful sleep somewhere between three and four o'clock this morning.

Only to be woken a couple of hours later by this telephone call.

But what if it was Ross? What could they possibly have left to say to each other? More to the point, what could Ross have left to say to her?

She would never know if she didn't answer the telephone call!

'Yes?' She spoke warily into the mouthpiece.

'Oh, you are there, after all,' a female voice answered warmly. 'I thought for a minute— I appreciate it's still early over there, and I obviously can't stay on the telephone for long. I didn't wake you, did I?' Sylvia Valentine added concernedly.

'Not at all,' Tazzy replied cautiously, wondering

what on earth Ross's mother was doing ringing her at this time of the morning; as far as she was aware, the other woman was still on a cruise in the Caribbean.

'Good. Only I know that you get up early in order to leave for work on time, and I did so want to be the first to give you our very best wishes,' Sylvia told her excitedly.

Tazzy was sitting up on the side of the bed now, her head thumping from lack of sleep. Maybe that was also the reason Sylvia's conversation was making no sense…?

'Sorry?' she muttered.

'Nigel and I are so very pleased,' Sylvia continued. 'The two of you are so perfect for each other.'

Tazzy blinked dazedly. 'We are?'

'But of course you are, my dear,' the other woman assured her.

'I knew that from the first moment I saw the two of you together. It's just taken Ross a little longer to see what was always in front of his nose. But I have to say, once he did realize…! Tell me, did Ross get down on one knee?' she prompted with gleeful interest.

Was it possible she was still asleep? Because if she wasn't dreaming, then she really didn't have a clue what Ross's mother was talking about!

'Er—'

'No, that was unfair of me.' Sylvia chuckled softly. 'I'm going to give Ross a ring in a minute, so I'll ask him myself. Is your ring gorgeous? Ross said he had chosen an emerald and diamonds because of your beautiful green eyes.'

Ring? What ring?

'But here I am chattering on, when you must be in a hurry to get to work. And Ross. But I did so want to welcome you into the family, my dear,' Sylvia added sincerely. 'And to assure you that I will be more than willing to help with the wedding arrangements.'

No, Tazzy was still asleep. She had to be.

'If you would like me to, of course,' Sylvia went on quickly. 'Nigel has told me I mustn't interfere, that if you want my help, you'll ask for it,' she confided wryly. 'I'm just so excited about it all.'

Welcome her into the family…? Wedding arrangements…?

Tazzy had missed something, she knew she had. She just wasn't sure what it was!

'I have to go,' Sylvia told her regretfully. 'But we can talk about all of this when we get back in a couple of weeks. We really are so pleased, Tazzy,' she repeated before ringing off.

Leaving Tazzy in a completely numbed state.

That really had to be the strangest conversation she had ever had. Conversation? It had been more like a monologue. A monologue where Sylvia Valentine seemed to be congratulating Tazzy on her engagement to her son Ross!

Someone—and she wasn't sure who—had completely the wrong idea about Ross's behaviour yesterday!

Could it possibly be her who was wrong about him?

But there hadn't been any ring. And Ross certainly hadn't asked her to marry him.

If he had, she wouldn't be feeling so utterly miserable. What—?

She stared at the telephone as it began to ring again. It was too much of a coincidence, too soon after Sylvia's puzzling call, for this second caller to be anyone other than Ross.

Did she want to talk to him?

CHAPTER TEN

SHE most certainly did!

'Tazzy, it's Ross,' he began cautiously once she had grabbed up the receiver. 'I understand my mother has just been on the telephone to you…?'

'Yes,' Tazzy replied just as guardedly.

He gave a heavy sigh. 'I'm really sorry about that. I had no idea— I didn't think— Please disregard anything she said to you that you may have found upsetting.' The grimace could be heard in his voice. 'It didn't even occur to me that she would telephone you like that. But once I had told her how I felt about you she seemed absolutely sure—but never mind that,' he dismissed briskly. 'Don't even think about coming in to work today,' he went on. 'I'm sure you've been bothered by the Valentine family enough for one day.'

'But—'

'I know, Tazzy, your sense of what's right dictates that you should come in to work today,' Ross acknowledged wearily. 'But I really think it's best if you don't.'

She wasn't so sure anymore, felt there were answers she needed to certain questions.

'And don't even think about giving me the ring back—because if you won't wear it then I have no use for it!' he growled before ringing off abruptly.

Two telephone calls. Neither of them making sense. And it wasn't even seven o'clock in the morning yet!

Ross had mentioned a ring too. An emerald and diamond ring? An engagement ring?

There had been a gold heart-shaped necklace in amongst the chocolates, could there possibly have been a ring in one of the other gifts?

Certainly not in with the nightgown, because she had taken that out of the box twice, once to look at it herself, the second time to indignantly show Ross. But if there had been an engagement ring in one of the previous gifts, that snowy white silk nightgown also took on another meaning…

The excitement began to build up inside Tazzy as she hurried down the stairs, the gifts once more on the kitchen table where she had placed them haphazardly after picking them up from the floor the evening before; she hadn't wanted Shadow to eat the chocolates during the night and make herself sick.

The teddy bear!

Ross had advised her not to throw away the teddy bear before opening up the Cellophane and looking inside…

Nestled behind the red heart with the words 'I love

you' sewn onto it that the bear held between its paws was a green ring box...

Tazzy's hands shook as she opened up the lid, giving an audible gasp as she stared down at the ring presented in green velvet, a large emerald surrounded by six diamonds...

An engagement ring?

Sylvia Valentine had certainly seemed to think so. And Ross had implied as much too when he'd spoken to her a short time ago.

But he hadn't asked her to marry him, only to—

No! The ring had been delivered *before* the nightgown, had arrived at four o'clock with the teddy bear, and Ross had arrived at seven forty-five hoping for a positive answer to what was meant to be a romantic marriage proposal. And instead she had thrown him out of the house, assuring him that he had read all the signals wrong if he had thought she would look favourably on any proposal he cared to make to her!

Oh, Ross...

Tazzy looked down once again at the beautiful emerald and diamond ring, tears blurring her vision. Ross might not have proposed yesterday, but he had done everything else he possibly could to show her he loved her: the dozens of red roses, the chocolates and necklace, the love-o-gram, the bear holding this beautiful ring, the white silk nightgown, which she was now sure he had meant as a gift for their wedding night. And all those lovely, lovely messages accompanying the gifts.

Ross loved her!

Not only that, he wanted to marry her!

All she had to do now, she realized, was go to him and tell him there had been a terrible mistake. All! What she really had to do was go to Ross and tell him she had behaved like an idiot, that she had completely misjudged him, and the type of proposal he'd been making.

And hope he would forgive her.

Mrs Brown was busy making scones when Tazzy let herself in by the back door two hours later. 'Mr Valentine said you wouldn't be in today,' she commented.

'Mr Valentine doesn't know everything,' Tazzy assured the other woman lightly. 'Is he in his office?'

The older woman nodded. 'Been there all night by the looks of him.' She frowned, totally disapproving of the way Ross sometimes became so engrossed in what he was doing that he worked twenty-four hours without a break.

But Tazzy hoped Ross's lack of rest meant he had no more been able to sleep last night than she had.

She had dressed carefully for this meeting, wearing a fitted green dress the same colour as her eyes—eyes the same colour as the emerald ring Ross had bought for her! She had washed her hair, brushing it loosely onto her shoulders in the style Ross had said he liked, applying make-up to hide the shadows under her eyes, blusher to hide the paleness of her cheeks. She only hoped Ross wouldn't throw her out before she had chance to say what she wanted to!

Ross was sitting behind his desk when Tazzy quietly let herself into the room, but he wasn't even pretending to work, his feet up on the desk as he lounged back in his chair, his eyes closed.

But those eyes opened as he sensed her presence in the room, taking his feet off the desk to straighten in his chair, his expression wary as he saw the teddy bear Tazzy carried.

His gaze flickered back to her face. 'I thought I told you I didn't want any of those things back,' he rasped defensively.

Tazzy's heart ached for the lines of weariness beside his eyes and mouth, the slight growth of beard on his face clear indication that he hadn't shaved yet this morning; in fact, he was still wearing the snowy white shirt and black trousers from last night, the dinner jacket draped over the back of his chair.

Tazzy took the green ring box from behind the heart in the bear's paw, holding it out to Ross. 'This is for you,' she told him huskily.

He made no move to take the box from her. 'I don't want it.' He scowled.

He sounded so much like a disgruntled little boy

that Tazzy couldn't help giving a rueful smile. 'You haven't seen what it is yet,' she reasoned gently.

His mouth tightened. 'Of course I've seen it—I chose it!'

She shook her head. 'I don't think so.'

Ross's eyes narrowed. 'You think I would let someone else choose what was supposed to be your engagement ring?' he growled.

Her heart gave a leap at these words, her resolve deepening as she placed the box in front of him on the desk. 'I wish you would open it,' she encouraged firmly.

He gave an impatient sigh. 'I told you—' He broke off as he opened the lid to the box, staring down at the ring inside. 'This isn't your ring...' He looked up at her and frowned.

'No,' she acknowledged lovingly. 'It's yours.'

His frown deepened. 'But—'

'I'm wearing mine. See?' She held up her left hand, the ring nestling on her third finger. 'That's your ring.' She nodded towards the open box on his desk. 'From me to you. If you'll wear it,' she added uncertainly.

It had taken her two hours to arrive here after Ross's telephone call, because she'd had to wait for the jewellery shop to open so that she could purchase the ring that now nestled in the box; a wide gold band with their names beautifully engraved on the inside.

She looked at Ross, once again unsure now that she was actually with him. What if she was wrong? What if—?

Ross stood up abruptly, moving quickly round the desk to sweep her into his arms. 'I have no idea what is going on,' he told her ruefully. 'But if that ring means you're asking me to marry you, then the answer is yes!' He groaned before his head lowered, his mouth taking fierce possession of hers before she could gasp a reply.

Did that ring mean she was asking Ross to marry her? She supposed that it did. But what did it matter who did the proposing, as long as Ross continued to kiss her like this?

Which he did, kissing her so passionately that Tazzy's head was spinning wildly when he released her some time later.

'How I love you, Anastasia Mabel Darling!' he murmured emotionally, his forehead resting against hers as he looked down at her with those warm sherry-coloured eyes, his arms possessive about the slenderness of her waist.

'I love you too,' she told him achingly. 'And I'm so sorry I misunderstood what was happening yesterday— You knew all the time that my middle name was Mabel!' She pouted in realization.

He nodded. 'Did I ever tell you that my grandmother, my father's mother, was called Mabel?'

'No.' She laughed softly, so full of love for this man she felt as if she would burst.

'Well, she was. She was also my most favourite person in the world,' he added huskily. 'Until eighteen months ago, when a certain Anastasia Mabel Darling walked into my life!'

Her eyes widened. 'Eighteen months ago...?'

'Ridiculous, isn't it?' Ross acknowledged self-derisively. 'I think I fell in love with you the first time I saw you. I was just too blind to know it at the time. It took your non-appearance at my parents' anniversary party to show me just how utterly blind I've been all this time.' He shook his head. 'I spent the whole evening moping about as I imagined your "previous engagement" was with some other man!'

Tazzy gave him a quizzical look. 'There was no previous engagement and no other man. I just didn't want to spend the whole evening looking at you with some other woman! You see, I've been in love with you for the last eighteen months too,' she admitted shyly.

'Oh, Tazzy!' His arms tightened about her almost painfully as he buried his face in her silken hair. 'The time we've wasted!' He shook his head in self-disgust. 'I would probably have carried on pining away for you if my mother hadn't told me not to be so stupid, that if I loved you I should tell you so and stop wasting time!'

Tazzy felt her previous liking for Sylvia Valentine

deepen into a much stronger affection; it wasn't every mother who would encourage her only son in his love for another woman.

'I'm really sorry about her telephone call this morning,' he added. 'Please don't think it was a family conspiracy or anything like that.' He frowned. 'It was just that—before they went away I told my mother—in my infinite wisdom!—that I intended asking you to marry me on Valentine's Day. I don't think it ever occurred to her that you might say no!'

Probably because Sylvia Valentine, with the wisdom of *her* own years, had already been able to see that Tazzy was in love with her son...

'So you decided it was a good idea to bombard me with gifts and love messages on Valentine's Day?' She smiled indulgently.

Ross grimaced. 'I thought I had completely blown it yesterday. What an idiot I was to think you would be impressed with those things!'

'Not an idiot at all.' Tazzy put silencing fingertips against his lips. 'The roses, the chocolates, the necklace...' she touched the delicate gold chain she had fastened about her neck before leaving the house earlier '...even the love-o-gram—'

'That damned love-o-gram,' he groaned. 'I tried to stop it, could see that I had already gone too far with the gold necklace, that you were becoming angry now rather than intrigued, as I had wanted you to be. So I excused myself before we went out so that I could quickly telephone the agency. They said they would try to contact the man and stop him before he reached the restaurant. The phone call in the restaurant was to tell me they hadn't been successful,' he remembered with a wince.

Tazzy chuckled softly. 'Ross, I would have been overjoyed if I had guessed that any of those gifts came from you, even the love-o-gram—'

'I didn't write it, you know,' he put in hastily. 'Merely told them your name and colouring, they said they would do the rest! Hearing that man singing about the beauty of your breasts—! I almost punched him!' he acknowledged grimly. 'As for Peter—! Despite what I might have said, I had actually booked that table for us two weeks ago. Something Peter was only too aware of.' He scowled slightly at the memory. 'He certainly made me pay for the privilege when he flirted so openly with you!'

He *had* been jealous of the other man. 'There's never been anyone else for me but you,' she assured him as she reached up to kiss him lingeringly on the lips, at the same time revelling in the freedom to do so. 'There never will be,' she added sincerely.

His arms tightened possessively. 'You really mean that, don't you.' It was a statement, not a question. 'That's what I meant yesterday when I said I valued your old-fashioned code of morality,' he told her huskily. 'You seemed to think I was criticizing you in some way, but I wasn't. I want to spend the rest of my life with you, want you with me for the rest of your life, and I know with certainty that if you ever make that sort of commitment to me that it will be for life. I won't settle for anything less!'

'I won't offer you anything less,' Tazzy responded softly.

Ross moved back slightly. 'Tazzy, darling, will you marry me?'

'Oh, yes,' she replied unhesitantly, her eyes glowing with love as she looked up at him. 'After all,' she added huskily, 'I already have the nightgown for our wedding night!'

'How I love you, Tazzy!' Ross bent to tenderly kiss her lips. 'I love everything about you, your honesty, your loyalty—'

'You make me sound like the family pet,' Tazzy protested laughingly.

'No.' He shook his head firmly. 'Please believe me when I say I just love being with you. Every moment of every day,' he said gruffly. 'Besides, we already have a pet in Shadow,' he teased. 'It's the family that may need a little working on!'

Her family and Ross's. She could imagine nothing more wonderful.

What a truly miraculous day Valentine's Day was…

The Bridesmaid's Proposal

by

Rebecca Winters

CHAPTER ONE

"MIRROR, mirror, on the wall. Who's been the biggest fool of all?

"*You* have, Reese Bringhurst. But not after today!"

Wavy black hair framed the oval of her face with her well-shaped nose and wide, passionate mouth, the kind the camera loved.

Unfortunately, too many weeks of crying into her pillow every night had taken its toll. A little more base to cover the blotches of red, a touch more liner to accentuate the haunted China-blue eyes staring back at her, and her stage makeup was perfect.

It ought to be.

For two years she'd been applying it herself before leaving for the TV studio to play the minor role of Carly Shaw on a daytime soap. But today it was vital she do a flawless job. It was her wedding day on the set...and her swan song.

When the writers of *Laguna Nights* found out she was leaving the show, they'd decided to marry her off to her romantic lead, Alex Kieris, who played the part of Fabio Andretti.

Of course it meant the timid Carly would have to

step out of character for the first time in her screen life and do something bold, like ask Fabio to marry *her*. But the writers didn't worry about things like that.

It would provide the perfect surprise ending for the innocent Carly, who, for a whole year, had fought against her attraction to the older, worldly Fabio because she believed he and the beautiful, cunning Melissa were in a relationship.

According to Phyllis, the director of the show, Carly would be killed off in a tragic disappearance in the jungle surrounding Cancun on their behind-the-scenes honeymoon. Her body would never be found. That way they could bring back another Carly at a later date if they wanted to.

For now it would be the fictional end of the fictional Carly. As for Fabio, the black-haired, black-eyed Adonis who'd received more fan mail in the last year than anyone else on the show, the writers would find him a new love interest to frustrate the out-of-control-manipulative Melissa.

Reese got up abruptly from the stool of her dressing table. "It's time for your real life to start. Say goodbye to Carly. In a little while, she'll no longer exist."

And she would never see her costar again…

Don't think about him, Reese.

She couldn't afford to remember the dozens of

times he'd kissed the daylights out of her while the cameras had been rolling.

It was imperative she forget those torrid love scenes on the beach with the director orchestrating every gasp, move and sigh.

But most of all, she had to stop dwelling on the many times off camera when she and Alex had talked quietly about life while they'd been waiting for their scenes to be taped.

During those stolen moments, they would discuss their favorite books, music, art. He would give her glimpses into his childhood spent in Athens where he had been raised by his grandparents. Reese had wanted those conversations to go on forever.

For those who didn't know, Alex was of Greek origin. He had come to America after his grandparents died. At twenty-five he'd gained U.S. citizenship. Apparently he'd done all kinds of work, even some local television in New York before coming out to the West Coast.

Though he acted the part of a flashy, cocky, self-important Italian on the screen, he wasn't like that in real life. Quite the opposite in fact. He was very patient with her while she asked endless questions about Greece and its history.

Many were the times she'd been so fascinated by what he said, she'd forgotten where they were until the director had suddenly called out, "Places, everyone!'' To her chagrin, those precious moments would be gone.

Alex would once again take on the persona of the seasoned charmer Fabio, who attempted to pursue Carly at every turn. For the last year on the show, it had been his mission in life to try to seduce the vulnerable, somewhat shy twenty-three-year-old with his experience and gorgeous male body.

Then six months ago Reese's aunt Lilian had passed away unexpectedly from an aneurysm. From that time on Alex had been aware of her grief and had encouraged her to talk to relieve the pain. He'd turned out to be a wonderful listener.

So wonderful in fact that their talks had caused something to change for Reese. She couldn't separate fantasy from reality. When the cameras were rolling and they got into those embraces where she would give in to Fabio before pushing him away, she might be kissing Fabio as the script dictated, but she found herself trying to reach the elusive Alex.

He was the person to whom she responded. She wanted their on-screen relationship to continue after they called it a day at the studio.

When she had realized what was happening, she had known it was time to leave the show. Without hesitation she had phoned her agent, who, after the proverbial weeping and wailing over a bad, bad career move, had taken care of the legalities.

To her surprise it had sent a minor shock wave through the cast and crew. She was no superstar. Far from it. Yet she and Alex had been voted the favorite couple at the soap opera awards. That had brought up the show's ratings.

In front of everyone, Phyllis had flat out told her she couldn't leave. Did she want more money? What? Phyllis hadn't accepted it, and had urged her to think about it some more over the Christmas break.

It was very flattering to be asked to reconsider her decision, but Reese was in love with Alex. Painfully in love. Seeing him again after being separated for the holidays, she could no longer stay with the show and be kissed by him week after week when she knew he had no interest in her off screen. Rumor had it he was in a committed relationship with an older woman. That didn't surprise Reese.

Certainly it would take a more mature, sophisticated woman than Reese to attract Alex and hold him. She would only be hurting herself to keep showing up for work wishing for something to happen between them when it couldn't possibly come true.

Though Alex was always congenial, both off and on camera, there was a remoteness about him at times. She knew he'd just come back from spending Christmas in Greece. No doubt the woman he loved lived there. If he'd been forced to endure a long-distance relationship, it would explain why his private life seemed to remain so mysterious.

She stifled the sob in her throat and checked her watch. Nine a.m. Time to go.

Dressed in her usual T-shirt and jeans, she left the Burbank condo her aunt had willed to her, and hurried down to the underground garage. It was only a couple of miles from there to Television Central in Los Angeles.

Her last trip to the studio. Everything she did today would be for the last time.

Before long she drove into the huge parking lot packed end to end with cars. After getting out of her aunt's old car, she sprinted on long, shapely legs past three sets of guards on her way into the building.

They called friendly greetings to her. As she turned and waved to each of them her ebony hair glistened in the rare January sun. The smog was almost nonexistent this morning, a good omen for what would be the most painful day of her life.

Though she'd known the loss of her parents in her early teens, and more recently had lost her aunt, she'd been forced to come to grips with their deaths. But Alex was alive, and the knowledge that he was involved with someone else was killing her.

More than ever she realized she had to remove

herself completely from the acting scene if she hoped to get Alex out of her system.

"Good morning, Reese!"

Jerked back to a cognizance of her surroundings, she smiled at her favorite security man standing next to the metal detector.

"Hi, Bob."

"Before you go inside, do you think you'd have time to autograph this for my daughter?"

She slowed down. "Of course. Is it for Julie or Chris?"

"Chris. She never misses your show." He handed her the latest copy of *Soap Craze*.

To make it easier for her, he'd opened it to the page featuring some of the cast of *Laguna Nights*. He used his finger to point to the picture of her in Fabio's hard-muscled arms.

There was Alex again. Big as life. As long as she came to this studio every day, she couldn't escape him.

"Sign there, will you? It'll make her day." Bob handed her a pen.

Hard to believe Reese's signature could make anyone's day, but it was a phenomenon she would never complain about. Being an actress had brought in a terrific income, and she could never complain about the great working hours.

But she'd promised herself she would finish college. After today's show, she was going back to school full-time at the University of California in San Diego to get her undergraduate degree in American History. It would take five more semesters. Then it was on to graduate school.

Anything to stop thinking about Alex, who was eight years older than her twenty-three. He was a self-made, hard-working man turned actor who because of his origins brought a fascinating dimension to his role as her would-be lover.

An awful emptiness stole through her at the thought of never seeing him again. This had to end. Thank heaven it was her last day. Their last taping.

Aware Bob was waiting, Reese signed the picture with a flourish, then handed everything back to him. Pasting another smile on her face, she hurried inside past the main foyer filled with pictures of famous television celebrities from the past. Her aunt's face made up part of the collection.

Lilian Jaynes, the elder sister of Reese's mother, had been one of the soap greats on *Laguna Nights,* playing the role of Kathryn Shaw right up to the week she died.

At fourteen, Reese had gone to live with Lilian after her parents had been killed in a car accident. Then halfway through college, just before she had turned twenty-one, she had got the surprise of her life. Her aunt had talked the producer into letting

Reese audition for the part of Kathryn's long-lost daughter Carly on the show.

Reese knew the storyline well. So often she and her aunt had laughed over the ridiculous scenarios the writers thought up.

Carly Shaw had been stolen by her father when she was a baby. Kathryn hadn't been able to find them. When he'd died, the twenty-year-old Carly had searched for her mother and eventually found her so they could be united.

The role of Carly had had immense appeal for Reese because she'd loved her aunt and it would be easy to play the part of her daughter on the set. But acting hadn't been Reese's interest. She'd only auditioned for the part to please her wonderful aunt. She had never dreamed anything would come of it.

Amazingly, Phyllis had listened to them read together and loved their interaction. She'd pronounced it a match made in heaven.

So Reese had taken time off from school to play the part. She had a hunch her aunt had used her considerable influence to get Reese hired so the two of them could spend more time together. Reese had been deeply touched by her aunt's desire to stay close to her and give her the love that her parents no longer could.

Lilian had been widowed early in life and never had children. As a result, she'd doted on her only niece. Theirs had been a loving relationship. Very special.

But now that her aunt had passed away, it was time for Reese to grow up and move on. Though she'd lost the people she'd loved, she'd never known anything but love from the three of them. Reese realized how lucky she was.

She was resolute in her determination to put this part of her life behind her; what she needed to do was get today's taping over with and concentrate on the many blessings in her life.

Forget Alex Kieris, she told herself as she entered the large hallway. It divided set thirty-one from set thirty-two, where another soap was being filmed.

Like running an obstacle course, she dodged a dozen waiting actors, and avoided the huge props and deconstructed sets being rolled from storage to stage and back again. The show's publicist wanted to talk to her, but she had to decline until after the taping.

With little time to lose she continued working her way to the other end of the hall. Wardrobe was up the stairs.

It was a good thing Reese always did her own hair and makeup before she came to work. She needed to change into her bridesmaid outfit pronto.

Patsy, the magician who dressed her and made everything work, was waiting for her. "Glad you decided to drop in. I was starting to get nervous. Heavy traffic?"

"The worst!" That was as good an excuse as any.

Reese averted her eyes before slipping out of her top and jeans. Patsy was right there to lower the sea-foam chiffon dress over her head. Like froth, it swept around her legs to the floor.

A matching broad-rimmed hat and three-inch pumps completed the outfit, bringing her height to five feet eight inches.

Costuming had made that decision. She was maid of honor, and she and Fabio, the best man who stood six feet three, would look better walking down the aisle together if she were taller.

"Your basket of flowers. The marriage license is rolled up and stuck in there with the roses."

"Real white roses?" Reese lowered her head to smell the marvelous fragrance.

"Yeah. They just arrived."

Reese turned to leave.

Patsy called her back. "Here's the ring to give the groom."

"Oh—can't forget that." She slid it on her pinky. "You're a miracle worker, Patsy," she said, taking it from the other woman. "I'm going to miss you."

"We hate to see you go, but a person's got to do what they've got to do." She put her hands on her hips. "You look scrumptious, but you're acting all quiet and jumpy. Something's wrong."

A small cry of surprise escaped Reese's lips because Patsy could sense anything at all.

"Hey? Are you okay? Do you have a headache? I can get you some water and painkillers."

She shook her head. "That's so nice of you, but I'm fine, Patsy. Just keyed up. You know. The last day on the set."

"I thought so. If you need anything, just let me know."

I need for this day to be over.

CHAPTER TWO

REESE thanked Patsy one more time, then headed for the door. She walked down the stairs as fast as her heels would allow. The first thing she did was check the call sheets outside the stage. Virtually everyone in the cast was on camera today for the big wedding scene.

The main couple on the show, Miranda and Carlo, was getting married for the second time. Carlo had asked Fabio, his nephew from Italy, to be his best man.

Kathryn Shaw—Carly's mother—and Miranda had been best friends. After Kathryn's sudden tragic passing, Miranda had treated Carly like another daughter. But by doing so, she'd alienated her own only daughter Melissa, who hated her mother and had been fathered by Miranda's first husband. He was in prison for embezzlement.

Melissa was in love with Fabio and so jealous of Carly, she'd tried to kill her several times. She'd adamantly refused to be the maid of honor at her mother's wedding. Thus Carly had been chosen.

Off the set, Elaine Hirsh, who played the part of Miranda, was a wonderful friend and support to

Reese. When her aunt had died, Elaine and her husband, along with Alex, had been right there to comfort her and make sure she wasn't alone.

The whole cast had honored Lilian's memory both on and off the set, but it was Elaine who'd taken Reese under her wing for real. Since the funeral they'd grown very close and had shared many private confidences despite their age difference.

Elaine knew the real reason Reese was leaving the show. Because she could remember how painful it was to be in love and not be able to do anything about it, she was the one person who hadn't tried to dissuade Reese from her plans. In front of the others she'd applauded her decision to go back to the university and get her degree.

"Hey, Reese!"

She looked over her shoulder and saw twenty-eight-year-old Leah headed toward her in one of those slinky dresses that made the most of her voluptuous figure.

"That's quite an outfit Wardrobe has put you in."

"I wouldn't be caught dead in it otherwise." They smiled at each other. "It's the pits you're leaving the show. You have no idea how much I'm going to miss trying to kill you off."

Reese chuckled in spite of her pain. "You'll be getting your last chance today."

"True, but as usual I won't succeed, and *you* will

get to fly off into the sunset with the breathtaking Fabio.''

''Don't envy me. On our honeymoon, I get lost in the jungle, never to be seen again. You'll have Mr Irresistible all to yourself.''

Her married friend grinned. ''Don't I wish. So what's the real deal on Alex?'' she asked, lowering her voice. ''Is he taken? Like in for keeps?''

''Who wants to know?'' Reese questioned non-committally.

''Sally. She's had a crush on him forever.''

Sally and a dozen other actresses.

A shiver ran down Reese's back. She rearranged the flowers in the basket she was carrying, making sure the certificate lay on top for easy access.

''I don't honestly know, Leah. Rumor has it there's another woman, but he doesn't share anything about his personal life with me.''

''Well, if *you* don't know, nobody else does, that's for sure. Since your aunt's funeral, he has seemed a lot more attentive around you. I thought maybe he confided in you.''

''Afraid not. My aunt gave him some acting tips when he first came on the show. He liked her a lot, and knows I've missed her, so he's been a good listening ear. That's all.''

''That's *not* all. Take a look at him in that tux.''

''I'm looking.'' Reese had already sensed him

coming before she'd actually caught sight of his tall, fit, male physique.

"So is every woman on both sets. Sally needs to cool it. You can tell he hates fawning women."

That was exactly why Reese was leaving the show, before she made a fool of herself over him as Sally was doing. With his dark attractive features and olive skin, her heart couldn't take much more.

"He's headed our way. Lucky you," Leah quipped. "If I were you, I'd make the most of that final clinch he gives you in the vestibule. After to-day's taping, there's not going to be any more of that to look forward to."

Thank you for reminding me.

"All the emotion he puts out is strictly for the camera."

"Come on," Leah baited her. "Admit there were times when the temperature heated up between you two."

"I admit he made our love scenes look passionate, but that's because he's a good actor."

"Whatever you say." Leah emphatically didn't believe her. At Alex's approach, the skin prickled on the back of Reese's neck.

"Good morning, ladies. Brushing up on your lines?" he asked in his deep, cultured voice. He spoke with a slight Greek accent but saved his deep Italian accent for the camera.

Somehow Reese found the courage to lift her guarded blue gaze to his. "It can't hurt. I'd like my final performance to go without a flaw."

His black eyes gleamed. "You always do perfect work. It has made my part easy."

"Thank you."

"It's true. You're Lilian Jaynes's flesh and blood. She was a master actress. So are you. When your fans find out you've left the cast of *Laguna Nights,* there'll be mass mourning."

But you won't mourn over my absence. Reese would only have been a blip on the screen of his life.

"They'll get over it as soon as the writers find you a new love interest."

"Word has it they're going to let me grieve for a few weeks, then I'll take up my original vocation as an Italian monk. Without Carly Shaw, I no longer want to live in the world."

"You made that up."

On occasion Alex could be a tease. Maybe this was one of those times. If Patsy had been able to tell Reese was uptight, surely it hadn't escaped Alex she was more nervous than usual this morning. No doubt he was trying to get her to lighten up.

But to her surprise he lifted his hands in defense. "I swear I'm telling the truth. Ask Stan. Melissa's going to pretend to be a priest and smuggle herself inside the monastery to make my life hell."

If that was true, then lucky, lucky Melissa. An ache passed through Reese's body more intense than before.

His eyes narrowed on her face. "You were supposed to laugh. Are you having seconds thoughts about leaving the show?"

Her head reared. "None!"

"You don't have to pretend around me. You wouldn't be human if you didn't have some misgivings about walking away from all your friends here."

"Of course I'll miss everyone, but acting's not for me. When Aunt Lilian died so suddenly, I'm afraid any thespian tendencies inside me died with her. If my aunt had done something else for a living, the idea of being an actress would never have occurred to me.

"Let's face it. My chance to play Carly Shaw on a soap opera was an absolute fluke. To be honest, I'm eager to get back to the university. In retrospect, two years away from the books makes me want to jump right into my studies again."

"Still planning a graduate degree in Archaeology afterwards?" he inquired.

"I don't know. My parents were hoping I'd follow them into their field, but I'm also thinking Anthropology. Maybe I liked this stab at acting as much as I did because I've always found people and their behavior fascinating.'' *Especially yours, Alex Kieris.*

''Carly, Fabio, Melissa—church scene coming up next!'' the stage manager announced.

Alex's gaze swept over her. ''Let's go do it, shall we?''

They walked the short distance to the vestibule of the church where Carly and Fabio would link arms for the walk down the aisle ahead of the bride. Melissa took her position behind the back door where she could eavesdrop on their conversation.

When they were in place, Alex whispered, ''Smile, Reese. It's our wedding day. All the grief and misunderstandings between us are about to come to an end. In a few minutes we're going to give the viewing audience a twist they're not expecting.''

''It's a twist with a sting,'' she murmured, hoping he couldn't hear her heart clogging up her throat.

He cocked his dark head. ''That's true. You've been on the show a year longer than I have. After losing Lilian, the fans are going to have a doubly hard time letting you go.''

He unexpectedly reached out to adjust her hat. At her questioning glance he said, ''Just making sure the rim doesn't get in the way of my kissing you at the altar. I don't understand why they gave you a hat to wear.''

With a grin he said, ''In Greece a bride wears a

garland of flowers so the poor grooms don't get injured before the honeymoon even starts.''

Reese had been right. The woman waiting for him in Greece was on his mind.

''This is L.A., and I'm the bridesmaid, remember? Normally I'm not the one who gets kissed at the altar.''

''You are this time! I may just remove your hat at the appropriate moment, so don't be surprised.''

''You mean inappropriate, don't you?'' she teased, trying to put on a happy, carefree face so she wouldn't give herself away completely. ''After all the stunts you've pulled on me that weren't written in the script, I don't think there's anything you could do that would shock me.''

His eyes glinted black fire. ''I have to admit you've been a real sport to put up with me for the last twelve months. It's proof of your great acting talent that every time I blundered, you covered for me without missing a heartbeat.''

That was where Alex was wrong. Around him her heart had stopped beating more times than he would ever know. It was the reason she was leaving the show now instead of putting off her studies for another year.

School seemed to be her only salvation. Being forced to immerse herself in her studies wouldn't cure her broken heart, but if she wanted to obtain decent grades she wouldn't have the time or luxury to wallow in pain. At least that was what she was telling herself right now.

He reached for her left hand.

"What are you doing?"

"Wardrobe handed me this gold band to put on your finger. Let's make sure it slides on easily, otherwise I'll have to put it on your baby finger."

Baby finger... She loved his little language mistakes.

"You did say you wanted our last scene to go without a hitch."

Biting her lip, Reese clutched the basket in her right hand while he checked the fit. She willed her body not to shake.

"Perfect sizing." He slipped it back off. "But your hand feels like ice," came the unexpected comment before he chafed it with his to warm her up.

"I have poor circulation." She snatched her hand away.

"That's news to me. I never noticed the problem while you were putting sunscreen on my back during our beach scenes."

Before she could find a logical response, the pre-wedding march music started to play in the background.

"Places, everyone! Action!"

With those words, the two of them became Carly and Fabio.

Reese immediately slipped into the role and peered at Fabio from beneath the rim of her hat. "Is it true you're going back to Italy after the wedding?"

His black eyes narrowed. "Why do you ask?"

Reese's whole body throbbed with pain. "Just answer me, dammit!" she cried in a hushed tone, her eyes filling with tears.

He put out a finger to catch a drop, then rubbed the moisture around with this thumb. "Tears. From you?" he mocked. "I didn't think it was possible."

"There's a lot you don't know about me."

"Did you ever give me the chance, *bellissima?*"

"I'm giving it to you now."

"What do you mean?"

"Don't listen to her!" Melissa broke in on them with a maniacal look in her eyes. "I heard her tell Miranda she was in love with you, but she was lying! All this time she's been sleeping with Carlo."

Carly gasped. "That's not true and you know it," she whispered, enraged.

"Give me a break—" Melissa fired back. "Think about it, Fabio. That's why you've never been able to get Carly in *your* bed."

"You're wrong, Melissa. The only reason I haven't slept with Fabio is because I knew *you* were in love with him. I didn't want to hurt you."

"Ooh. You really know how to play hardball, don't you?" Melissa's furious gaze switched to Fabio. "The only reason she's hitting on you now is so she can get her hands on your portion of the Andretti fortune."

"There is no fortune, Melissa," Fabio declared with quiet menace. "I gave it to the church when I entered the priesthood."

"I wouldn't want it anyway!" Carly cried. "Money means nothing without love. How can you stand there and accuse me of such lies? Carlo's old enough to be my father. He's always been in love with your mother. They've been like parents to me. Don't listen to her, Fabio."

"Don't listen to her, Fabio," Melissa mimicked brutally. "Get ready to die, Carly!"

Melissa pulled a gun from the thigh holster beneath her dress. But before she could shoot it, Fabio wrenched it from her hand.

"I might have known you'd try to ruin your mother's wedding day," he said with cold fury. "My uncle told me how their first wedding ended in disaster because of you, but you're not going to get away with it a second time. Get out of here, Melissa!"

Two ushers seating people rushed into the vestibule. "What's going on? The guests are waiting."

"Escort this woman from the church and call the

police to pick her up for threatening Carly with a deadly weapon.''

While one of the ushers dragged Melissa, who went kicking and screaming, the other one relieved Fabio of the gun.

After he disappeared, Fabio turned to crush Carly in his arms. ''Are you all right?''

''Yes.'' She struggled for breath. ''Fabio—you didn't believe her, did you?''

''What do you think? According to Carlo, she's been unstable for years. Maybe she'll finally get the psychiatric help she needs.''

''She was actually going to kill me.''

''Don't think about that now.''

''How can I not?'' she cried. ''Oh, no—the wedding march has started up!''

CHAPTER THREE

"Let it!" Fabio fired back. "You were about to say something important before she tried to kill you."

"There's no time to go into that now."

"Carly—Melissa just said that you told Miranda you loved me. Is it true? Tell me." He shook her gently.

She swallowed hard. "Yes!" she cried at long last. "Even though you're too old for me and I'm too young for you, it's true. The difference in our ages no longer matters to me. I don't care that Melissa loved you first. I can't live without you, Fabio. W-what would you say if we got married today? We could make it a double wedding with Carlo and Miranda. She knows how I feel about you."

A stillness ensued. "You're asking me to marry you?"

"Yes." Her voice trembled.

"You're not joking."

"No."

"I didn't know women in America did things like this."

"They do when it's a leap year. Today is February

twenty-ninth, the day when a woman can ask a man to marry her.''

''That's right…it really is the twenty-ninth. You *do* love me!'' he cried.

''Yes, darling. In fact I took out a wedding license and signed it. All you have to do is sign it in front of the pastor after the ceremony, and our marriage will be legal.''

''Let me see it.''

She plucked it from the basket. He unrolled it and examined it, then lifted his head as if dazed.

''This is the real thing… All those times you told me you hated me and begged me to leave you alone, you were lying?''

''Yes!''

He folded the certificate and put it in his pocket. ''I want to hear you say those words to me. Look at me, Carly, and tell me you love me.''

Don't call him Alex, Reese. Whatever you do, don't call him by his real name!

She finally lifted her eyes to his. ''I'm in love with you, Fabio. I always have been, from the moment Miranda first introduced us. But I knew Melissa was in love with you, too.

''Out of respect for both of them, I didn't dare let you know how I really felt. Also, I didn't think you could be interested in someone like me who's lived such a sheltered life. But the thought of living without you is unthinkable at this point." Reese's heart was on fire for him. "Will you marry me today? Right now?"

He flashed her the heart stopping smile for which he was famous. "That all depends. How long do you intend our marriage to last?"

Reese had been waiting for him to slip in a line that wasn't in the script. With that last question, he hadn't disappointed her. It was his way of having some fun with her for the last time.

"Forever," she whispered fervently.

"Do you have any idea how long I've waited to hear those words?" His voice rang with raw emotion. "Here's my answer."

He pulled her into his arms and kissed her as he'd always kissed her for the camera, as if he really meant it. But it was a stage kiss, pure and simple. Unfortunately his acting ability was so incredible, Reese almost forgot the scene was being taped.

"I love you, Fabio, but we're holding up your uncle's wedding."

"I don't care. When he finds out we're getting married, too, he'll understand."

"Fabio? Please—we mustn't make Miranda any more nervous than she already is. By now she probably knows Melissa tried to kill me. We can't do this to her!"

"Do what?" He captured her mouth again.

"We have to think of everyone in the church waiting for the wedding to begin," she cried when he eventually let her catch her breath. "It wouldn't be fair to hold it up any longer."

"You're right." He slowly relinquished his hold. His eyes played over her in adoration. "After the ceremony, we've got the rest of our lives to be together. Come on, *bellissima*. I can't wait to say our vows in front of everyone."

With her whole body throbbing from the hungry kiss he'd given her, Reese slipped her arm through his. Alex clamped it tightly against him. They began their walk past the vestibule doors and down the aisle. The guests seated in the pews stood up.

Reese knew her cheeks were on fire from the heat of her emotions. Since that last kiss they were spinning out of control.

She studied the smiling faces of all the cast members who were dressed up for the occasion looking splendid. Every face was dear to her.

As memories of two wonderful years flashed through her mind, she smiled back through the tears. Her aunt would have loved this scene. She would have been sitting on the front row beaming at the two of them.

Alex gave her hand a little squeeze before she took her place at the left of the altar. No doubt the hidden gesture was meant to congratulate her for improvising a line at the last second.

He took his place next to Carlo, and the wedding march began.

They turned to watch Titian-haired Miranda, who approached the altar with paced steps. She was dressed in a white silk suit. Every woman should look so beautiful at forty-five. She carried a sheaf of fresh white flowers and had eyes only for Carlo.

Many times during an emotional scene, the cast members forgot they were acting. This was one of those moments. Reese could believe Miranda and Carlo were getting married for real.

When Miranda reached Carlo's side, the pastor entered the front of the chapel through a side door. Reese didn't recognize him. Evidently Phil was sick today and someone from the acting pool had been called in.

The pastor looked out over the crowd. "Please be seated," he said with solemnity.

When the congregation did his bidding, his gaze fell on the people standing directly before him.

"Dearly Beloved, we've assembled in this place to witness the marriage of two of God's children. There is no holier union on earth as Carlo and Miranda have already discovered. It's the reason they're renewing the vows they spoke to each other five years ago.

"The bond between them has grown stronger through adversity. Today they wish to celebrate their great happiness with their friends.

"Miranda? If you'll let Carly hold your flowers?"

Carly reached for the bouquet.

"That's fine. Now, Miranda? I want you and Carlo to take each other by both hands and look at each other while you repeat your vows."

For the next few minutes Reese listened to the words. The ceremony was as stirring as some of the real weddings she'd attended at church.

"Pastor Wood?" Fabio broke the silence.

A cry of surprise echoed through the congregation.

"Forgive me for interrupting, but when you hear what I have to say, I know Carlo and Miranda will understand."

He cleared his throat, as if he was having trouble keeping a rein on his emotions. "A few minutes ago, Carly did me the great honor of asking me to marry her, and I said yes. She has made me the happiest man in the world."

Cries of delight came from the congregation. Everyone looked at Carly, but the only eyes she saw were those of Fabio, staring at her with burning intensity.

Alex was a magnificent actor all right.

His gaze finally swerved to the pastor. "Carly and I have been listening to the ceremony as if it were our own. With your blessing, Pastor, we would like to say our final vows with Carlo and Miranda. I have the marriage license in my pocket for you to witness and sign afterwards.''

Reese's pulse started to run away with her. Even though this was all scripted, more than anything in the world, part of her wished it were really happening.

The pastor smiled. "I can't think of anything that would please me more, Fabio. There had to be a reason you left the monastery to enter the world again. Your union with Carly will be holy, too. The children born to you will bless that union even more.

"Carly, my child? I've felt your love for Fabio. I've seen it in a dozen subtle ways over the past year. I know what has been in your heart. Therefore I couldn't be happier to marry you to the man you've loved in secret. Now that love can be let out into the open where everyone can rejoice with you.

"If you'll give the flowers and the basket to Christine, I'll ask you to join Fabio over here.''

Christine, played by one of Reese's favorite actresses on the set, was seated on the first row. She relieved her of her props.

With each step Reese took toward Alex, her heart thudded harder.

"Carly? Take Fabio by both hands."

At the moment of contact, she felt light-headed.

To lift her eyes and look at him without giving herself away was the hardest acting she'd ever had to do. The pastor took them through the vows.

"Repeat after me. I, Carly Shaw, take thee, Fabio Andretti, to be my lawfully wedded husband, to love and adore from this day forth."

Long ago the line between Fabio and Alex had blurred for her. Looking into his jet-black eyes, she said, "I, C-Carly Shaw, take thee, Fabio Andretti, to be my lawfully wedded husband, to love and adore from this day forth."

"Fabio? Repeat after me, I, Fabio Andretti, take thee, Carly Shaw, to be my lawfully wedded wife, to love and adore from this day forth."

He gripped her hands tighter. "I, Fabio Andretti, take thee, Carly Shaw, the most beautiful love of my life, to be my lawfully wedded wife. I promise to watch over you, to care for you in sickness and in health, to love and adore you from this day forth, and forever."

Alex's elongated speech was his second deviation from the script. It sounded heartfelt. Every fan out there would melt on the spot.

The pastor smiled at all four of them. "Now, by the power invested in me by the church, I pronounce both Miranda and Carlo, and Carly and Fabio, man and wife.

"What God has joined together, let no man put

asunder. You may exchange rings, then kiss your brides.''

Alex swept Reese in his arms first, as the script directed. The force of his embrace dislodged her hat, which fell to the floor. He'd warned her.

After he'd kissed her long and hard, he slid the band on her finger. She in turn removed his ring from her pinky and, with a trembling hand, pushed it onto his ring finger.

''You're mine now,'' Fabio said, before kissing her hands.

After Carlo and Miranda had exchanged rings, the pastor raised his hands in benediction.

''Members of the congregation? May I present the two Mr and Mrs Andrettis. You may give them your best wishes in the vestibule of the church.''

Wedding music accompanied their joyous walk down the aisle behind Carlo and Miranda. Alex kissed her neck several times, playing the part of the besotted bridegroom to the hilt.

The cameras stayed on them as everyone followed them into the vestibule. Immediately both couples were converged upon with kisses and congratulations.

While Carlo hugged Miranda, the pastor, who stood at the offerings table, took Fabio and Carly aside for them to put their signatures on the license and certificates. When their business was concluded, Fabio waved the papers in the air.

"It's official, *cara*. You're my wife now."

"Fabio—I love you so much!"

Again the newlyweds embraced.

"Ah-h-h," everyone murmured.

The cameras stopped rolling.

"Great take, guys!" Phyllis declared. "I'm in tears, and that's never happened before. After you get changed, come on back to the set. It's party time for Reese. One day I might forgive her for leaving us, but I'm not making any promises."

CHAPTER FOUR

REESE pulled her hand from Alex's grasp and left the set before anyone could detain her. She passed Leah on her way up to Wardrobe. The actress who'd gone off stage earlier had already changed into slacks and a knit top.

"You look comfortable, Leah. I have to admit I can't wait to get out of these heels."

"I know what you mean. Those spikes they made me wear almost killed me before I could pull the gun on you."

"You know something? You had a wild look in your eyes that could have scared me under other circumstances. You deserve to get the best villainess award again this year."

"We'll see."

"I'm not kidding. You're so good at being bad, it's frightening."

"Thanks. Let's talk after you get changed."

"I'll be down in a few minutes."

It didn't take long for Reese to divest herself of the dress and shoes. Soon she was back in her jeans and T-shirt.

She returned everything to Patsy, including the

ring Fabio had put on her finger. One of the assistants in Wardrobe would sweep the set for any props left around.

"You're coming down to the party, I hope?"

"Wouldn't miss it," Patsy declared. "Thanks for the beautiful flowers, Reese. They arrived a few minutes ago. What a surprise!"

"Good. I'm glad they got here before I left. No one deserves them more than you. In fact I'm going to see if a best service award can't be given out on the night of the soap awards. You'd win it hands down, Patsy."

She smiled. "That's sweet for you to say. You've made my day."

"You've made mine every morning for the last two years. I'll never forget." After hugging her, Reese walked over to the dressing table to remove her makeup.

Patsy followed. "Do you know something? You're just like your aunt Lilian. She always remembered everybody, too. I bet you miss her."

Reese blinked back the tears threatening. "You'll never know." Especially right now. When she'd never been in such pain in her life, how could she possibly go home to an empty condo and pretend everything was going to be all right?

After every bit of makeup had been removed, she applied lotion to her skin and put on her own pink frost lipstick. With a flick of the brush through her thick black hair, there was nothing else to do but go downstairs and face her peers with a happy face.

Little did they know she would be putting on the greatest performance of her existence in front of them.

Patsy had already left by the time Reese jumped up from the chair and hurried downstairs. When she entered the set, she noticed everyone congregated around a couple of banquet tables enjoying a catered lunch smorgasbord style. On another table were half a dozen bottles of champagne and glasses.

Elaine started clapping when she saw Reese. Pretty soon she was surrounded by cast and crew alike with more hugs and best wishes for the future.

While she was filling her plate with Swedish meatballs and pasta, she saw Alex walk in. Through veiled lashes she noticed he'd changed into a white polo shirt and navy cargo pants.

He was such a striking man, Reese purposely struck up a conversation to avoid looking at him. But she was feverishly aware of him working his way through the crowd, smiling and talking with everyone.

Leah walked over to her with the mike. "It's time for speeches! Let's hear it from you, Reese."

For once Reese was center stage without a script. "This is scarier than acting." Her comment provoked laughter. "Whoa… I knew this was going to be hard." Her throat had swelled.

She could feel Alex's dark gaze. "I've had the time of my life with all of you. You've been like a family to me. When Aunt Lilian passed away, you were there to support me. I couldn't have gotten through some of those difficult hours without you."

Emotion got in the way. She waited for a minute to gather her composure. "My parents were big on academics. They both got their doctorates in a field they loved. Though they would have supported me as an actress, I know they had other dreams for me.

"Even Aunt Lilian knew I wouldn't stay with acting, but I'm so glad I was given the opportunity to work with her. Thank you for that, Phyllis."

"You're welcome, darling. You're a natural. If you ever decide to come back, we'll always be here."

"Thank you. Thanks, everybody. Be assured that when I'm home studying, my TV set will be permanently turned on to *Laguna Nights*. Among other things, I have to watch Melissa's reaction when she finds out I disappeared in the jungle."

Another lie. Reese had no intention of ever watching the soap again. It would be too painful, but the cast members didn't need to know it. They laughed and cheered.

"In fact I can't wait to learn what horrible scheme

she has in mind for the next man unlucky enough to be her obsession. Do we know who that is yet, Stan?''

The head writer nodded.

''Obviously you're not going to give out any secrets today.'' She would have to wait two months to find out if Alex had been teasing her about the new storyline or not.

''Sorry.''

''That's all right. Now that I'm out of the loop, I'll just have to be patient like our fans.'' She flicked her gaze to the attractive man she wouldn't be seeing again.

''Alex? I couldn't leave without letting you know it has been a great thrill for me to be cast opposite you. I'm the envy of every woman with a television set.''

All the women cheered loudly.

''Ladies? I'll let you in on a little secret. Leah? Are you listening?''

''Yes,'' her friend said with a broad smile.

''I cannot tell a lie. He could heat it up all right. I've been in meltdown the entire year.''

''I knew it!''

The place went wild. There was more cheering and clapping and good-natured funning as everyone teased her and Alex.

''From now on the guys I date are going to have

to pass the Alex Kieris test or they're out of the running.''

There was an enigmatic smile on Alex's face as he approached her and grabbed the mike. ''Unlike my costar here, I'll never kiss and tell. But I will say that playing opposite Reese has been an unforgettable experience. One I wouldn't have missed.

''Between her and Lilian, I was able to get my feet wet in this business without completely floundering.'' He turned to Reese. ''I'm going to miss you, Carly Andretti.''

A strange glint in his eye made her suddenly nervous.

''I hope I can be forgiven for doing something that hasn't been scripted. You guys are getting a preview of our off-the-set honeymoon. After all, she *is* my wife now!''

In front of everyone, he pulled her into his arms and gave her the kind of passionate kiss for which Fabio Andretti was famous. It went on and on until there was thunderous applause and wolf calls.

Since he was hamming it up, she decided to let herself go this once and really kiss him back. No one would know this farewell kiss was for Alex, not Fabio.

''Go, Carly!'' some of the cast chanted.

When it appeared Alex was enjoying her abandoned response and had no intention of ending it, Reese had to be the one to break it off.

"Whew!" She turned a flushed, smiling countenance to the audience and fanned herself. "In your face, Melissa!"

The cast roared with laughter.

At this point Leah took over the mike. "Don't anyone leave until we raise our glasses to Reese in a toast."

To Reese's dismay, she'd left hers behind on the table. Maybe it was just as well. She would have choked on her champagne.

"To Reese. Health, happiness and a long life wherever your road takes you."

While the others clicked glasses and finished off their drinks, Alex made another surprise move by sipping his champagne, then putting the glass to Reese's lips. She had no choice but to drink a little of it from the same place on the glass where his lips had been.

Her legs wobbled like jelly.

"Hey, Reese?" Brad called to her. "I need to talk to you for a minute."

For once she was thankful the show's publicist never gave up. "Coming!"

Without daring another glance at Alex, she handed back the empty glass to him and followed Brad into the hall. But once she'd moved past the doors, instead of stopping to chat, she kept on walking down the hall toward the front entrance of the building.

While she made her escape, Brad had to run to keep up with her. "Where's the fire?"

"To be honest, I don't have time for an interview right now. I'm sorry." She wiped her eyes so he wouldn't see the tears.

"I know it's tough to leave. Just give me a few words while I walk you to your car."

She whipped out of the front door and kept up her fast pace clear across the parking lot.

"Where will you be going to school? I need a little information for the show's Web site. The word's going to leak out that you're no longer a cast member. *Soap Craze* will start hounding me. You know how that goes. I'm going to be besieged with questions."

"I'd rather not say. The sooner I'm anonymous, the better."

"Winter semester won't start for another week. What'll you do in the meantime?"

"Volunteer work."

"What kind?"

"Hospitals. Kids."

"Who's the latest man in your life?"

She climbed in her car. "I don't have one, Brad. If you value your job, don't quote me wrong."

"Would I do that?"

"Yes. That's what you're paid to do. Go pick on Alex. Maybe you can find out the name of the secret woman in his life."

His brows lifted. "Oh, yeah? You know something I don't?"

"No. That's your department. I'm out of here." Flashing him a bright smile, she shut the door, turned on the ignition and started to back up.

Brad shouted something to her but she kept on going. Right into another car.

"Oh, no!" she cried as she heard the clank of metal against metal. For once in her life she'd forgotten to look first.

With her adrenalin surging, she jumped out of the car to see how much damage she'd done and ran straight into Alex. He steadied her with his hands. What was he doing out here?

"I hit *you?*" She half gasped the question.

His lips twitched. "Let's just say you caught the rear bumper of my truck."

"I'm so sorry—" She tore her eyes from his and moved away from him to see how bad it was.

She couldn't find anything but a scrape mark on his fender, but the back left door of her car had a good-sized dent.

"It's my fault," she moaned. "For once I didn't look where I was going."

"It's both our faults," he muttered. "I wanted to block you off before you got away."

With those words Alex had her full attention. Her heart started to race. She turned toward him. "Why would you want to do that?"

He eyed her intently for a moment. "After you call your insurance company, I'll tell you. But first we need to get our vehicles out of the way. Why don't you park yours? Then I'll join you."

Without waiting for her response, he got in his truck and moved it to the nearest parking space while Reese moved her car back where she'd parked it before. In another minute he'd climbed into her passenger seat.

She'd already pulled out the insurance card she carried in her wallet and had started to make the call. Soon she was able to give out the details. "Yes. It was my fault. I forgot to look."

The man on the phone asked for her opinion of the damage to Alex's truck. Reese bit her lip before looking at him. "How much do you think it will cost to fix your bumper?"

"The scrape mark can be rubbed out. Don't worry about it."

"But—"

"Here. Let me talk to them." He took her phone from her. "This is Alex Kieris. I'm the one who caused the accident, not Ms Bringhurst. Send the bill to my insurance company.''

Reese listened as Alex gave the man the particulars. After hanging up, he handed her back the phone. ''Why don't I follow you to your car dealership? Then we'll talk.''

She shook her head. ''I don't want to put you out any more than I already have. These things take forever.''

''Work's over for me today. I have no plans. Are you in a big hurry to be someplace special?''

''I was.''

''Then let me help you.''

''Why would you do that?''

''Because you're not nearly as brave as the front you put on for everyone today. You may not want to be an actress, but it still couldn't be easy to walk away from all the people your aunt loved, only to go back to her empty condo.''

''You're right.'' Reese's voice throbbed. ''I was going to take a long drive.''

''Then let's do it together.''

''Why?'' she asked him again because, so help her, she couldn't think, let alone speak when he was sitting in the intimate confines of the car with her.

''Would you believe me if I told you, 'I've grown accustomed to your face?''' He sang the last. Alex had a nice singing voice.

"No." She laughed to hide her chaotic emotions. "With a talent like that, you could perform on Broadway."

"Wrong side of the country. I'd rather spend the rest of the day with you."

"And?" she prompted him.

His mouth curved upward. "You know me well, don't you? Actually, I'd like your opinion about something. What do you say? It would be doing me a great favor."

She found herself staring at him. "Considering that I ran into you, you've put me in a position where I can hardly afford to turn you down."

His eyes flickered in satisfaction. "Good. I'll meet you at the dealership."

This time Reese looked before backing out. Only now did she notice that Brad had disappeared a long time ago. By the time she reached the gate of the studio parking lot, Alex was right behind her.

She knew why he was doing this. He was the sort of man who didn't forget a kindness. Her aunt had taken a special liking to Alex. In the early days, she'd invited him to the condo where she could teach him some of the acting tricks of the trade. The fact that he was a quick study artist was a testament to his natural acting prowess.

Reese had looked on with great interest and pleasure, occasionally being pressed to act a part to help

Lilian put over a point. Now that she had passed away, he felt it incumbent to be Reese's friend on this day of transition from actress to ordinary mortal waiting for school to start.

It was his way of paying Lilian back for those hours of friendship and instruction that had bonded the two of them. But some time during that period, Reese had also grown attached to the charismatic man who'd treated her as he might treat a sister.

He showed her the greatest respect. It was a tribute to his professionalism that he was careful how he handled their love scenes. Off the set, he never touched her or made comments that could be misconstrued.

Except for scenes shot on location at the beach in Laguna, he'd never gone anywhere with her after the taping of a scene was over.

No question about it. Alex had always been the complete gentleman. Only today at the party had he acted out of character and kissed her in front of everyone. Nobody thought anything of it.

But Reese still hadn't recovered. Was it any wonder she'd backed straight into him?

CHAPTER FIVE

THE five-mile drive took a good twenty minutes in the lunch-hour traffic. When Reese pulled into the bay of the dealership, Alex stopped his truck short of the overhead door to wait for her.

The guy in charge came over to get her paperwork done. During the litany of questions, he kept glancing at her.

"You're Carly!"

She nodded. "I'm surprised you recognized me without my makeup."

"I'd notice you anywhere, any time. We have a TV in the office. Most weekdays we watch the soaps. *Laguna Nights* is the favorite around here."

"The producer will be happy to hear it."

"You're even better looking in person."

"Thank you."

"Would you be willing to come inside and sign a couple of autographs for the guys? I'd consider it a personal favor." The male interest in his eyes almost blinded her.

"Sorry," sounded a deep, familiar voice with the fake Italian accent that sounded authentic. "She has other plans for the rest of the day."

Alex had joined them. Without hesitation he opened the door and helped her out. "We're in a hurry. You know how it is." He kissed her unsuspecting lips in proprietorial fashion.

"You're Fabio!" The other man sounded dazed. He wasn't the only one in that condition.

"That's right. She'll call you later to find out when she can expect her car to be repaired. Let's go."

Alex put his arm around her shoulders and ushered her to his truck. "I couldn't resist," he confessed as he helped her into the passenger side. "If that guy's eyes had gotten any bigger, they would have fallen out."

The picture he'd painted made Reese chuckle. "Except that he was even more excited to discover your identity. You're as famous as any movie star with top billing."

"Don't kid yourself. He was getting ready to make his big move on you. I bet it happens to you all the time," he said as he got in his side and backed the truck around.

"Not as often as you think. From what I hear, you're the one who has the most trouble in that department."

"Where we're going, neither of us will have to worry about our privacy being invaded."

"I didn't know we could go to the moon."

A smile hovered at the corner of his sensuous mouth. "The destination I have in mind isn't quite that far away."

"If you mean the rental car place, the closest one is about three blocks from here."

"I'll take you there later. For now let's just relax and enjoy this unexpected sunny day."

His suggestion sounded heavenly.

She fastened her seat belt. If she was dreaming, then so be it. "What did you do during the holidays?"

Alex made a U-turn out of the lot and headed for the street bordering the dealership. "I had a lot of unfinished projects around here." He flicked her a glance. "What did you do?"

"I spent it with a friend in La Jolla."

"Cammy?" he asked once they'd merged with the traffic.

He had an amazing memory. Cammy was Reese's childhood friend. They'd grown up together on the same street in La Jolla. Now she was married and had a baby.

"Yes. We drove around looking for a rental home for me near the university."

"Did you find one?"

She nodded. "I've decided to let someone lease my aunt's condo. It will pay my rent and feed me so I won't have to work while I'm going to school full-time."

"What are you planning to do for the next week until classes start?"

Brad had asked her the same question. "Volunteer at the hospital."

"That's a noble way to pass your time."

"Aunt Lilian was the one who got me interested. She did it for years."

"Your aunt was a remarkable woman. So are you."

"Thank you." His compliments were making her nervous. "Look, Alex—I know you're trying to pay my aunt back by looking out for me today, but it really isn't necessary. I'll be twenty-four on my next birthday and am a big girl now."

"I've noticed," he inserted in a tone that sent a wild shiver of excitement through her body. "I waited a whole year for the kind of kiss you gave me at the party."

Her breath caught. "That was for fun."

"It felt like a lot more than that to me, and I ought to know better than any man...unless you've been seeing someone behind my back."

"What do you mean behind your back?"

"Exactly what I said. Who's the man in your life who has opened you up and made you give more freely of yourself? I thought I knew everything about you.''

She blinked. "There isn't another man."

"The guy at the dealership would never believe it.''

"I don't care what he believes." She eyed Alex covertly. "I could ask you the same question. Who's your secret woman?"

"If you really want to know, I'll tell you about her later. How's that?"

"Is it serious between you two?" She could have shot herself for asking the question, but it was out now and she couldn't take it back.

"Very."

She clutched her hands together and stared blindly through the side window, away from him. "I see. Is she an actress, too?"

"No."

They'd come to the Pacific Coast Highway. He turned right and joined the stream of traffic headed north. Suddenly the mood between them had darkened. With every mile, her agony increased.

Agreeing to spend the rest of the day with him was the worst mistake of her life.

"Alex, I—"

"Don't worry," he cut her off. "We don't have a long drive. I promise to feed you."

"I ate at the party."

"One mouthful. I watched."

She took a ragged breath, not knowing what to say. His behavior was so different than usual. Always before he'd treated her like a cherished sister. But ever since she'd backed into his truck, it felt as if everything had changed. In some indefinable way, he'd changed.

The next sign came into view. Malibu lay just around the curve in the highway.

Like many Hollywood stars, Clark Robison, the actor who played Carlo on the show, lived there with his wife and family. One evening soon after Reese had gotten the part of Carly, he'd invited the cast to a party at his fabulous house in Topanga Canyon.

Reese could still remember standing on his deck, trying to imagine what it would be like to live in such a paradise with the man you loved. At that point in time, Alex hadn't arrived on the scene yet.

What an irony that, almost two years later, she discovered herself sitting next to the man of her dreams at the very moment the truck passed the turn-off for Clark's home.

She studied the landscape. Amazingly, the chaparral-type vegetation that had gone up in flames from the terrible fires of the recent past had grown back a lot since she'd come to Malibu for the party.

"Here we are," Alex broke in on her thoughts. He'd turned left at the light and had driven them into the parking area of a one-story building on the ocean side of the highway. There were a dozen workmen moving about. The place was obviously undergoing major renovations.

He read the question in her eyes.

"Once this was an art gallery. As you can see, a lot of it was scorched, and some of the rooms partially destroyed by fire. I bought it for a good price over the holidays."

This was one of his unfinished projects?

A good price in Malibu was probably three to four million dollars. But her aunt had told her that because three different television networks had wanted to sign up Alex, he'd been offered the kind of a salary to afford the very best, and he'd taken it.

Alex got out of the truck and walked around her side to help her down. Every time he touched her, even if it was just to assist her to the ground as he was doing now, she felt it to the very bones of her body.

"Come inside. One of the rooms has been dry-walled so I can use it to work."

"Are you a famous artist I should know about? Or maybe an art dealer who's planning a new opening?"

He stared at her through veiled eyes. "Neither one." He extended his hand. "Hold on to me while we make our way through—it's a maze of building materials at the moment.''

Reese was glad for his support. With almost every step she needed to be careful as he guided her past the weathered-looking stones a workman was fitting into place in front of the building. Two men worked in harmony tiling the roof.

With Alex's help, she reached some wooden steps leading into the shell of a rectangular room with a stone fireplace at one end. The bank of windows facing the ocean was covered by plastic so you couldn't see the view. Another group of workmen were putting in dark wooden beams across the ceiling. They nodded to Alex.

''Watch your step,'' he cautioned Reese as they stepped down another makeshift wooden staircase at the opposite end of the room. It led into a smaller room with a patio table and a couple of lawn chairs. Plastic sheeting prevented her from looking out at the ocean.

Alex seated her. ''Take a look through this. I'll be right back.''

Intrigued, she opened the looseleaf binder he pushed in front of her. It was full of photographs mounted beneath transparent overlays. The yellowish color on the edges of the pictures told her they'd been taken a long time ago.

Though she'd never been to Greece, the charming,

centuries-old country house hidden by greenery couldn't be located anywhere else. Many exterior and interior angles revealed the detail of beamed ceilings and stone walls with niches containing icons.

She loved the ancient stone fireplace and indoor tile trim running the length of the heavy beams that curved with age.

In the front of the off-white villa was a delightful patio and fountain inlaid with stone. The whole place was smothered with overgrown vines and trees.

By the time she'd looked at the last set of photos, which included a much younger Alex and his grandparents, she marveled to realize he was recreating that same villa here in Malibu, the kind that looked several hundred years old.

He came up behind her and put a can of cola on the table next to her. "What do you think?"

Her heart gave a strong kick. "When this is finished, you will have captured the enchantment of your grandparents' home. I absolutely adore it. How long do you think it will be before you and the woman you love can live here?"

She'd decided to come right out with it so he wouldn't think she was getting any romantic ideas about him.

He sat down opposite her and began drinking from his can. She watched his throat work, enjoying the sight of him relaxed and seemingly content. She studied his long, powerful legs stretched out in front of him. His fingers were long and lean, too. Everything about him was beautiful. Too beautiful.

After he put his empty can on the table, she felt his penetrating gaze. "We won't be living here."

His comment set her straight with a vengeance. "I don't understand."

"This is going to be a Greek restaurant."

"Restaurant?"

"That's right. I'll do the cooking. She'll help me run the place."

"You *cook?*"

"I do." He pulled the looseleaf binder toward him and pointed to one of the pictures. "You see that patio with all the tables?"

"Yes?"

"My grandparents enlarged their house and ran a taverna there for many years."

"You never told me that before."

"I thought I did. I learned to cook in my grandmother's kitchen."

"Well, I remember you saying something about that, but I had no idea you meant she turned it into a business."

He nodded. "She taught me how to make everything according to her exact specifications. It was a sad day when she passed away. My grandfather stopped wanting to live. He died within the year."

She lowered her head for a moment. "How hard that must have been for you."

"You would know," he murmured. "The place was so full of memories, and so empty, I couldn't stay there alone. So I put it in the hands of a Realtor to rent, and I left for New York on a worker's visa."

"I can relate to wanting to leave." No wonder Alex was being so solicitous of her today. His ties to his grandparents were as great as hers to Lilian. She loved him that much more for being sensitive to her needs.

No man she'd ever met could measure up to Alex. Reese was shattered by his admission that he was deeply in love with someone else.

"There are plenty of Greek restaurants in New York in need of a good cook," he continued to explain, unaware of her agony. "I had all the work I wanted while I continued to study English and begin the arduous process of becoming a citizen."

How come he'd waited all these months before confiding this kind of personal information to her? When she thought of the many talks they'd had...

"What brought you to Los Angeles?" Even though she knew there was this important woman in his life, Reese couldn't prevent herself from asking more questions. As long as he was giving her the opportunity, she had this incurable need to learn everything and anything about him.

CHAPTER SIX

BENEATH his dark brows, Alex's black gaze trapped Reese's. "You fell into acting because of a fluke. So did I."

"How did it happen?"

"I worked under a famous Greek chef at the Athena Plaza in downtown Manhattan. Someone suggested he do a pilot for a television show. He needed an assistant and asked me to help. It meant more money for me, which I badly needed to support myself."

"That's how you got on TV? A cooking show? Fabio Andretti?" She couldn't believe it.

His smile reached his eyes. "Not Fabio. The upshot is, the pilot did well, but the weekly series didn't. My boss didn't have the personality of a Chef Emeril, who's been a great success on American television."

"I love his show!"

"You and everyone else who changed channels to watch him instead of my boss. But it was my lucky day because a Hollywood soap producer happened to catch a few of the episodes, and he contacted someone at the network doing our show. I was asked to fly out to LA to read for a part.''

''I'd call that destiny,'' she whispered in a shaky voice.

''I didn't know it at the time, but I do now. You're absolutely right. It *was* destiny.''

She had an idea he wasn't talking about his career alone. ''Then this woman you love isn't from Greece?''

''Who told you she was?''

''No one. But you know how people gossip. I heard you were committed to someone, so I just assumed as much.''

He leveled his all-encompassing gaze on her. ''If that were the case, I would never have left Greece in the first place. As it was, I needed a total change of scene. New York seemed the right destination for me.

''When the offer came, I jumped at the chance to see another part of the country and make a decent salary. But the producer of the network in New York warned me not to do anything until I'd found myself the right agent.''

''Nobody in the performing arts should make a move without one.''

Alex nodded. ''He gave me a name. That favor turned out to be critical for me. This agent wouldn't let me sign any contracts until I'd auditioned for as many soaps as I could. He wanted me to hold out for the top salary.

"Naturally the money was important, but I also realized that if I was asked to play a part I couldn't abide, then it wouldn't have mattered how much I was offered."

"I know what you mean," Reese inserted. "If I'd been asked to play the role of Melissa, I wouldn't have done it. I'm not an actress at heart. I couldn't act the part of a person of whom I didn't approve, even if it was all for pretense."

"That makes sense. The first few scripts I read didn't interest me either. In both cases I was supposed to play a mobster from the underworld. I didn't want to start out like that and then be typecast forever doing the same roles."

"You were smart."

"Not really. The truth is, they held no appeal. I wanted something different. Out of the blue my agent asked me if I could do an Italian accent. Since one of my good friends was Italian, that was easy. I just mimicked him for my agent, and he took matters from there."

Reese smiled. "As my aunt told me, you're the quickest study she ever met." She'd said a lot of other wonderful things about him, too, but Reese didn't dare tell Alex or he would realize how deep her feelings for him went.

''It's because of that accent I got the part of Fabio Andretti, the priest who left the monastery because his soul was conflicted.''

''Just as yours was,'' she said quietly.

He studied her for a minute before nodding his dark head. ''It tore me apart to leave Greece. It tore me apart to stay.''

''I'm sorry you had to be in that kind of pain, Alex. No wonder you played the part of Fabio so convincingly. Many times during our scenes I felt it and knew it had to come from someplace deep within you.''

She kneaded her hands beneath the table. ''Has your sorrow diminished at all?''

''Of course. No one stays in that dark place forever. One day I took a drive and ended up here. The minute I saw this damaged gallery, I could envision my grandparents' villa. It would be like planting an old vine in new ground.

''Once that idea took hold, I never let go of it. By December, I had enough money saved to make an offer on the property. A Christmas present to myself.''

Her eyelids prickled with unshed tears. ''It's a fantastic plan. But—''

''But what?'' he broke in.

''There's always a fire danger here. Malibu's not

protected from the worst of the Santa Ana winds like Orange County or San Diego.''

''I'm aware of that fact. The Realtor warned me I might find myself having to remodel again in a few years, or even be forced to build an entire new restaurant.''

He leaned toward her. ''It doesn't worry me. As long as I have my memories, I can rebuild anywhere.''

She averted her eyes. ''I'm sorry I brought it up. Believe me, I didn't mean to sound negative. More than anything I want your project to be a great success.''

''I know you do, and I appreciate your concern.''

''What are you going to call your restaurant?''

''Kousina Sofia.''

''Your grandmother's name.'' Her eyes lifted to his face once more.

''That's right. Sophie's Kitchen.''

''She'll be overjoyed.''

One black brow lifted expressively. ''You believe in the afterlife?''

''Don't you?''

''Yes. As a matter of fact I do.''

Reese was enjoying their exchange too much. ''So...how will you fulfill your dreams to run a busy restaurant and balance your acting career at the same time?''

He closed the cover of the looseleaf binder before flashing her a piercing glance. "No one told you yet?"

She frowned. "Told me what?"

"I didn't renew my contract. I've left the show, just like you."

Alex had left the show?

"Today was my last day, too." He answered the question she hadn't voiced yet because she was so stunned.

"Your news has to be this year's best kept secret—" she blurted.

"That surprises me. Usually everything leaks out."

"Not this time!"

She took a deep breath while she tried to sort through this new development. Except that what he did or didn't do was no longer supposed to be of any consequence to her. He was in love with someone else!

"What are the writers going to do about Fabio?"

"As I told you earlier today, he'll go back to the monastery. Melissa will manage to infiltrate, believing she is torturing Fabio. But when he finally removes his hood, she'll discover she's been harassing the wrong monk.

"He'll tell her Fabio has gone, and no one knows

where he went." Alex spread his hands. "That's as much as Stan would tell me."

Reese started to laugh. "Oh, boy. I can't wait to watch when she hears the news."

Alex chuckled. "I can't either. Leah's the best at being the worst."

Though they shared an amusing moment, Reese was dying inside. He wouldn't be on the show anymore. From here on out the woman who loved him and had the right to love him would claim his undivided attention.

It was still too much for her to process all at once. She had dozens more questions to ask, not knowing where to start first.

"H-how soon do you expect to open for business?" she stammered.

"Two months. Hopefully six weeks, but that would probably be pushing it."

"I see. Are you going to live in Malibu, or commute from Culver City?" Her aunt had contacted a friend who'd helped him find a good apartment there.

"That depends on a variety of factors. I'll worry about it later. Right now my main concern is to get this place ready. I'm of two minds how to treat the windows. I've known you quite a while and have discovered we have similar tastes in a lot of things. I'd like your opinion."

"But I'm not Greek!"

"You're a woman with a woman's instincts for what works."

"What does your girlfriend think?"

"I'm asking *you*," he asserted. "When you walk in here two months from now, do you want to be able to see the ocean through a wall of glass?"

"That sounds very contemporary."

"It would be a concession for those tourists who've come from all over the world to visit Malibu and eat by the water."

"That's true. But I thought the whole idea was to reproduce your grandparents' Greek villa."

"It is."

She frowned. "Don't you see that the great charm of their home lies in the small-paned windows peeking out from plants and flowers growing all around?"

"Then much of the ocean view would be shut out."

"They'll get the view coming and going from your place. But when I think of Greece, I imagine an inn that's a little darker on the inside. You know. Cozy and intimate. Take a look at this one picture."

She reached for the looseleaf binder and opened it to the page she wanted him to see. "It's so delightful to discover this adorable patio room partially hidden by all the greenery.

"That's the secret of a place like this. You feel like you've come across this rare treasure suddenly. The element of surprise causes you to forget what's outside. You want to go in and shut out the world for a little while. The small-paned windows give it the feel of an enchanted cottage."

"Enchanted is an interesting choice of word."

"People love to be transported by the atmosphere when they dine out. If I were you, I'd reproduce every square inch of their wonderful house. Let your guests get a real taste of what it's like to eat in Sophie's kitchen."

"So you believe my idea will work?"

"You don't need me to tell you that. After they leave your restaurant, they'll savor the memory of it while they watch the ocean on their way to wherever they're going.

"As for the locals, they live next to the water. They see it every day and crave a different ambience while they eat. I think I'd be a lot more concerned about finding me the best landscape artist there is to make your slice of Greek living look exactly like it does here."

"That's the next item on my agenda."

"You shouldn't have any trouble finding a good one. California's nurseries are the best! They have everything you'll need to make this authentic. Dad and Mom had one of the most beautiful yards in our neighborhood where I grew up.''

''Did you help?''

''Yes. My parents might have been workaholics, but when they took time off, they were outside weeding and making the garden more beautiful. I spent hours with them going to nurseries looking for the right plants and ground cover.

''If you let a professional study these photographs, I know you could make this one of the most sought after dining spots in Cali—''

Reese stopped talking because it had just dawned on her she'd been babbling on enthusiastically for the last couple of minutes. Alex couldn't have gotten a word in if he'd wanted to. A smile lurked around his lips. She felt like an idiot.

''Sorry, Alex. I got carried away. When you asked for my opinion, you didn't know you were going to be treated to a full-blown lecture.''

His hand reached across the table to cover hers. He squeezed gently before letting it go again, but the warmth of his touch remained.

''After playing opposite the timid Carly, who was always fearful of letting herself go, it's refreshing to be with Reese Bringhurst, whose zest for life is contagious. Your instinctive response was exactly what I needed to hear. I happen to agree with you about everything you said.''

"I'm glad. What you're going to achieve here will automatically guarantee you success."

His white smile turned her heart over. "A majority of two. That's all I've been waiting for to go full speed ahead with the rest of my plans. Come on." He got up from the table and came around to help her. "Let's make use of the rest of this day and find me a landscape artist."

He took the looseleaf binder from the table and tucked it under his free arm. "After we're through with our business, I'll take you to dinner as my way of saying thank you for your input.

"I know a place near the Santa Monica Pier that fixes the best mahimahi you ever tasted. I remember how much you and Lilian liked it when the cast ate at that seafood restaurant in Laguna."

Alex kept astonishing her with what he knew and remembered about her and her aunt. For him to go to this much trouble to help her get through this difficult day, he truly must have felt indebted to Lilian.

But since Alex was in love with someone else, Reese decided that their going out to dinner together was the wrong thing to do for everyone concerned.

"If you really want to pay me back, I can think of a better way to do it."

She felt his body tauten. "Name it."

"Why don't you bring your girlfriend to my condo this evening and cook us a real Greek meal?

Not only do I want to test out your chef skills, I'd like to meet the woman who captured the heart of the man behind Fabio Andretti's persona.''

There—now he would know Reese wasn't living in some fantasy world where he was attainable.

His eyes seemed to glitter for a moment. ''You'd really like to meet her?''

''Of course. More important, I would imagine she would like to meet me. At least *I* would if I were in her shoes.''

''She's never said.''

''Maybe not, but it couldn't have been easy to watch you kissing me all these months.''

''She doesn't watch soaps.''

''I wouldn't either if the man I loved were acting in one. I could forgive it because it was the career he'd chosen. But I couldn't forgive him for going out to dinner alone with his romantic costar. Not even if he felt obliged to be nice to her because of Lilian Jaynes's kindness to him.''

His chest heaved. ''You're an exceptional woman, Reese. Are you acquainted with authentic Greek cuisine?''

''No. Only fast food gyros. What about your girlfriend?''

''Her experience has been the same as yours.''

Reese was stunned. ''You haven't cooked for her yet?''

"I've been waiting for her to ask me."

"But you're a chef!"

"There's an expression in English. A prophet is without nobility in his own country."

"You mean 'honor.'"

"Thank you. That's the word. I still make a lot of mistakes."

"Your English is remarkable. Did you study it in school?"

"Twelve years. My grandparents insisted."

She bit her lip before looking at him. "Has it hurt your feelings that your girlfriend hasn't shown an interest in your cooking?"

He hunched his broad shoulders. "We've had more important things on our minds than food."

"But it's what you do! It's part of who you are!" she cried as he helped her across the courtyard into the truck.

"I'm touched that you care." He placed the loose-leaf binder between them.

"Of course I care! We've put in full days together at the studio on a weekly basis for the past year. I've spent more time with you than any boyfriends who've come and gone from my life."

"Have there been many?"

"A few, but naturally you're important to me in a completely different way. I can't wait to taste your grandmother's cooking."

Her comments seemed to make him happy. "In that case, I can promise the three of us a real treat."

The three of us.

You've done it now, Reese.

But meeting the woman he loved was the only way to cure her illness. In war time you cauterized a wound to prevent death and infection on the battlefield.

That was what she had to do. Walk through the fire tonight so she'd be able to survive the rest of her life.

CHAPTER SEVEN

Two hours later they left the office of an established landscape artist in Malibu who promised to have some renditions of Alex's ideas completed in a few days.

Unfortunately Reese would never see the drawings. In order to put Alex in the past where he belonged, she couldn't afford to do anything that reminded her of him. Under no circumstances would she drive by his restaurant months from now to see the finished product. It would hurt too much.

"Hungry?" he asked as they passed a drive-in.

"I'm starving. I'm sure you are, too. But this is like Thanksgiving for me. I want to be ready to enjoy my first real Greek meal to the fullest, so I'm not going to do anything to take the edge off my appetite."

His dark eyes gleamed. "Then we'll hurry and buy our groceries. On the way to your condo we'll pick up a rental car for you."

"That's right! I forgot all about it. Thank you for reminding me."

"You're welcome."

In relatively little time they pulled into the parking

lot of a Greek market in Burbank. By now it was five o'clock. Once again he came around and helped her down. It seemed automatic for him to cup her elbow as he guided her into the neighborhood grocery store.

An auburn-haired woman at the cheese counter called out greetings to them. Alex answered in Greek and a short conversation in his native language ensued. The clerk nodded several times.

"She's going to wrap up some lamb chops and feta cheese I need while we pick out items for our salad and dessert."

Reese watched in fascination as he chose his produce with infinite care, explaining as he went that only the best kos and romaine lettuce would do. Kalamata black olives were a must, and fresh dill.

In the fruit section he picked out the finest figs. From there they walked over to the dairy products. He reached for cream. In another area of the store he put several scoops of fresh walnuts and peanuts in a sack.

They left the checkout counter with their arms full of groceries. He put the sacks in the built-in toolbox behind the cab of his truck and they took off for the closest car rental place.

"I'll follow you back to your condo."

She paused before getting out of the truck. "What about your girlfriend? Aren't you going to pick her up first?"

"It's more important to get our meal started. At some point she'll join us."

"All right," she said in a quiet voice. "I'll hurry."

It was a good thing Reese had been so upset last night. In the hope of working off enough excess energy to fall asleep, she'd given the condo a thorough cleaning. Little had she realized she would be entertaining Alex and his intended tonight.

Never had she missed her aunt's presence more. Lilian would have helped Reese get through the coming evening's agonizing experience with grace.

If she had one thing to be grateful for, her aunt's kitchen was well equipped. They'd both enjoyed cooking, so Alex shouldn't have too much trouble finding the things he needed to prepare their dinner.

Since it was near closing time, the rental place didn't have a lot of cars for her to choose from. She ended up with a compact, but she couldn't complain at the reasonable price.

By the time she'd parked in the garage and let herself in the condo, Alex was buzzing her from the foyer to let him come up.

"Hi," he said when Reese greeted him at the front door. His low, attractive voice permeated her entire being.

"Come on in." She took one of the sacks from him. He followed her through the traditionally decorated condo to the kitchen where they set everything down on the countertop.

"Since you've been here many times before, you know your way around. Please feel free to freshen up while I empty the sacks."

"Thank you."

How different their situation at this point in time. Her aunt was gone, and his girlfriend would be joining them at any minute. The sooner she got here, the better.

Being alone with Alex was not a good idea at all...

As she was removing the last of the items from the sack he entered the kitchen and came to stand next to her. His nearness had the effect of changing the rhythm of her breathing.

"What can I do to help?" she blurted.

He plucked the olive oil from the rest of the items. "For Frikassee of Lamb, I'll need a deep skillet and a whisk."

In a jerky movement, she opened one of the bottom cupboards and rummaged around for the kind of pan he wanted. The whisk was in the second drawer.

"Here you go. What else can I do?"

"Slice those onions for me."

While she found the chopping board and a knife, he poured some oil in the pan and set it on the burner. Then he reached for a mixing bowl and started cracking eggs.

He worked fast. It was fascinating to watch him use the whisk so expertly while he added lemon juice. She felt his total concentration on what he was doing.

After washing her hands, she got started on her task. Pretty soon tears were streaming down her face. He glanced at her out of the corner of his eye and chuckled.

"I should have told you to put a little piece of bread in your mouth. It helps prevent the fumes from tickling your nose."

"I didn't know that! Was it one of your grandmother's tricks?"

"No. My grandfather's. Otherwise he couldn't stay in the kitchen to help."

She wiped her eyes with her arms. "How fun those times must have been."

He opened the package of chops and started salting them. "You know how it is when you're young. You don't appreciate how happy you are until those times are gone."

"You're right. I didn't particularly love to weed, but, when I look back on it now, those times with Daddy were priceless." She took the board of onions over to him.

He darted her an intense look. "Are you sure you're not a professional cook? You did those just right." He poured them into the hot oil to soften them up.

That was how his compliment made her feel. Soft and eager for the attention he showered on her. So far it had been a magical day. But reality would hit as soon as his girlfriend arrived.

She needed to get here before Reese forgot Alex had been entertaining her for the sole purpose of making her cut-off day from the studio bearable.

With deft movements, he placed the chops in the skillet and browned them on both sides. Then he washed the kos lettuce. With the leaves still wet, he placed them on top of the meat and added fresh dill before covering the pan.

While it simmered, he prepared a green salad, and a side dish of rice with a tomato sauce made of a dozen ingredients.

When the lamb was ready, he poured in the egg mixture. "Now for the most important ingredient."

He knew she was mesmerized by everything he said and did.

"What is it?"

"A few teaspoons of Mavrodaphne wine. It smells and tastes like the sugar-sweet plums and black raisins growing around my grandparents' villa. We're about ready to sit down to a meal I promise you will enjoy."

"Then I'd better hurry and set the table."

She put out three place mats and her aunt's best

china and silver. Alex had searched until he'd found an imported dry white wine from Crete. No doubt it went superbly with the meal he'd planned, so she placed three wineglasses next to their water glasses.

They worked in harmony getting everything ready to put on the table. Faint from hunger, she could have eaten the whole ball of crusty bread he called Psomi.

Reese had placed him at the head of the table. She flicked him a glance after he'd seated her. "I feel honored the master chef is dining with me, too."

"I'm the one who's honored." He poured wine into both their glasses.

"Alex—we really shouldn't start until your girl-friend gets here."

"Yes, we should," he came back forcefully. "This meal is ready to be eaten. To wait would ruin it. Try the lamb before you taste anything else, even your wine. That way you'll detect its unique flavor. I want your opinion."

She looked at him with pleading. "Is this another test to decide if you'll be offering this dish to cus-tomers?"

"Yes."

"You don't really mean that."

The glimmer in his eyes unsettled her. "You're my first customer. It may be one of my favorite dishes, but if you find it an acquired taste, I need to know immediately."

She lowered her head. "I don't think I want the responsibility."

"Now you're sounding like Carly. I thought she'd gone away."

"I'm afraid there's more Carly in me than you realize."

"You mean the one who asked Fabio to marry you?"

"No. That part was totally out of character thanks to Stan and his writing staff."

"But you have to admit it got her what she wanted in the end."

"True."

"Come on. Live dangerously and take a bite," he said in a husky tone.

One taste before swallowing and Reese said, "You don't need me or anyone to tell you how delicious this is. The flavor and texture are out of this world."

He gave her a smile she'd never seen before, as if her opinion truly mattered to him. For a moment she caught a glimpse of the little boy he once was who would have been so anxious to please his grandparents.

"Now drink a little wine, then try the rice."

Prepared to do anything for him, she obeyed his command.

"The sauce—it's pure ambrosia, as my aunt would say. That was her favorite word for food too good to be true. Wouldn't you know it has a Greek origin?''

''That's right. Food for the gods.''

''Yours tastes like that, Alex. Now, if you don't mind, I'd like to enjoy it the way I want.''

He threw back his head and laughed while she proceeded to eat everything in sight.

''You eat too fast,'' he observed when she finally put down her fork with a sigh of contentment.

''I couldn't help it. It was your fault. Oh, Alex— I don't care if you believe me or not. That was the best meal I've ever eaten in my life. You know what I think?''

One black brow quirked.

''When people call in for reservations, you should tell them not to eat or drink anything at least six hours before arriving. That way they'll feel just like I do.''

''And how is that?''

''Like there's not one thing wrong with my world right this minute. Did I ever tell you about this book I read called *The Cook?*''

''I'm sure I would have remembered if you had,'' he teased.

She flushed. ''That goes without saying, doesn't it?'' After a pause, ''It was a mystery. This wealthy, dysfunctional family advertised for a cook. There was a feisty grandfather, an ambitious father, a twenty-four-year-old slaggard son, and a twenty-year-old selfish daughter all living under the same roof.''

''Nice.''

She chuckled. ''The cook was after the family money. He got to know each member very well, and catered to their needs by fixing them the kind of food they adored.

''One by one he had them eating out of his hand, so to speak. They'd do anything for him. It got to the point where they couldn't live without him. He solved their problems, suggested what they should or should not do, the friends they should keep, the friends they should get rid of.

''In time he ran the whole house and eventually controlled the purse strings. Everyone trusted him. In the end the old man left everything to him in his will.

''When the other family members found out, they tried to contest it, but it was too late. The cook booted everyone out of the house and lived happily ever after.''

Alex finished his wine without taking his eyes off her. ''That's quite a story. Are you assuming I have ulterior motives for feeding your fancy?''

CHAPTER EIGHT

WHAT an odd question.

"Of course not, Alex. I was using it as an illustration to compliment you. Obviously the author understood the effect of the perfect meal on the senses and made a fascinating tale out of it."

He wiped the corner of his mouth with his napkin. "With adulation like that, am I to presume you're ready for dessert? It was my grandfather's favorite."

"Not yet!" Reese cried. "I couldn't. There's no room. Maybe when your girlfriend gets here."

"I expected her before now. It appears she's not coming after all."

"Because of me?"

He nodded slowly.

"But that's absurd, Alex!"

"Not really. The truth is, she's a lot like Carly, too timid and hesitant to fight for what she wants. I'm afraid our relationship is over."

Aghast, Reese pushed herself away from the table and stood up. "If she's jealous of me, she shouldn't be. I'd be happy to call her and tell her that nothing has ever gone on between us."

"She doesn't see it that way," Alex explained.

"You'd never convince her otherwise. Frankly, neither does anyone else who knows you or me."

Her heart thudded sickeningly. "It doesn't matter what other people think. It's human nature to gossip. But I wouldn't hurt your girlfriend for anything in the world. We should never have spent this day together, Alex. It's only made matters worse for you." Her voice shook.

"You're wrong. The break had to come. Today was the right time to call it quits."

She clung to the chair back. "But earlier you told me it was very serious between you two."

"It was. However there's a big difference between serious, and doing something about it."

"Like what?"

"Like getting married."

"You don't want to marry her?"

"No."

"I thought she was going to help you run the restaurant."

"I thought so, too, but obviously things have changed."

Reese started clearing the table. At the doorway to the kitchen she paused. "How long have you known her?"

"As long as I've known you."

"If you didn't want to marry her, why have you stayed in the relationship?"

"We'd both made a commitment and didn't want to go back on it."

"A-are you devastated that it's over?" she stammered.

"Not at all. If you want to know the truth, I'm relieved. Which brings me to the question I've been wanting to ask you since you ran into my truck."

At the mention of the accident, her pulse rate picked up speed. "Just a minute while I put these plates in the dishwasher."

"I'll finish clearing."

The moment he got to his feet, she darted into the kitchen and started loading. With several trips he'd brought everything in from the dining room. He put the remaining food in the fridge. Soon she'd started the machine.

In the act of wiping off the counter, she turned her head toward him. "What did you want to ask me?"

He studied her features for a moment. "Since you have a week before your school starts, how would you like to spend it with me?"

She blinked. "You mean like help you pick out things for your restaurant?"

"We could do that. I could help you find someone to rent this condo. If you need a mover to transport some things to La Jolla, I'm your man. I've got a truck and am ready to go."

"Aren't you being a little impetuous? Your girl-friend must be shattered to think things are over between you."

"If she is, someone else is already waiting in the wings."

Reese stared at him. "Are you implying she was unfaithful to you?"

"No."

"Then maybe if you gave it a little more time—"

He shook his head. "It's finished, Reese. I'm ready to move on. You and I have both severed ties with the studio. Something tells me you are as much at a loose end as I am right now."

His comment was so patently true, there was no point in denying it.

She drew in a deep breath. "I'm going to be honest with you about something, Alex."

He'd propped himself against the counter. "What's that?"

"I don't think we should see each other again after tonight."

"Give me a reason."

She folded the dishcloth. "Because it's not a good idea."

"That's not specific enough."

"For one thing, you're just coming out of a relationship."

"Meaning what?"

"Meaning you're feeling vulnerable and...lonely."

"So I've turned to you because you're the most handy female around, is that what you think?" He smoothed a strand of her hair off her forehead. It caused her to tremble.

"It's true."

"What's so bad about two lonely, vulnerable people seeking each other out? We've been friends for a long time."

In a panic, she backed away from him. "That's the whole point. We're friends. Nothing more."

"Would you like it to be more?"

"Stop using Fabio's lines!"

"Is that what I'm doing?"

Heat suffused her face. "Except for the part about him feeling alone because he left the monastery, it's *his* script verbatim."

"Like I said. I related to Fabio in a lot of ways. The part was perfect for me. Sometimes it's hard to separate fantasy from reality."

She folded her arms. "Well, in our case you're going to have to. If Alex Kieris and Reese Bringhurst were meant to have had an off-screen love affair, it would have happened long before now.

"The fact that you waited until breaking up with your girlfriend before turning to me proves that what you felt for her was what you *should* feel if you're really in love.

"I don't want to be a woman you've decided to spend time with because you can't have the one you really wanted. A year's a long time to devote to one person, Alex. You can't tell me you didn't have hopes of marrying her when you first met her."

He cocked his head. "You're right. She changed my world."

"You see?" Reese cried. "That's what I'm talking about. Even if it didn't work out in the end, you felt that way about her when you first met."

"That's true."

"Thank you for being honest about that at least."

"I wouldn't be anything else with you."

"Then you understand where I'm coming from."

"I think I do. You're a lot like your aunt Lilian."

Reese jerked her head toward him. "Did she tell you about her husband?"

He nodded. "She also confided that after she'd been widowed, there were several men who'd been friends with her a long time before they proposed to her. Two of them were costars on the show like you and me. But she didn't say yes to any of them because the fire wasn't there from the start."

"One of these days I'm going to meet a man who's so on fire for me, nothing else matters and he can't live without me."

"You mean like my grandfather."

"Yes. He loved your grandmother so much, he lost the will to live after she died. My parents felt the same way about each other. So did Lilian and her husband. That's the kind of love I intend to have. When the right man comes along, I'll know it."

"So you have no interest in even keeping up a friendship with me?"

"For what purpose? We're no longer costars. I don't believe men and women can be friends. Either we're lovers, or we're nothing. If I want friendship I can call Leah or Cammy."

He rubbed his thumb across his lips thoughtfully. "I'm glad you made that clear. Once again it appears you and I are in agreement and hold to the same philosophy about men and women. I would never spend time with a woman I didn't desire.

"Furthermore, I couldn't costar with a woman I didn't find appealing. If Leah or Sally had been playing the part of Carly, I would have turned down the role of Fabio."

"As long as we're being honest, that works both ways, Alex. If you'd been unattractive to me, I would have told Phyllis I wanted out of my contract a year ago."

His gaze played over her face. "That's because neither of us is an actor at heart. We can't pretend something we don't feel."

"No." *I can't go on pretending I don't care around you.*

"Tell you what, I'm going to fix our dessert."

"Can I watch?" she asked brightly. Until he left the condo, she had to act as if she weren't dying from pain. "I promise not to give away any of your secret recipes."

"I wasn't worried. You can help me if you want."

"I'd love to."

"Bring me two dessert plates, and get the cream out of the fridge."

He was like a magician. One minute there was a bunch of isolated ingredients on the counter. In the next, he'd made a beautiful arrangement of figs, bananas, walnuts and peanuts.

After sprinkling them with cinnamon powder, he put a little brandy in the cream and poured it over the top.

"This dessert is a nice change from Filo pastries. Not as heavy." He pulled a fork from the drawer. "Here. See what you think."

Before she could stop him, he'd put a mouthful of the concoction to her lips. She had no choice but to open up and eat.

Incredible.

That was what it was. Incredible.

"You like it?"

She made a moaning sound.

"I take it that's a yes."

Reese nodded.

"Just a minute. Don't move. You've got cream on your mouth." He removed it with his index finger and tasted it. "It could use a little more brandy. What do you think?"

"I—I think it's perfec— Oh—there's my phone. Excuse me for a minute."

She turned to reach for the phone on the wall, but she was trembling so hard, she had to brace herself against the counter.

"Hello?"

"Hi. I thought I'd call and see if everything is okay? If it's not, maybe go to a movie or something."

"Leah—"

Alex moved around to her side so he could watch her while he ate the dessert he'd made.

"You sound funny. Are you all right?"

"Yes. Of course I am."

"Have you got company?"

"Yes."

"A man?"

"Yes."

"Let me guess. It wouldn't be Alex Kieris, would it?"

Heat filled her cheeks. "Why do you say that?"

"Because when you left the set, he raced after you

like a bat out of you know where. I'm just putting two and two together. It's okay. Obviously you can't talk right now. How about lunch tomorrow?''

"I'd like that. Arturo's at twelve-thirty?''

"Perfect. See you then you, lucky, lucky girl.''

"Bye.''

Alex took the receiver from her and put it on the hook. ''Did Leah want to do something with you tonight?''

"Yes.''

"Then why did you let my presence stop you?''

She averted her eyes. ''Because I'm not in the mood for a movie.''

"What *are* you in the mood for?''

He'd finished his dessert. She put hers in the fridge, and washed his plate. Anything to give her hands something to do.

"After the most fabulous meal of my life, I'm too full to do much of anything except lounge in the other room and watch a little TV before I go to bed.''

"That sounds good to me too. Shall we see what's showing on the cooking channel?''

She was amused by the suggestion, a smile broke the corners of her mouth. She headed for the living room and picked up the remote from the coffee table. ''Do you watch it often?''

"Sometimes when I can't sleep.''

Reese purposely sat down in a chair next to the

couch so they'd be separated. "If you want to stretch out, make yourself comfortable."

He eyed her intently. "You don't mind?"

"Of course not. After working so hard in my kitchen, you deserve a rest before you have to go home."

"Then I'll take you up on your offer."

CHAPTER NINE

TONIGHT the Japanese chefs were having some kind of contest. Though it was entertaining, Reese couldn't possibly concentrate. Her eyes kept straying to the sight of Alex's hard-muscled physique lying on his side. He'd propped his dark head on one of the cushions, the picture of virile male contentment.

They made desultory conversation and chuckled over some of the chefs' antics. At one point she made another comment, but Alex didn't answer.

He'd fallen asleep. The problem was, Reese had never been more wide awake.

Too restless, she went to the kitchen for the fabulous dessert he'd made. While she ate it, she switched channels to a movie classic made in the forties. One her aunt had particularly loved. But it didn't hold her interest. When it was over and the ten o'clock news started, she realized this situation couldn't go on any longer.

After turning off the TV, she got up from the chair and walked over to the couch.

"Alex?"

There was no answer.

"Alex?" She bent down and nudged him gently.

His eyes suddenly opened. "Reese?"

"Yes. You've been asleep for the last hour. It's getting late."

"You want me to leave?"

What a question. "I need to go to bed. If you're too tired to get up, you're welcome to stay on the couch tonight. I'll bring you a blanket and a pillow."

"I'd rather go to bed with you." He reached up and pulled her down so she half lay on top of him. His mouth closed over hers. "Umm. You taste of brandy and figs. Could anything be sweeter or more luscious?"

His hungry mouth sought hers until her own passion started to spiral out of control. Unlike their last kiss at the party, they didn't have an audience. He might just decide this could go on indefinitely. That was because he was missing his girlfriend. No way was Reese going to be a substitute!

"We're not being taped, Alex," she cried, wrenching her lips from his. "Wake up."

"I know the difference between fantasy and reality," he murmured. "For your information I'm very much awake and am looking forward to spending my wedding night with my new bride."

He kissed her mouth again as if his desire for her was insatiable.

"Enough's enough, Alex," she said crossly. "I

enjoyed this day with you very much. The food was divine. But now it's over and you need to go home.''

She eased herself away and stood up on rubber legs.

He stared at her through slightly glassy eyes. ''From here on out, my home is with you, wherever you are.''

''Be serious, please.''

''I've never been more serious in my life. You're my wife now.''

''Obviously you're in one of those dream-like trances and can't wake up. Lie back down while I get you some covers.''

''Only if you lie down with me.''

He started to reach for her again, but she backed further away from him. ''You're beginning to make me nervous.''

''I'm nervous, too. I've never been a husband before. It appears I have a very reluctant bride on my hands.''

''Stop it, Alex!''

''Stop what? If you don't believe you're Mrs Alex Kieris, then take a good look at our marriage license and certificate.'' He pulled two folded papers out of the pocket of his cargo pants and handed them to her.

In a daze, she opened them to see what he was talking about. The license looked like the prop she'd used during the taping. But when she saw the names, they read Reese Bringhurst and Alex Kieris.

The marriage certificate had their real names typed in, dated with today's date. A Pastor Martin Rippon had signed both papers. She also noted the names of two of the cast members who'd used their real names to be witnesses.

She lifted her head and stared at him. "What is all this about?"

He rose to his full, intimidating height. "We were married today by a real pastor, not an actor. The vows we took in front of our friends are sacred and binding."

Reese's body started to tremble. "I don't believe you," she whispered.

"That's fine. Pastor Rippon's number is in the phone directory. You're welcome to call him right now."

She swallowed hard. "What kind of strange joke is this?"

"It's no joke. During the taping, you put your own signature on these papers. That makes them legal."

"Alex? I don't understand anything. What's going on?"

"I'm the man you were talking about earlier, a man who's on fire for you. What else? If you don't want to be married to me, you'll have to hire an attorney. Should you decide you want to be my wife, you know where I live. Maybe this will help you make up your mind, *agape mou.*''

He caught her face between his hands and gave her a deep, searing kiss before leaving the condo.

Long after she heard the door click, she stood there shaken and confused.

Finally, when she could gather her wits, she dashed in her bedroom and reached for the phone.

Be home, Elaine. Please be home.

''Hirsh residence.''

''Oh, thank goodness it's you, Elaine!''

''Reese?'' She sounded surprised.

''D-did I waken you?''

''Heavens, no. I rarely get to bed before midnight.'' There was a slight hesitation. ''What are you doing calling me tonight of all nights?''

Reese sank down on the side of her bed, torturing the phone cord. ''What do you mean, tonight of all nights?''

''Leah phoned to tell me Alex was there. I thought of course everything had gone according to plan.''

She jumped to her feet, unable to sit still. ''What plan?''

''I take it Alex isn't there now,'' Elaine said in a quiet voice.

''No. He just left after telling me the craziest thing I've ever heard in my life.''

''What was that, darling?''

"He said we got married on the set today. *For real.*"

"It *was* for real."

"I mean legally."

"That's right. The man is madly in love with you."

No. He couldn't be... The blood started to pound in her ears.

"Darling? Are you still there?"

"Yes," her voice squeaked.

"The moment he found out you were leaving the show, he set everything up with Stan to rewrite the script so you could be married in front of all of us."

Her heart was pounding out of rhythm. "You're telling me the truth?"

"I would never lie to you, Reese. The whole leap year thing was Alex's idea. After waiting so long to claim you, he loved the idea that you would end up proposing to him."

Reese could still hear him saying, "I didn't know women in America did things like this."

It sounded exactly like something the real Alex would say.

"Phil was upset that he had to stay home so a bona fide pastor could come to officiate, but he understood the situation. He wasn't about to let anything stand in the way of true love."

"Phil did that for Alex?"

"Everyone helped. Brad's job was to distract you until Alex caught up to you in the parking lot."

"He accomplished his mission. I ran straight into Alex's truck."

"Brad came running back inside to tell us."

Reese's face went hot. "I was crying so hard I didn't look where I was going."

"It was the perfect ending to a perfect wedding ceremony, darling. The cast and crew, Phyllis, the producers, everyone was in on it, and they're so happy for you."

Unbelievable.

"Surely you caught on while you were eating. Alex planned that champagne brunch with all your favorite foods."

That was why there were meatballs and pasta?

"The roses were his idea. Honestly, Reese. It's the most romantic thing I ever heard of in my life! The way he looked at you today, those vows he said to you at the altar—they melted my heart. Why aren't you with him when I know how much you love him?"

Reese was so incredulous, she couldn't speak.

"For months that man has been in agony waiting for you to leave the show so you two could be married."

She shook her head. "If that's true, then I'm the

last person on the face of the earth to know it. Why didn't he ever say anything to me?''

''He said it every time he took Carly in his arms. Couldn't you feel it? When he kissed you at the altar, every woman on the set stopped breathing. Your lovely hat fell off and you didn't even notice because you were too enthralled with that gorgeous new husband of yours.''

''He warned me the hat might get in his way when it came time to kiss me.'' *The brides in Greece wear garlands.* That should have been a clue. ''But honestly, Elaine, I thought it was all play-acting from beginning to end.''

''No man is that great an actor, Reese. Or woman. The way you responded to him, everyone on the show knew how you two felt about each other. Your great love affair has been the only topic of conversation on the set for the last year!''

''All this time everyone's known how I've felt about him?''

''If you could see your eyes when you look at him… It's something you can't hide. What's so wonderful is that he can't see anyone else but you when he comes on the set. Like Phyllis said today, the love between you and Alex has been a beautiful thing to watch.''

''I still can't believe it. He told me he'd been in love with another woman all of last year.''

"He was. That woman was you! You were his secret girlfriend—until you became his wife today!"

Good heavens.

"If this has come as a complete surprise to you, blame it on Lilian. From what I understand, he made a promise to her a long time ago. I don't know the details. That's something private between the two of them. I'm sure he'll tell you when he's ready. You didn't fight with him tonight, did you?"

"No." Her voice wobbled. "I asked him what kind of strange joke he was playing. That's when he left."

"So he's still in agony…" Elaine's voice trailed.

At this point, Reese needed answers only one man could give her.

"Elaine? I've got to hang up."

"Call me when you get back from your honeymoon."

Honeymoon…

Should you decide you want to be my wife, you know where I live.

CHAPTER TEN

ALEX stepped out of the shower and hitched a towel around his hips to shave. It had been forty-five minutes since he'd left Reese's condo.

Obviously it was going to take more than one kiss from Prince Charming to bring Sleeping Beauty awake. He would give her another twenty minutes, then he wou—

The ringing of his cell phone was the most satisfying sound he'd heard in a long time.

He picked it up and checked the caller ID. R Bringhurst. After clicking on he said, "Reese?"

"Hi." She sounded breathless.

"Hello yourself."

"We...need to talk."

"I couldn't agree more."

"Are you at your apartment?"

"Yes. Where are you?"

"In the foyer of your building."

Alex sucked in his breath. "I'll let you in."

After ringing off, he pulled his robe from the hook of the bathroom door and shrugged into it. Then he walked down the hall to the living room. This day had been a long time in coming, but, as his grandfather had taught him, anything worth having meant you had to work hard for it. "Patience, my boy."

For a full year, patience had been his mantra. Now if the gods were kind, it would pay off.

The knock on the door coincided with the thundering of his heart. He opened it immediately and there she stood, his raven-haired, blue-eyed beauty. Her fragrance filled the aperture.

She'd changed into a periwinkle-blue top with a kelly-green skirt. The dynamite combination brought out her coloring and the voluptuous mold of her body.

Her gaze studied him as if she were seeing him for the first time. In a way he supposed she was. Always before she'd thought of him as her costar.

Tonight she was finally seeing him as Alex Kieris, the flesh and blood man who had shown up on the set every weekday morning as she had. One moreover who wanted her with every fiber of his being.

"Come in."

He stepped back, giving her the space she needed. Up to this point he'd done all the running. The rest was up to her now. In the next little while he would discover whether she couldn't live without him either. If he'd misread the signs...

After shutting the door, he followed her alluring figure into his living room. His furnished apartment was half the size of Lilian's. The man who'd lived here before had decorated it in a neo-contemporary style, but Alex found it sterile and lacking a woman's touch. He couldn't wait to vacate.

She swung around. It caused her hair to swish against her cheeks. "I called Elaine."

Her admission came as no surprise. Since Lilian's death, Reese had drawn closer to the other actress.

"You needed verification that we were legally married today?"

He watched the flush that broke out on her face. "She told me it was a real pastor who performed the ceremony."

Alex cocked his head. "We're married in the eyes of the law, but only if you want to be. If not, then I'll give you an uncontested divorce. My intention wasn't to cause you grief.

"The last thing I would want to do is force you to fight me in court because you didn't know you were taking vows in front of a certified clergyman."

She rubbed her arms, a gesture she only did when she was nervous or unsure of something. "Elaine found the whole thing very romantic."

"But you didn't."

"I'm still in shock, Alex. What possessed you?"

"I'm surprised you would even ask that question. Surely it's obvious I'm in love with you."

In the still of the room, he could hear her shallow breathing. "Since when?"

"Since the day we met on the set and read our lines to get a feel for each other. It was love at first sight for Carly on Fabio's part. I don't know about you, but I'm afraid the same thing happened to me."

The woman trembling in front of him remained silent. It could be an answer of sorts. He had yet to find out.

"If there's any truth to what *Soap Craze* says about us being the magic couple, I owe it all to the fact that Reese Bringhurst sprang into my world full blown and I haven't been the same since. Before I left Greece, if someone had told me an American television actress would be the woman who set me on fire, I would have scoffed at the mere idea."

She shook her head. "You have a very strange way of showing your interest."

"There was a reason for that."

Reese stared at him with a baffled look in her eyes. "I'd like to hear it."

"Would you like to sit down first?"

"No."

He folded his arms. "After two weeks of working together, I approached your aunt about asking you out."

"Why would you do that?" she demanded. "I'm my own person."

"Probably because in Greece it's the way to do things in polite society. If you were a Greek girl, my

grandparents would have talked to your aunt first, or
your parents, of course. It may be old-fashioned, but
I was raised in a traditional home and it's the nice
way to do things."

"I agree," she admitted in a quiet voice.

"It didn't surprise me when she told me she would
rather I left you alone."

Reese's head flew back. "She didn't!"

"Oh, yes, she did. But I wasn't alarmed. It happens that way in Greece, too. You have to woo the
parents, or, in your case, your aunt. So I began asking her to give me acting tips."

The beautiful blue eyes fastened on him grew
huge. "That's the real reason why you came over to
the condo all those times?"

The corner of his mouth lifted. "It was my main
agenda. Not that I didn't need all the acting help I
could get. But *you* were the reason, and your aunt
knew it."

A gasp came out of Reese.

"Lilian was a wonderful woman, but very shrewd.
She knew exactly what she was doing. It was a game
we played. The longer we played it, the more I realized I was gaining ground with her and getting
closer to my goal of taking you out."

There was a long pause before she said, "My aunt
liked you very much."

"The feeling was mutual, believe me. Before she

died, she told me she approved of me, but she made me promise her something.''

Reese clasped her hands. "I'm almost afraid to hear it.''

"In essence she told me she'd seen everything from her vantage point as an actress, and, on the whole, she worried that if both people in a marriage were actors, it was hard to make it work.

"I told her I had other aspirations in life and would only continue to play the part of Fabio until I'd made enough money to get me started in business. That reassured her. However, she was still concerned about you.''

"But she knew I wouldn't stay with acting!"

He eyed Reese soberly. "She was dying, Reese. She feared her death might be too hard on you after losing your parents. She worried you would stay with acting because it was something you knew, something comfortable. Though I didn't like to admit it, her fears made a great deal of sense to me.''

Again there was quiet before Reese asked in a tremulous voice, "What did she make you promise?''

"That I would do nothing about my feelings for you unless you left acting of your own free will. She wanted you to carve out your own destiny, whatever it was, without any influence from me.''

A hand went to her throat. "I can't believe what

I'm hearing.'' Her eyes impaled him like lasers. "So if I hadn't left the show—"

He shrugged his shoulders with unknowing elegance. "Then I wouldn't have left either. It was my only way to have my cake without eating it, too. Tell me something, Reese. What made you decide not to renew your contract?"

She half turned away from him. "After Aunt Lilian died, my heart wasn't in the show. She made it fun and exciting. It was something we could do together that brought us so close, but without her I realized it wasn't for me. So I held on until I could leave without causing more upheaval than necessary."

His jaw hardened. "Obviously you didn't live for those moments when we could be on the set together. You weren't like me, eager for the work day to start so I could hold you in my arms. Because of you I had a reason to get up in the mornings. The worst part of the day was having to get in my car and drive away from you. The weekends were a living hell for me."

Reese swung back toward him. "They were for me, too!" she cried, hot faced. "You want to talk about pain? I knew I was in love with you after the first day of being with you on the set. Nothing like that had ever happened to me before.

"I told Aunt Lilian how I felt. She warned me it

happened to every actress who was given a role opposite an attractive costar. A kind of in love with love thing. It would pass.

"But it didn't pass, Alex. My love for you deepened. Talk about living for every day. Once you started coming to the condo, I prayed you would stay and talk to me, be with me. Alone. It never happened."

"Now you know why," he said in his deep voice.

"Because you never sought me out, I knew I had to leave the show. I couldn't take loving you like I did, knowing I meant nothing to you. In fact I'd just decided to break my contract when Aunt Lilian suddenly took ill and died. After her funeral I realized I needed to stay on until renewal time came up. It wouldn't have been fair to walk out."

"I agree."

"But these last few months…" She shook her head. "They've been a literal hell for me, too."

Lines marred his handsome features. "When I heard you were leaving the show, I asked Stan to write some new lines for you so we could be married surrounded by all our friends. I wasn't about to let you get away from me. Not after waiting an entire year for you."

Her eyes filled with tears, making them shine like deep blue pools. "Elaine said she thought it was the most romantic thing she'd ever heard of in her whole life.''

His heart skittered all over the place. ''What I'm concerned about is what *you* think. No one else matters. Do you want to stay married to me?''

She started moving toward him with a mysterious smile on her lips. He'd never seen that exact look on her face before.

''For how long?'' she demanded.

''Into the afterlife and beyond.''

''Alex—''

He felt her arms go around his neck, felt her luscious mouth search avidly for his. Their legs tangled. Exquisite pleasure-pain shot through his body that this woman was really his at last.

''I love you, Reese. I'll live wherever you want to live, support you in any way you wish. Give you all the children you want. You're my life.''

''You're mine.'' She moaned the words before they began kissing each other into oblivion.

For twelve months they'd given each other kisses and embraces day in and day out on the set. But it was nothing like this total communion of mind, soul and body.

Without conscious thought he carried her into the bedroom and followed her down on the mattress. The warmth, the beauty of her took his breath.

Before any more time passed, he reached in his robe pocket and slid a ring on her finger.

Her eyes shone like pulsating stars as she lifted her hand to look at it.

"It was my grandmother's. My grandfather gave it to me with the charge that I find a woman to bring home." He kissed her long and hard.

When he lifted his mouth he whispered, "How would you like to get on a plane to Greece tomorrow? I want to take you home for a week."

"There's nothing I'd love more," she whispered back against his lips. "You don't know how many times I've dreamed of traveling there with you. The pictures you painted. Your memories. I've forgotten nothing you've ever told me."

His response was to crush her in his arms. "I'd give anything if they could have met you."

She covered his face with kisses. "I know how you feel. My parents would have adored you. But right now I'm just thankful Aunt Lilian was an actress. Otherwise I would never have met you."

He groaned as he followed the sensuous curve of her lips with his finger. "Don't think about it. I can't comprehend life without you now."

"Nor I, darling," she cried, smothering him with kisses. "I'm so thankful we're already married. It was perfect. Trust my amazing husband to plan out such a fantastic wedding. There was a very special feeling on the set today. It felt like we really were getting married. The pastor was so solemn. Now I know why.''

''I had to twist his arm.''

She smiled at him. It was a woman's smile, full of mystery and the knowledge of the ages. ''Obviously not too hard. Aunt Lilian would have loved every second of it. In fact I have to believe she was looking on.''

''I'm sure of it,'' he agreed as he buried his face in her glistening black hair.

Reese had always been a giver, but her response to him now made him thank God he'd been born a man.

His grandfather had been right. ''All things come to him who waits.''

His wife was all things to him. The long wait was over.

The Billionaire's Blind Date

by

Jessica Hart

CHAPTER ONE

'COME *on,* Mum…we're going to be late!'

'I'm coming, I'm coming…' Nell scrabbled feverishly through her bag, checking to see that she had everything she needed. She had been so forgetful recently, and it had all been such a rush this morning that if she wasn't careful she would have to go to the meeting this afternoon without any make-up on, and that was the last thing her confidence needed right now.

Ah, there was her comb. At least she'd be able to do something about her hair when she got to the office. Now, where was her cosmetic bag? Had she left it in the bathroom after all?

'Mu-um…' sighed Clara.

'I've got to get myself a decent bag,' Nell muttered to herself. 'I can't find anything in here… Oh!'

She broke off in consternation as the bag slipped from her grasp and landed with a splat on the doorstep, spilling keys and pens and tissues and lipsticks and the odd coins that always seemed to be lurking in its depths onto the path.

Clara bent to help pick them all up. 'Mum, what is the matter with you at the moment?' she asked, ten going on forty-five. Anyone would think that she was the mother, and Nell her awkward child. 'You're not usually this muddled.'

'I'm not that bad, am I?' asked Nell absently, shoving everything back into her bag. There was that compact mirror she had been looking for everywhere.

'You lost your keys the other day.'

'That could happen to anybody,' Nell protested as they headed down the pavement at last.

'And when you came to pick me up at Charlotte's the other day, you went to the wrong house although you've been there millions of times.'

'The doors were the same colour.' Nell tried to defend herself, but Clara hadn't finished.

'*And* you forgot that Sophie was coming last Saturday.'

'I'm sorry,' she apologised before Clara could come up with any more examples of what a bad mother she was.

Her daughter was right, though. She wasn't usually this vague. 'There just seems to be a lot to think about at the moment,' she tried to explain. 'I'm not really settled into my new job yet.'

It was true that moving jobs had been more stressful than she had imagined, but that wasn't the real reason she was so unsettled at the moment, was it? Deep down, Nell knew that what had really thrown her was being reminded about P.J. after all these years.

It was all Thea's fault. Nothing had been the same since she had got in touch with P.J.'s sister on some internet site. There was no need for people to go contacting old school friends, Nell thought crossly as she waited with Clara at the lights. It just made you remember all the things you had tried so hard to forget for the last sixteen years.

P.J. was part of her past. He had gone to the States, she had stayed here. They had both moved on. She hadn't thought of him for years. Well, not very often, anyway.

Sometimes she didn't think of him for weeks at a time.

But now he was back.

'Guess who's back in town?' Thea had said, bursting with news, and Nell had been taken aback at the way her heart had clenched at the sound of his name.

'Janey says he's been incredibly successful,' Thea told her. 'Something to do with electronics. We should have known. He always was a bit geeky, wasn't he?'

'He wasn't *geeky*,' Nell objected, annoyed. 'People just used to say that because he was clever.' She defended him, just as she had all those years ago.

'I wish we'd known just how clever,' said Thea. 'It's a pity you didn't stick with him, Nell.

According to Janey, he's practically a billionaire now.'

P.J., a billionaire? Nell couldn't get her head round the idea. In her mind he was still the P.J. she had loved, a bit gawky, very young and very lanky, with that thin, intelligent face and the unexpected smile. The thought of him as a thrusting tycoon was vaguely unsettling. It didn't fit with her image of him at all. She had always pictured him as a scientist rather than a businessman.

But then, she had never imagined that she would become a struggling single mother, either.

'Janey says that he's not with anyone at the moment,' Thea went on, oh so casually. 'You should get in touch.'

'That would look subtle, wouldn't it?' Nell said sarcastically. 'Hi, P.J., I haven't been in touch for sixteen years, but I've just heard that you're incredibly rich, so I wondered if you fancied meeting up?'

'You could say that you'd just heard that he was back in London,' Thea suggested. 'You wouldn't need to mention the rich bit.'

'No, and of course P.J. would never guess that I knew that he had all that money, him being so stupid and all!'

Thea sighed. 'It wouldn't be like that with P.J. It's not as if you'd be a remote acquaintance coming out of the woodwork. You were engaged once, after all.'

'That just makes it worse!' said Nell, recoiling from the very idea.

Her sister looked at her speculatively. 'It's a shame. You two were always good together. Still, maybe Janey will tell him that you're divorced, and he'll get in touch with you.'

Nell doubted it very much. P.J. had been nicer about Simon than she deserved, but no one liked being rejected, and presumably now that he had made his millions he had no trouble finding a girl-friend.

Good luck to him, she thought. He deserved his success, but his life and hers were worlds apart now. It was nice to know that he was well and successful, but there was no point in thinking about him any-more, she decided. She would put him out of her mind completely.

Absorbed in her thoughts, Nell didn't realise that the green man was beeping at the lights until Clara dug her in the ribs. 'Wake up, Mum!'

Nell started, and let her daughter bustle her across the road. Really, she must pull herself together. She was supposed to be looking after Clara, not the other way round.

Clara was eyeing her thoughtfully as they turned down a side street. They had walked to school so many times now that they followed the route automatically. Nell was sure that she could do it in her sleep.

'Are you nervous about your date tonight?'

Nell sighed. She had been so busy thinking about P.J. that she had forgotten all about her blind date. 'I wish I'd never agreed to go,' she grumbled. 'I don't know why I let you and Thea bully me into these things!'

'It would be nice for you to have a boyfriend.'

'Clara, I'm thirty-seven! I'm too old for boy-friends.'

'You're not,' said Clara loyally. 'You're not much older than Thea, and she's just got married.'

That was unarguable. Her sister had been thirty-four when she'd met Rhys, and ready to give up on ever finding the right man for her.

'Sometimes you just have to wait for fate to put the right person your way,' said Nell, thinking that fate had done the best it could twenty-one years ago. It wasn't fate's fault that she had been too young and too silly to recognise the right person for her.

Not for the first time she wished that her daughter weren't quite so interested in adult relationships. It was hard to explain some of the complexities to a ten-year-old, but from a very small child Clara had been fascinated by people and why they behaved the way they did.

She had been hardly more than a baby when her

father had left, and took having divorced parents in her stride, but Nell really wanted to give her the example of a loving relationship, so that she could see that it was possible for adults to live together and be happy. That was the main reason why she had let Thea talk her into making an effort to meet men again, but so far her blind dates had not been a success, to say the least.

There had been Neil, who had, according to his own confession, thrived on a double life, Nick with the appalling table manners, Paul who had talked about himself all evening, and Lawrie, the latest disaster, who had spent the entire date describing his red sports car, apparently believing that it would be enough to make any woman fall at his feet. Thea had assured her that tonight would be different, but Nell wasn't convinced.

'I never really had boyfriends even when I was young,' she told Clara now. 'I married your father when I was twenty-one and before that there was only—'

She stopped. Somehow she had ended up back at P.J. It was uncanny the way all her thoughts seemed to lead back to him, in spite of the fact that she had decided so utterly and definitely that she absolutely was not, no way, going to think about him anymore.

'Oh, look at that puppy,' she said quickly as a scatty Labrador with huge paws and an eager expression gambolled along the pavement towards them, towing its owner in its wake.

'Ah-h-h…cute…' Clara cooed and let the puppy slurp at her fingers, quivering in ecstasy at all the attention, but the moment it had been dragged on its way she fixed a beady look on her mother, who had just begun to hope that she had been successfully distracted.

'Only who?'

'Only who what?' Nell prevaricated. Clara was a darling, but sometimes she could be just a little too perceptive and persistent for comfort.

'You said you'd only had one boyfriend before Dad,' Clara reminded her.

'Oh, yes, that's right,' she said as carelessly as she could. 'Just a boy I knew at school.'

'What was his name?'

'P.J.,' she admitted reluctantly.

'What, like in pyjamas?' said Clara, unimpressed.

'Yes.' Nell was conscious of a slightly defensive tinge to her voice. She had thought of P.J. as P.J. for so long that the initials no longer seemed odd to her.

'Why was he called that?'

'His real name was Peter John Smith,' she explained. 'He used to say that using his initials was the only way he could make himself sound interesting.'

Clara looked puzzled. 'Was he really boring, then?'

'No, he wasn't boring.' Nell couldn't help smiling as she shook her head. P.J. had been a lot of things, but never boring.

His image rose before her, long and lanky, with that humorous, beaky face and eyes that were blue and very alert. P.J. would never have made it as a model, that was for sure, but he had been kind and clever and funny, and everybody had liked him.

'He was...nice,' she told Clara. 'He was very easy to talk to. We had good fun together.'

The other girls had mooned over the better-looking boys in the year above, but P.J. had been much more fun. And it wasn't as if he had been exactly ugly. He had had a stubborn jaw and laughing eyes and an unexpected, slightly lopsided smile that would suddenly make him seem much more attractive than he actually was.

Without meaning to, Nell sighed. If only she couldn't remember him quite so vividly.

'What happened?' asked Clara. 'Did you have a fight?'

'No.' Nell hesitated. It was hard to explain what had happened when she couldn't even explain it to herself now. 'We'd been going out since I was sixteen and he was seventeen. We'd been away to different universities and…well, I suppose we'd started to grow apart.'

They had been so young, too, she thought. She had been just twenty-one, and desperate to get married and have a family, while P.J. had wanted to wait. It had begun to seem as if they were just staying together out of force of habit.

'And then I met your father…'

She trailed off, remembering how glamorous Simon had seemed at the time. A few years older, he had had all the swagger and sophistication that P.J. had lacked, while she had been too naive to realise that kindness was worth so much more than sophistication, or that good looks and self-confidence counted for little compared to someone you could rely on absolutely.

Like P.J., in fact.

'Your dad swept me off my feet,' she told Clara.

And he had. Simon had promised her everything she had ever wanted…and then spent the next eight years crushing her bright hopes one by one.

Clara swung her bag thoughtfully. 'Do you wish you'd married P.J. instead of Dad?'

'Of course not.' Nell stopped dead in the middle of the pavement, and gave her daughter a hug. 'If I hadn't married Dad, I wouldn't have you. How could I possibly be sorry about that?'

She couldn't let Clara think that she ever regretted

the choice she had made. Her marriage to Simon hadn't been a success, but they had had Clara, and she was worth everything.

'It's all a long time ago,' she said. 'I shouldn't think P.J. even remembers me now.'

Somehow it was a depressing thought. Nell made herself push it away and squared her shoulders mentally. It was ridiculous the way she had let thoughts of P.J. unsettle her recently. She had been fine when she'd thought he was in the States, but, really, what difference did it make if he was back in London or not? It wasn't as if she mixed with a wealthy crowd, let alone with billionaires, so she was hardly any more likely to bump into him.

So she might as well put him out of her mind. Again.

The trouble was, her life just wasn't big enough at the moment. That was the only reason P.J. suddenly seemed so important. Thea was right, she needed to get out there and meet someone new, or failing that take up a hobby. Basket-weaving, or train spotting or something… There must be some interest out there for her. There was no use hankering after what-might-have-beens.

They crossed the last road and turned into the busy street where Clara went to school. There was still a cluster of parents and children at the gate, so they weren't too late, thank goodness.

Nell glanced at her watch. She might get the earlier tube after all. It would give her time to pick up her suit from the dry-cleaner's and get changed and made up before she had to face her boss. Eve was always banging on about the importance of professional image, and she wouldn't think much of Nell in old track-suit pants, faded sweatshirt and trainers, with a naked face and hair all over the place. This *would* be the morning she had slept through her alarm.

This was better, thinking about work instead of about P.J., Nell congratulated herself. A motorised wheelchair was buzzing busily towards her along the pavement, and, her mind still on not thinking about P.J., Nell stepped automatically out of the way.

Only to misjudge the kerb and stumble into the road, right into the path of a passing car. There was a glancing blow on her arm and a squeal of brakes, but all Nell could see was her daughter's white, horrified face.

'Mum!'

The car practically stood on its nose and Nell reeled away from it, feeling sick with shock at the narrowness of her escape.

'It's OK… I'm OK…' she said as Clara flung herself at her, and she hugged the little girl tightly to reassure her.

A car door slammed and quick footsteps came towards them. 'Are you all right?' a male voice asked, sharp with concern. 'I didn't hit you, did I?'

Clara pulled herself away from her mother and turned on him furiously, venting her fright in shrill anger. 'You should be more careful! You could have knocked her over!'

Nell braced herself for a mouthful of abuse. A lot of drivers would react aggressively in a near accident, and it had been her fault, after all. Fortunately, this man seemed to take in Clara's distress and was calm enough not to take out his own fright on a little girl.

'Yes, I could,' he said to Clara, sounding almost as shaken as Nell felt. 'I'm really sorry. I wasn't expecting your mother to step out into the road like that, but that's no excuse, I know.' He turned to Nell, who was rubbing her arm. '*Did* I hurt you?'

'No, I…I…' She trailed off in disbelief.

He looked just like P.J.

Older, tougher, more solid, but yes, exactly like P.J. He looked like him, he even sounded like him, but clearly he couldn't *be* P.J. That would be too weird. Coincidences like that just didn't happen. It was just that she'd been thinking about him.

Nell shook her head slightly to clear it. Perhaps she had been knocked over after all and was having some bizarre out-of-body experience? But he was staring back at her and the blue eyes that were uncannily like P.J.'s widened with incredulous recognition.

'Nell?' he asked in a tentative voice.

'Hello, P.J.,' she said weakly.

CHAPTER TWO

P.J. STARED at her, trying to take in the fact that it was actually Nell. Janey had been doing her best to drop her name into every conversation they had had since he had come back to London, and he had been disturbed by how vividly he could remember her.

Nell was divorced now, Janey had said pointedly. Why didn't he give her a ring?

P.J. had been hesitant. It wasn't as if he had been pining for Nell all these years, but the memory of the look in her eyes as she gave him back his ring still had a surprising power to hurt. The raw pain had faded to the merest twinge now, of course, but he didn't want to go through that again.

Still, the idea of seeing her again had both intrigued and unnerved him, and he had been thinking about it more than he should have done. That was probably why he hadn't been concentrating as well as he should, until she had stumbled out into the road in front of him.

And now here she was, his first love, his lost love, standing in a busy London street, while the passers-by, hopeful at first of some gory incident, had quickly lost interest and were now surging impersonally past them once more, oblivious to the fact that his world had just turned upside down.

Nell.

She was older, of course, and thinner, he thought, and she had lost the golden bloom that had so entranced him as an adolescent. There was a wariness and a weariness in the lines around her eyes that hadn't been there before, but it was unmistakably Nell. She had the same wide grey gaze, the same sweetness in her expression, the same air of deceptive fragility.

'Nell…' He ran his hands through his hair a little helplessly. 'This is bizarre… I always hoped I'd bump into you again one day, but not literally! Are you sure I didn't hurt you?'

Nell looked down at herself as if to check, becoming aware for the first time of a dull throb in her ankle. She must have wrenched her bad foot as she'd tried to right herself.

'I think my arm just caught your wing mirror,' she said, feeling more shaken by coming face to face with P.J. than by the accident.

It was disconcerting to find him so familiar, and yet so changed. She had been right in thinking that he would grow into his looks, but she hadn't expected him to turn into quite such an attractive man. Where the young P.J.'s face had been thin and beaky, now it was strong and angular. His neck and

shoulders had broadened as he had thickened out
with age, and he had acquired a solidity and a presence that was almost unnerving, but the crooked
smile and the blue dancing eyes were just the same.

'Let me see.' Unaware of the train of her thoughts,
P.J. took her arm and felt it gently. 'It doesn't seem
to be broken, anyway.'

Nell was unaccountably flustered by the feel of
his hands, and miserably conscious of her bare face,
and scruffy clothes. If fate had wanted her to meet
P.J. again against all the odds, it could at least have
waited until she was looking more presentable.

'Honestly, it's fine,' she said almost sharply, and
pulled out of his grasp, only to wince as she stepped
back onto her twisted ankle.

'You're limping,' said Clara protectively. 'It's
your bad foot, too.' She cast P.J. an accusing glance.
'She broke it last year.'

'And now I've made it worse. I'm sorry...' P.J.
looked enquiring, and Nell had no choice but to
make the introduction.

'This is my daughter, Clara,' she said. 'Clara, this
is—'

'P.J.,' supplied Clara before she could finish. She
looked assessingly at P.J. as she held out her hand,
and quite suddenly she smiled, as if he had passed
some rigorous test. 'Hello,' she said.

'Hello, Clara.' P.J. shook her hand gravely, but

his eyes twinkled. 'It's nice to meet you, but I'm really sorry I had to nearly knock your mother over to do it. We're old friends.'

'I know,' said Clara. 'Mum was just telling me about you. She said you were nice.'

P.J. glanced at Nell, his eyes warm with amusement, and to her chagrin Nell could feel herself blushing.

'We were just talking old boyfriends and how I met you at school,' she said as casually as she could. She didn't want him thinking that she spent her days boring on about him. 'Clara doesn't believe that I was ever that young, of course!'

'Oh, she was,' P.J. told Clara with a grin. 'She was the prettiest girl in the school. I couldn't believe how lucky I was, I can tell you!'

Clara beamed approvingly at him, and Nell's heart sank. Her daughter was an incurable matchmaker, especially since she had taken such a successful hand in her aunt Thea's affairs the previous year, and now she had evidently decided that it was time that her mother had some romance in her life, too. It was clear that she was eyeing P.J. up as prospective candidate.

Heaven only knew what she would say if she discovered that P.J. was not only eligible but rich enough to solve all her mother's financial problems without even noticing a blip in his bank account! She had to nip her plans in the bud right now, Nell decided.

'Clara, we're going to be really late,' she said quickly. 'We'd better get on.' She turned to P.J. 'Nice to see you again, P.J.,' she said with a bright smile and what she hoped was an air of finality.

If P.J. heard it, he ignored it. 'Let me give you a lift,' he said.

'There's no need,' Nell said firmly, and pointed to the school gates. 'We're just going along here.'

'What about your ankle, Mum?' Clara put in. 'You won't be able to walk on it. How are you going to get to work?'

'I'll be fine when I get to the tube.'

'Where do you work?' asked P.J.

'In the city,' said Clara, disregarding Nell's attempt at a quelling look. 'It takes ages to get there,' she added, blatantly fishing.

P.J. didn't disappoint her. 'Oh, well, that's easy, then,' he said. 'I'm going that way myself. I just have to drop off the kids first.'

Kids?

Jolted out of her annoyance at the way the two of them were calmly organising her life for her, Nell turned belatedly to where a car with sleek, expensive lines was pulled up, half on, half off the pavement. Three small, curious faces were staring through the back window at them.

Three? And this was the man who hadn't been ready for children at all! An extraordinary mixture of emotions—none of them explicable—churned around in Nell's chest. Surprise, regret, disappointment, and worst of all something that felt suspiciously like jealousy.

She didn't know why she was so taken aback. Why shouldn't P.J. have married and had a family just as she had? What had she expected? That he would have spent the last sixteen years pining for her?

Janey had told Thea that he was single at the moment, and somehow it had never occurred to Nell that he might be divorced, like her. She had always thought of P.J. as someone who would make a commitment and stick by it, no matter what.

Of course, Thea might have misunderstood. Why not accept the more obvious explanation? Nell asked herself. That P.J. was happily married with three gorgeous children, and a phenomenally successful career, while she was single, with one gorgeous child, and her career was best not thought about too much.

'It won't take long,' P.J. was saying. 'Their school is just round the corner.'

Nell knew the one. It was an extortionately expensive private school, the kind of place she would never have been able to send Clara, even if she and Simon were still married. Not that expense would be an issue for P.J. now. You only had to look at that car and the immaculately tailored suit he was wearing to know that he could afford whatever he wanted.

He had a very different life from her now, that was for sure. Not that it made any difference to her, Nell reminded herself. There was no reason for her to feel prickly and defensive the way she suddenly *was* feeling for some reason.

'Really, there's no need for you to give me a lift,' she said shortly, and saw Clara looking puzzled at her tone. 'I'm quite capable of walking, and anyway, the tube is much quicker than sitting in traffic. Thank you for the offer, but we really should go. Come along, Clara.'

Sadly, her attempt at a dignified exit was ruined by the way her ankle buckled the moment she tried to take a step.

'Mum, you can't walk,' cried Clara, obviously exasperated by her mother's stubbornness. 'Don't be silly!'

'Clara's right,' said P.J., and gave Nell a smile that made her heart do an alarming somersault. 'You always used to be so sensible, Nell. Don't tell me you've changed that much!'

'You have,' she said without thinking.

'I'm sixteen years older and wearing a suit,' he acknowledged, 'but otherwise I'm just the same. I'm not suggesting you get into a car with a stranger. We used to be friends.'

And lovers…

The unspoken words hung in the air, and for Nell it was like a series of pictures flicking through her mind. P.J. reaching confidently for her hand, smiling as he drew her towards him. Lying by the river in the long, sweet grass, drowsy with sunshine, feeling the tickle of a feather on her nose, opening her eyes to see him leaning above her with that wicked grin. P.J. turning up at her door, half hidden behind a huge bunch of roses, when she passed her finals; holding her as she wept and wept for a lost dog.

'Come on, Nell,' he said with a smile that told her he remembered just as much as she did. 'Get in the car and stop being silly like Clara says!'

Clara giggled and hugged Nell, evidently taking it for granted that the matter was now decided. 'Bye, Mum. See you tonight.' She turned brightly to her new ally. 'Bye, P.J. Don't let Mum do anything she shouldn't!'

'Goodbye, Clara.' He grinned. 'Don't worry, I'll look after her.'

Nell shook her head ruefully as her daughter ran off, school bag bumping against her back. 'That girl…!'

'She's great,' said P.J. 'I like children with personality.'

'She's got that all right,' said Nell with feeling.

'Well, she's issued her instructions, and I wouldn't want to be in your shoes if she finds out that you haven't done as you were told!' He held open the passenger door. 'Come on, in you get.'

It would be ridiculous to refuse now, and she could hardly run off with her ankle like this. With the distinct feeling that she was being managed, and not at all sure that she liked it, Nell limped over to the car and got in. Turning with a little difficulty, she smiled a hello at the children in the back.

'Jake, Emily and Flora,' said P.J., pointing affectionately at each one. 'Kids, this lady I almost knocked over is an old friend of mine, Nell Martindale.'

It was odd hearing her maiden name again. 'Nell Shea now,' she reminded him.

'Of course. Sorry.'

P.J. switched on the engine abruptly. He had forgotten Simon Shea there for a moment. Of course Nell had taken his name. She had been besotted with him. Stupid to think she would have changed it back.

'We're divorced, but I kept Shea so that I'd have the same surname as Clara,' she said, almost as if she could read his mind.

'Oh. Sure.'

P.J. felt a bit better for some reason. He checked the mirror and pulled out into the heavy traffic as

Nell engaged the children in conversation, discovering that they were nine, seven, and five and a quarter respectively, that they didn't mind school but that they all hated Mrs Tarbuck, who shouted at them if they were naughty.

Nell had always been good with children, he remembered, and had longed to have a baby of her own. He was the one who had resisted the idea, thinking that they were too young and that there would be plenty of time to start a family. More fool him, he thought bitterly. While he had still been hesitating, Simon Shea had swept Nell off her feet with his easy promises.

P.J. was a quick learner. After that, he had seized every opportunity that had come his way. It had led to astonishing success and wealth beyond anything he had ever been able to imagine, but somehow none of it had ever quite compensated for the bitterness of that first hard lesson.

In the back seat, the children were still chatting happily to Nell about the contents of their lunch boxes.

'It sounds yummy,' said Nell, thinking what engaging children they were. They didn't look exactly like P.J., but there was a definite family resemblance and Jake, the boy, had the same alert blue eyes. Would their children have looked like this if they had married? she wondered a little wistfully.

'But I don't like banana,' little Flora was grumbling, sticking out her lower lip. 'Mummy *always* makes me have one. She says I have to have a bit of fruit, but I don't see why I should.'

'I'm afraid I make Clara have fruit every day, too,' Nell confessed to Flora's disgust. She might not like the idea of P.J. having a wife, but on some things mothers had to stick together.

'Here we are.' P.J. pulled up outside the school and opened his door to get out. 'Out you get.'

The three children scrambled out of the back seat and he stooped, giving the girls a kiss and Jake an affectionate tweak on the nose, and then they were gone, running into school with their friends.

'They've forgotten us already,' he said wryly to Nell as he got back into the car, and she nodded, grasping at the chance to fill up this first moment when they were alone with polite chit-chat.

'Clara's like that. The moment she meets up with her friends, she's completely absorbed in their own world. I'm sure she never gives me a thought when she's with them.'

P.J. sent her a sidelong glance. 'You should be pleased that she's not clinging to you. You want your child to grow up well balanced and independent, don't you?'

'Of course, but sometimes it's a little hard when

you spend your whole life thinking about them and you realise it's all one way.'

'That's your job as a parent, isn't it?' he said with a lopsided smile. 'And Clara's the kind of child who'll go far. She's got charm in spades.'

'When she wants to use it,' said Nell in a dry voice. 'She's like her father that way,' she added without thinking.

'Ah, yes, Simon,' said P.J. evenly. 'How is he?'

'He's well. He's got a new wife and a new family now, though, and I don't see much of him.'

'Janey told me that you were divorced,' he said. 'I'm sorry. It must have been hard for you. I know how much you loved him.'

Had she loved Simon, or had she just been carried away by an illusion? Nell wondered. It was hard to remember now.

'You were right,' she said abruptly.

'*I* was right?' P.J. glanced at her in surprise. 'What about?'

'You said that Simon didn't really know me, so he couldn't really love me. You said I didn't really know him, so I couldn't trust him. You said he'd break my heart and leave me…and he did.' Nell's smile was twisted. 'I think you're fully entitled to say "I told you so!"'

'Nell…' P.J. wished he could say something to help, but he couldn't think of anything. 'I'm sorry,' he said at last, quite simply. 'I shouldn't have said those things to you. I was just lashing out because I was raw and bitter. I suppose I wanted to hurt you because you'd hurt me, but I swear I never wanted to be proved right.'

'I know. I'm sorry, too,' said Nell quietly. 'I never wanted to hurt you, P.J., but I know that I did.'

'Hey, I survived.' The corner of P.J.'s mouth turned up in his crooked smile as he tried to lighten the atmosphere, and Nell found herself remembering with piercing clarity exactly what his lips had felt like against her skin. Shivering a little, she turned away.

'I can't say I thought so at the time,' he admitted, hoping to take some of the sadness from her expression, 'but it didn't take long for me to realise that it was all for the best.' He hated the thought that she had spent years feeling guilty about the way their relationship had ended. She had had enough to bear without that.

'Oh?' Nell kept her eyes on the car ahead as they inched towards a busy junction. Naturally, she was pleased to know that P.J. hadn't been heartbroken, but surely he ought to have had *some* regrets?

Or had he been wanting to end things himself, so that her decision had come as a huge relief? For some reason, that thought was worse than feeling guilty about the way she had hurt him.

'You were right, too,' P.J. told her, one eye on the traffic, the other on Nell's suddenly rigid profile. 'We'd been together too long, and our relationship was stale. It was time for us to be braver and get out there on our own. If we'd got married then, we would have been tied down with a mortgage and babies straight away. We would never have gone to Africa or done all those things we'd planned to do, would we? We'd still be there, regretting the opportunities we'd missed, and resenting each other for it. I certainly don't think I'd have taken the risks I did to start my company if I'd had a family to think about.'

They had made it to the junction, and P.J. waited, looking for an opportunity to cut across the traffic. Nell studied him sideways under her lashes as he concentrated on driving. The set of his jaw was achingly familiar, and the line of his cheek and the curl of his mouth made her feel hollow inside.

He could have been hers. They could have spent the last sixteen years loving and laughing. They could have gone to Africa, and taken any babies with them. They would have been able to do anything as long as they were together. It wouldn't have had to end in bitterness and resentment the way P.J. thought it would.

'So you think it all worked out for the best?' she asked.

CHAPTER THREE

AN ONCOMING car flashed its lights, and P.J. pulled out, easing the car in the long line of traffic and lifting a hand in acknowledgement. 'Yes, I do.' He glanced at Nell. 'Don't you?'

'I'm sure you're right about us,' she said quickly, in case he thought she had more regrets about their broken engagement than he did.

'But?' he prompted.

Nell sighed. 'But when your marriage ends in a mess, it's hard sometimes to think that it was all for the best.'

'I can imagine,' said P.J., contrite. He hesitated. 'Does it still hurt?'

'About Simon?'

He nodded, keeping his eyes firmly on the road ahead.

'Not really. Not now. At the time it was horrible,' she told him, surprised at how easily she had slipped back into the way of talking to P.J. about the things she would normally keep to herself. 'But by the end it was just such a relief not to have to pretend and argue anymore.

'I didn't want Clara to grow up with us shouting

273

at each other,' she said, remembering how Simon had lied and blustered and finally left. 'It wasn't how I imagined having a family,' she went on a little sadly. 'I'd dreamt about giving my children a loving home with two parents but…well, it didn't work out like that, and I think it's better this way. At least Clara has a "normal" life when she's with Simon and Elaine.'

'How often does she see her father?' asked P.J. after a while.

'Not as often as she needs.' Nell watched a young man walking along the pavement, a small boy perched, delighted, on his shoulders. The sight of a father being tender and loving with his children always gave her a pang, thinking about how uninterested Simon had been with Clara.

'Simon's not a cruel father. He pays his maintenance for Clara on time, and he does his duty by her…but that's just what it feels like, a duty. It's as if she's a tiresome obligation now that he's got a new family. And I don't think Elaine feels comfortable with Clara. She's always changing the arrangements when Clara is due to go over there, and they never include her in their family holidays.'

'That's hard,' commented P.J.

'I don't mind not being part of Simon's life anymore,' Nell tried to explain, 'but I do mind for Clara.

She's always been an incredibly sensible child and
she never complains, but she's only ten.'

'I can't imagine having a daughter like Clara and
not wanting to spend as much time with her as possible,' said P.J., stopping at a pedestrian crossing.

'I know. That's why I—' Nell caught herself up
just in time. She had been about to tell P.J. about
her efforts to find a man who would be a better male
influence in Clara's life, but that would be taking
confidences a bit too far. P.J. had only been back in
her life for a matter of minutes, and a girl had her
pride, after all.

'Why you what?'

'Oh, nothing.'

P.J. sent her an uncomfortably searching glance.
'You've never thought about marrying again?'

Nell had never liked his habit of being able to
follow her train of thought even when she was trying
to be her most inscrutable.

Nell thought about asking him if he had any idea
how difficult it was to find someone new when you
were in your thirties, and had a child, and couldn't
afford to go out, and in any case were too dog-tired
after working all day and then looking after your
daughter to dream about anything more exciting than
a hot bath and an early night. And that was before
you started looking at the single men who were
available!

'No,' was all she said in the end, though.

It was definitely time to change the subject. 'What nice children Jake and Emily and Flora are,' she said, and meaning it. 'You must be very proud of them.'

'I am,' said P.J. 'Although I must admit that I haven't really had that much to do with them over the last few years.'

Nell couldn't help staring at him. How could he sound so casual about not spending enough time with his own children? She would have expected that P.J., once he became a father, would take his role very seriously.

'Their mother deserves all the credit for bringing them up, I think,' he was saying. 'She doesn't get as much support as she should.'

Nell's brows drew together. 'In that case, perhaps you could do a bit more to help her?' she suggested coolly.

'I'd like to,' said P.J., 'but it's difficult…and I have got a business to run.'

That had always been Simon's excuse too, she thought bitterly. 'I haven't got time,' he had used to say. 'I can't afford to take time off. I can't support you and Clara unless I work, can I?' His job, it seemed, was always more important than giving his daughter some attention.

'Oh, well, if your business needs you…' she said,

not bothering to disguise her sarcasm, and P.J. looked at her with a puzzled frown.

'It probably doesn't need me as much as I'd like,' he admitted.

'Does it need you more than your children?'

P.J.'s brow cleared. 'Are you thinking about Flora and Emily and Jake, by any chance?'

'Of course.'

'They're not mine,' he told her with a grin.

'But I thought...' Nell trailed off, trying to remember exactly what he had said about the children.

'They're Janey's. You remember my sister, don't you?'

'Yes,' she said a little stiffly, feeling foolish. It was an easy enough mistake to make, but, still, she shouldn't have leapt to conclusions.

And did this mean that P.J. did not in fact have the perfect marriage and the perfect family after all? Nell fought down the flicker of excitement that came with the thought.

'You obviously get on very well with them, anyway,' she said.

'I've been based in the States for the last few years, so I just saw them occasionally, but I've tried to make more of an effort since I got back to London,' P.J. told her. 'I still haven't sorted out a house, so I quite often spend the night with Janey. It gives me a chance to get to know the kids, and, as Janey's husband is away on business a lot, I think she's glad of the company.'

He grinned. 'Of course, the kids only like me because I give them a lift to school in the morning. Janey normally makes them walk.'

Janey had been just another giggling friend of Thea's when she and P.J. had been going out, but the more Nell heard about her now, the more she thought the two of them would get on. Not that she would get a chance to find out, Nell reminded herself quickly. She and P.J. had very different lives now, and it would be best to keep them that way.

Still, she thought P.J.'s nieces and nephew probably liked him as more than a chauffeur.

'It's a lovely car,' she said, stroking the soft leather seat appreciatively. 'I'm not surprised they like being chauffered around in it!'

'She's a beauty, isn't she?' P.J. gave the dashboard an affectionate pat, and Nell was submerged in a wash of memory so powerful that she clutched onto the seat as if it were all that stopped her being swept straight back into the past.

P.J. had always loved cars. She could see him now, showing off the first car he had ever owned, the one he had worked so hard to buy. His face had been alight with pride as he'd pointed out wheel trims and carburettors and propeller shafts, none of which had meant anything to Nell, who had only been able to see a battered old car. But she had nodded and looked suitably impressed, happy because he had been.

'She's a beauty, isn't she?' That was what he had said then, too, and Nell had smiled and agreed.

Now she couldn't help smiling. 'She's absolutely gorgeous,' she teased, exactly as she had then.

P.J. laughed and glanced at her as she sat beside him, and as their eyes met the air was suddenly charged with the memory of what had happened next.

'She's not as gorgeous as you,' he had said, pulling her towards him and turning her so that he could press her against the car door and cup her face between his hands. 'She's not beautiful the way you are,' he said, his young man's voice low and husky, and then he kissed her the way he had never kissed her before, a boy no longer but a man with seductive lips and sure hands.

Nell could still feel the way the door handle had pressed into her back. His urgency had taken her aback at first, until her own body had risen to meet it and match it, and she had wound her arms around his neck and kissed him back.

Her mouth was dry, her throat tight, and she swallowed as the memories pulsed and pounded through her. His hands had been so persuasive, his mouth so warm against her skin as they had explored each other, tentatively at first and then with increasing urgency, as they had discovered new sensations that had been thrilling and almost frightening in their intensity.

How could she have thrown all that away? Nell tried to remember when it had all changed. When had she started to take that excitement for granted? Had it been when P.J. had gone away to university, or when she had a year later? By the time she had graduated, they had been going out for five years. She had been ready to start a family, but P.J. had wanted to be sensible and wait until he was established in his new career.

Then Simon had turned up, and everything had changed again. He had been so confident, so dangerous and intriguing and exciting, and P.J. had been dear and familiar and not there.

And she had been young and silly, Nell knew that now. Too young to appreciate what she had in P.J. and too silly to understand the risk she was taking in throwing in her lot with a man she hardly knew.

Now the air was crackling with the memory of that first car, and the good times she and P.J. had shared. Nell bit her lip. She had known that getting in the car with P.J. was a mistake. She should have taken the tube, and to hell with her ankle, whatever Clara might have said.

The past was past. There was no point in sitting

here and remembering how much she had loved P.J. now, not when he had turned into someone so attractive and so successful and so out of reach.

P.J.'s eyes had gone back to the road, and Nell stared fiercely out at the traffic and willed the memories down as she tried to think of something to say.

In the end it was P.J. who spoke. The silence between that glance and his words had probably only lasted a few seconds, but it felt like an eternity to Nell.

'This car was the first thing I bought when I came back to London,' he said. 'Janey said it was typical of me to buy a car before a house.'

Nell was pathetically grateful to him for turning the conversation into neutral channels. She cleared her throat and tried to pretend that she had met him for the first time a few minutes ago, that they had never loved each other.

'Have you come back to London permanently?'

'Yes…I think so, anyway. I had a great few years in the States but I started to feel…well, restless, I suppose.'

P.J. couldn't really explain how that feeling of faint dissatisfaction had crept over him, as if his life were missing something, and he couldn't work out what it was. 'I kept thinking about coming home,' he said at last, 'but, of course, I haven't got a home here, at least not yet. I'm renting an apartment at the moment, but it's not the same as having your own home.'

'You could buy a house, couldn't you?' said Nell, thinking that, if he was half as rich as Thea said he was, London property prices weren't going to be a problem.

'I guess so.'

The trouble was that P.J. couldn't muster much enthusiasm for the idea. He would just have to hand a house over to designers and decorators, who would make it too smart. 'I'm not sure where I want to be yet, though.'

'You could take your pick of properties, couldn't you?' said Nell. 'I hear you've done well for your-self.' To say the least.

P.J. glanced at her again. 'Where did you hear that? I never thought of you as an avid reader of the business pages.'

'I hardly have time to read the headlines, let alone the business section,' she told him dryly. 'No, I had it from Thea, who had it from Janey when they met up on that internet site. It sounds as if Janey's very proud of you.'

'That's not what she tells me,' said P.J. with a wry smile. 'She's usually giving me a hard time about something.'

Building up a billion-dollar business meant noth-ing to his sister. 'What's the point of all that money if you haven't got someone to share it with?' she would demand. 'You need to get married and have a family.'

'It's not that easy,' P.J. complained. 'I don't want to get married unless I'm sure I've found the right woman.'

'Well, I can tell you you're never going to find her until you stop hankering after Nell Martindale!' Janey said.

'I got over Nell years ago,' P.J. protested, but Janey only smiled in that knowing—and particularly annoying—manner she had sometimes.

'Oh, yes? Has it never occurred to you that every single one of your girlfriends has looked a bit like her, and somehow none of them has ever quite measured up to her?'

P.J. had always pooh-poohed the whole idea. 'Rubbish,' he always said firmly. 'It's got nothing whatsoever to do with Nell at all.'

But Janey wouldn't let it go. She couldn't wait to tell him about her conversation with Nell's sister, and that Nell herself was free.

'That slimeball Simon Shea made her life hell for a few years, and then he dumped her and left her high and dry with a baby to look after and minimal maintenance. Thea says that she's been struggling on her own ever since. You should look her up,' she went on airily. 'Maybe you could finally get her out of your system.'

'She's not *in* my system,' P.J. said through gritted teeth. 'Nell was great, but it was over years ago,' he told his sister firmly. 'I've moved on since then.'

'Sure you have,' Janey scoffed, and he was so incensed that he ended up letting her set him up on some stupid blind date just to prove to her that he was perfectly ready to meet someone who bore not the slightest resemblance to Nell.

But now, extraordinarily, Nell was here, sitting beside him, and he could smell the faint drift of her perfume and see the curve of her cheek and the downward sweep of her lashes. He yearned suddenly to be able to reach out and touch her and feel her warmth, for her to smile at him and make the lost years disappear. But years didn't just disappear like that, P.J. knew. They were gone, and nothing could get them back.

Nell's voice brought him back to the present. 'Isn't it true, then?' she asked.

'Isn't what true?'

'That you've made your fortune?'

'Yes, I've made a lot of money,' said P.J. in a down-to-earth voice. 'Janey says it's an obscene amount of money.' He half smiled. 'I didn't set out to be rich, though. I wanted to build a business, and that was the exciting part. The money just came along with the success.'

'Must be nice, though,' said Nell, thinking of the bills and the mortgage and the credit card payments that loomed over her every month.

'Sure. It's great to be able to buy a car like this without thinking about it but…'

'You're not going to tell me that money isn't everything, are you, P.J.?'

P.J. laughed a little ruefully at the dangerous sweetness of her tone. 'Guilty as accused!' he confessed. 'It's a horrible cliché, I know, but it really *isn't* enough on its own. The best thing is knowing that you don't need to worry about it anymore, but after a while you're not even risking anything when you try something new, because you're always safe and have got money to fall back on.

'I miss that feeling,' he told her. Nearly as much as he had missed her, and being able to talk to her like this. 'Going out on a limb, trying something new, working flat out to make your idea succeed because the alternative is just too dire to contemplate… Now I've got a huge business, but I've got nothing to do! I employ thousands of people to do what I once did by myself, and it's all a bit…I don't know…dull, I guess. I've been feeling recently as if I need a new challenge, or something new to get excited about.'

'You should have a family,' said Nell lightly. 'It's hard to be bored with kids around. And you'd soon find a use for all that money you've got sitting around. You have no idea how expensive children are!'

'So Janey is always telling me,' said P.J.

There was a pause. 'Have you ever thought about having a family?' she asked, trying to sound casual, as if having children weren't the issue that had pushed them apart all those years ago.

He nodded slowly. 'Yes, I've thought about it a lot. I guess I made the classic mistake of thinking that I should wait until the time was right, and then found that the time was right, but my relationship wasn't.'

'You've never married?'

'No...I've come close, but...no.'

And it wasn't anything to do with Nell, whatever Janey said, P.J. swore to himself. It was just that he had never found another woman who was as easy to talk to as she was, who had felt quite as right in his arms, or who could offer him the same sense of peace when she lay warm against him.

'So you're still looking for the right woman?' Nell asked.

P.J. took his eyes off the road to glance at her, and their eyes met for a jarring moment as he re-membered how desolate he had felt when she had told him that she was going to marry Simon Shea. 'We belong together,' he had told her, not too proud to plead.

'You'll find someone else,' she had said, her voice shaking with tears. 'Somewhere out there is the perfect woman for you.'

'No, there isn't.' His voice had been as bleak as his heart. 'It'll only ever be you.'

All rubbish, naturally. How melodramatic he had been, P.J. thought indulgently. Of course there would be someone for him, just as Nell had said. He just hadn't found her yet.

'Yes,' he said, striving to sound suitably cheerful. 'Still looking.'

CHAPTER FOUR

'I WOULDN'T have thought it would be that difficult,' said Nell, thinking that she couldn't be the only woman who had noticed what an attractive man he had grown into. 'Surely billionaires get to have their pick of beautiful women?' she added with an ironic look.

'You'd be surprised,' said P.J. 'Janey says I'm impossible to please.'

He hadn't been hard to please before, thought Nell. All she had had to do was to be herself. Her gaze slid sideways to rest on his profile, lingering on the corner of his cool mouth, before drifting down to the lean, tough body and the competent hands on the steering wheel, and something turned over inside her.

She looked away. Inside the car, the silence seemed suddenly loud, and she could hear her heart thumping.

P.J. seemed aware of the same constraint. 'That's enough about my financially rewarding but ultimately empty life,' he said, mocking himself. 'Tell me what you've been doing.'

'Oh…' Nell lifted her shoulders a little helplessly.

'What is there to say? My life has been very unglamorous compared to yours. I've taken no risks and had no staggering success. I can't boast about my transatlantic lifestyle. I haven't even got a car, let alone one like this. I've just spent the last sixteen years getting through the days and bringing up my daughter as best I can. Not very exciting, I'm afraid.'

'I hate to sound like a walking cliché,' said P.J. with an ironic glance, 'but bringing up a happy, healthy child has to be more worthwhile in the long run than making millions.'

'It's probably as hard work, especially when you're on your own,' said Nell in a wry voice. 'Clara was hardly more than a baby when Simon left, so it was difficult to find a job that I could fit around looking after her.'

About to tell him about the expense of childcare, Nell caught herself just in time. She didn't want to sound like a sad, single mother, consumed with bitterness about her divorce and perpetually moaning about money. If she couldn't compete with him in the glamorous lifestyle stakes, she could at least convince him that she had a good life and no regrets.

Least of all about him.

'Anyway, that's the story of my life,' she said with a bright smile. 'No glittering prizes for me, but Clara and I have fun together, my family have been fantastically supportive, I've got lots of friends... I think I've been pretty lucky. And now I've even got a good job, so things are definitely looking up.'

Was that enough to convince P.J. that she was perfectly happy with her life? Nell wondered. If only he hadn't been quite so successful! It would be much easier to be honest and open with him if she didn't know how stupendously wealthy he was. As it was, she was terrified that he would think that she was hinting that she regretted having left him and was angling to re-establish their relationship just because of his money.

But P.J. showed no sign of thinking any such thing. He asked about her job instead. 'I was wondering what you did.'

'I'm in recruitment,' said Nell, allowing herself to relax a bit. Talking about work was good. Work made for an excellent neutral topic of conversation. She should stick with it from now on, and not let herself get diverted by memories.

'I used to work for an agency,' she told him. 'I dealt with mostly secretarial and clerical positions, but I've just got a new job with a firm of head hunters. It's very small but very prestigious, so it's a good move for me, but a bit scary at the same time. Everything is much more pressurised. I find it a bit stressful, to be honest.'

'Can't you go back to what you were doing before?'

There spoke someone who hadn't had to worry about money for a while! 'I've got this quaint little notion about paying my mortgage,' said Nell, a little more sharply than she intended.

'The brutal truth is that I need the money,' she went on, with less of an edge to her voice. 'And I want to prove myself, too. I've never had a chance to work like this before. Everything is much more professional and high-powered.'

'In what way?' asked P.J.

'I've got a very demanding boss. She always looks immaculate, and I'm supposed to look the same.' Nell's mouth turned down at the corners as she thought about Eve and the impossible standards she set. 'It's all about the company's image, she says, but it's a bit of a strain having to look perfectly groomed the whole time.'

P.J.'s blue eyes rested for a moment on Nell in her jogging pants and trainers and old sweatshirt, and his mouth quirked.

Nell flushed. He didn't need to say anything. 'I change when I get there,' she told him a shade defensively. 'I had an accident last year and broke my ankle and my wrist. I'm fine now, but walking long distances is hard except in sensible shoes, so I tend to wear these for the commute and put on my work shoes when I get there.'

'Very sensible,' said P.J. gravely, but his eyes

danced in a way that made Nell feel distinctly ruffled.

'Normally I'd be dressed properly by now,' she told him, even as she wondered why she was bothering to justify her appearance to him. 'But I've got an important meeting this afternoon, and I'm going to pick up my suit from the dry-cleaner's on the way in.'

If she hadn't overslept, she would have had her make-up on by now, too. It wasn't fair. If she had to bump into P.J. she could at least have been looking her best. That was just typical of her life at the moment, thought Nell fatalistically. It was about time something started to go right for a change.

'How is your ankle now?' he asked.

'It's fine,' she said truthfully. The rest had done it good, and she could only feel a slight throb now. 'I won't have to walk much further on it today, anyway. We've got an important meeting this afternoon, but fortunately my boss is a great believer in taxis, so we'll probably get driven door-to-door.'

P.J. looked interested. 'What's the meeting about?'

'I don't know much about it, to tell you the truth,' Nell admitted. 'I know that we've got an important contract to recruit someone for a senior position in some big company, and Eve—my boss—seems to think that if we do a good job, we'll be in a good position to do a lot more recruitment work for them. She wants me to go along and learn the ropes about finding out what they *really* want—which is apparently not always what they *say* they want! Fortunately I'm not going to be called upon to do more than look cool and professional and as if I know what's going on.'

'And won't you?'

'No,' said Nell frankly. 'I'm terrified that someone will ask me a question, but I'm hoping that if I keep my mouth closed and look enigmatic enough, it won't be too obvious that I haven't got a clue about what's happening.'

'Ah, then you have already learnt the secret of professional success!' said P.J., amused. 'I can tell you'll go far!'

They both laughed, but found their smiles fading at exactly the same moment, as if both unnerved by how quickly they had slipped back into the old, easy ways.

Constraint seeped back into the air. Nell stared desperately out of her window at the commuters streaming out of the tube station they were just passing. She was one of them usually. That was her life, not sitting in this luxurious car, cocooned in comfort with P.J. beside her. She belonged in the crowd, glancing enviously at those who could travel in such comfort. She didn't belong with P.J., not now.

She must remember that.

It would be too easy to forget if she were to spend any longer in P.J.'s company. The tug of attraction, the tug of the past, was very strong. Nell was conscious of having to dig in her heels mentally to stop herself falling back under the old spell, the one that made it seem as if everything were easy and natural between them.

But how could it be after all this time? This was just a chance encounter, a brief interlude, and it would be a mistake to pretend that it could always be like this. P.J. was a different man, one whose assurance and attractiveness had left her feeling flustered and more disturbed than she wanted to admit. Things might feel the same, but they weren't, and if she forgot that it would make going back to her real life so much harder. The past was the past. Better if it stayed that way.

As the silence lengthened in the car, and the memory of their shared laughter thrummed in the air, P.J. drummed his fingers on the steering wheel and thought about what Janey had said.

'You'll never move on until you've got Nell Martindale out of your system. Look her up. She won't be the same pretty young girl, and you won't feel the same about her.'

P.J. hadn't wanted to do that. He hadn't wanted to see that Nell had grown older, or to think that she had lost her charm. He hadn't wanted to face the fact that the old dream had died.

But now fate had put her in his way, and she was older, just as he had feared. Older and warier, with faint lines starring her eyes, but she was still beautiful, and the warmth and the charm were still there. Why not see if the spark could be rekindled?

They were edging over Waterloo Bridge now. They would be in the city soon, and then this strange meeting would be over. Why not take advantage of coincidence?

'What are you doing tonight?' he asked, breaking the silence so abruptly that Nell started in her seat.

'Tonight?' she echoed a little breathlessly.

'I was wondering if I could take you out to dinner to make up for almost knocking you over,' said P.J., hating himself for sounding so stiff and awkward. This was Nell, for heaven's sake. They had been friends and lovers for years. He ought to be able to ask her to dinner without stumbling over his words or making up an excuse to want to see her again.

'I can't tonight.' Nell didn't know whether to be glad or sorry that she had a real excuse. 'I've got a date.'

'A date?'

P.J. looked so taken aback that Nell was ruffled. 'There's no need to sound so surprised!' she said shortly, wondering if he had been expecting her to fall at his feet with gratitude at his casual invitation. 'It's allowed. I'm a free agent.'

'I didn't mean that…' P.J. wasn't sure what he *had* meant. He had always thought of Nell as essentially homely, he supposed. She was someone warm and comfortable to curl up with on a sofa, not someone who dressed up and went out on dates.

'It's just that you said very firmly that you hadn't married again,' he tried to explain, 'and I assumed…'

'…that I was too old?' Nell finished his sentence for him, and P.J. could tell from the brilliance of her smile that he had somehow made things worse for himself.

'No, of course not—'

'I *am* only thirty-seven,' she said huffily. 'Not all men fantasise about eighteen-year-old girls, you know. Some even find women my age attractive and desirable.'

'I know. I'm one of them.' It was P.J.'s turn to be provoked. He had just asked her out, hadn't he?

There was an antagonistic pause.

'So, who's your date tonight?' he asked after a moment, wanting to sound casual but afraid that he might have sounded belligerent and sulky instead.

'His name's John.' Nell was feeling spiky and defensive for some reason.

'Have you been seeing him long?'

There was a distinct edge to P.J.'s voice now, which only made her more determined not to admit that John was a blind date. She didn't need to account to P.J. for what she did, or whom she met, did she?

'No, not long, but it's going very well,' she said, spotting an opportunity to impress on P.J. that she stood in no need of charitable invitations to dinner from him or anyone else. She wasn't a sad divorcee, desperate for a night out, whatever he thought.

A muscle tightened in P.J.'s jaw. 'So, what's he like, this John?'

'He's lovely,' said Nell, improvising freely. 'Very kind and funny and intelligent. We get on really well.' At least, Thea had said that they would. 'I'm beginning to think he might be the one for me. We've started to talk about the future, and, well…it's still all very new, but I feel quite excited.'

Which would be news to poor John.

'How did you meet this paragon?' asked P.J. tightly.

'Through Thea.' It was a relief to get back to the truth. 'She actually set us up on a kind of blind date.' Nell even managed a laugh as if the very idea of her going on a blind date was absurd. 'She said we'd be perfect for each other, and we are.'

'Well, I'm glad you're happy,' P.J. made himself say, although privately he couldn't help thinking that her precious John sounded too perfect to be real. He just hoped Nell wasn't setting herself up for another bitter disappointment. He hated the thought of her being hurt again.

'I am,' said Nell, lifting her chin defiantly, and spotting a familiar row of shops with relief. She didn't want P.J. interrogating her about her supposedly wonderful relationship with John. She wasn't cut out for elaborate fibs.

'Oh, that's the dry-cleaner!' She pointed gratefully. 'Could you possibly drop me there, P.J.? I need to pick up my suit.'

P.J. pulled over obligingly, and turned in his seat to watch her as she gathered up her bag. 'Shall I wait for you?'

'There's no need. I just work down there.' Nell gestured in the direction of some office blocks along the road. 'I'll walk from here.'

To P.J. it was as if she were deliberately being vague so that he wouldn't be able to note where she worked. Obviously she had moved on, he thought with a trace of bitterness. There was no place for him in her life anymore, and if he had any sense he would leave it there, but somehow the thought of saying goodbye and losing her as soon as he had found her again was unendurable.

'What about another evening?' he asked, and she paused with her hand on the door.

'For dinner,' he said as she looked at him uncertainly. 'I wouldn't want to come between you and your hot date, of course, but there's no reason we shouldn't meet as old friends, is there?'

Only that it was too hard to think of him as an old friend now that he had thickened out and grown into a disturbingly attractive man. But how could she say that?

'I...don't think so, P.J.,' she managed after a moment. 'We can't go back. It was good to see you again, and I'm really grateful for the lift, but the past is the past, and I think we'd better leave it that way.'

She opened her car door, and got out, leaning back in to give him a final word of thanks before she shut it firmly on his hopes and turned quickly away.

A taxi swung past, blaring its horn at P.J. for blocking the road, but he hardly noticed. He just sat there and watched as Nell walked away from him all over again.

CHAPTER FIVE

As soon as she could, Nell rang Thea. 'Guess who I ran into this morning?'

'Um...Hugh Grant?'

'No.'

'Brad Pitt?'

'No.'

'More or less exciting?'

Nell hesitated.

'P.J.,' said Thea, and it wasn't even a question.

Nell held the receiver away from her and gaped at it. Sometimes her sister astounded her. 'How on earth did you guess?'

'Let's face it, Nell, most of the men we know aren't exactly up there with Brad Pitt when it comes to exciting!' said Thea. 'P.J. is the only one I can think of who'd give you a moment's pause if you had to compare him.'

'I wasn't thinking of him being exciting,' said Nell, still more than a little unnerved by her sister's perspicacity. 'I was just going to say that meeting him was just as unlikely as meeting Brad Pitt... I can't *believe* you guessed it was him!'

'I suppose it's just because we've been talking

about him recently,' said Thea soothingly. 'I knew he was back in London and it would be a surprise to run into him, that's all. Tell me what happened.'

'It was so weird, Thea,' Nell said. 'I still can't really take it in. One minute I was walking along with Clara, and the next he was *there*.' She told Thea about falling off the kerb into P.J.'s car. 'I thought I was imagining things at first. I thought it was the shock of the accident, but it really was him.'

Thea was delighted. 'Ooh, Nell, you know what this means, don't you? It's fate, literally throwing you together again!'

Nell sighed. She might have known Thea would start on that line. 'It was a coincidence, Thea, that's all.'

'A pretty amazing one, though! Well, go on, what's he like now?'

'He's just the same...' P.J.'s image rose before Nell with startling clarity. Those blue, blue eyes with their lurking laughter, the strong nose and jaw and the humorous mouth that seemed constantly about to quirk into a smile, and something clenched inside her. 'But he's...well, he's different, too,' she finished lamely. 'He's sixteen years older, for a start.'

'Has he grown into his looks, then?' asked Thea, straightforward as ever. 'I always thought he would look better when he was older.'

'Well...'

'Oh, Nell, he was gorgeous, wasn't he? I can hear it in your voice!'

'Not *gorgeous* exactly,' Nell protested, before her sister got too carried away. 'But, yes, he's quite attractive,' she added, rather proud of her cool and casual manner.

Sadly, it didn't fool her sister. 'Gorgeous, then,' she said with satisfaction. 'Are you going to see him again?'

'No, I don't think so,' said Nell, trying to sound as if she didn't care one way or another. 'He asked me to have dinner with him but...'

'But what?' demanded Thea ominously.

'But I said I didn't think it was a good idea.'

There was a pause while Thea made an audible attempt to contain her exasperation. 'Why not?'

'Thea, there's no point,' said Nell.

'No point in meeting a single, straight, attractive billionaire who just happens to have been in love with you?'

'He's certainly not in love with me now,' said Nell, alarmed to hear, too late, the unconsciously wistful note in her voice.

She made an effort to sound more casual and upbeat. 'You should see him now, Thea. He wears a suit and tie now, drives an incredibly flash car. He's very...assured.'

'P.J. was always like that,' said Thea to her surprise. 'Even when he was a teenager, and all legs and nose, he always seemed quietly confident and at ease in his own skin. You don't meet many people like that, especially not at school!'

'Well, he's even more like that now,' Nell admitted. 'It was so…odd. I felt as if I knew him, but at the same time it was obvious that I didn't know him at all. Maybe it was just that I'd changed too much.'

'You haven't changed at all.'

'Yes, I have. I used to be so young and so confident…' She trailed off a little sadly. 'I haven't felt like that for a long time.'

'I know what you mean,' Thea conceded thoughtfully. 'Back then, it was P.J. who seemed to be the lucky one, wasn't it? Everyone liked him, but he was a bit of a nerd, wasn't he? And you were always the pretty one with all the boys after you.'

'He used to say that he couldn't believe I would even look at him,' Nell confessed. 'He made me feel like I was some kind of goddess…and then, this morning… Oh. Thea, I just felt so dowdy and inadequate and a failure compared to him!'

'I don't suppose he'd ask you out if he thought that,' said Thea.

'I expect he just felt sorry for me,' said Nell gloomily.

Thea clicked her tongue in exasperation. 'Nell,

you're still gorgeous! If he asks you out again, you're to say yes.'

'He won't. Anyway, he doesn't know how to contact me.'

'That's not going to be much of a challenge to an intelligent man like P.J., is it? He just needs to ring Janey, who'll ring me.'

Nell sat up straight in alarm. 'Thea, you're not to give her my phone number!'

'I most certainly will!' said Thea in her most uncompromising voice. 'You may want to throw away the chance of getting back together with a wonderful man who'd solve all your problems, but I'm not going to help you do it!'

'Anyway, he won't call,' said Nell perversely. 'I made it very clear I didn't want to see him again.'

'Oh, well, it seems a pity.'

Rather to Nell's surprise, Thea left it there. 'Now, what are you wearing tonight?'

'Oh, I don't know... My black trousers?'

'You're not wearing those trousers again, Nell,' said Thea bossily. 'You can wear that dress you bought for my wedding. You look wonderful in that.'

Nell sighed. 'Do I have to go?' she asked, thinking that if she hadn't had this blind date Thea had set her up on, she wouldn't have had to refuse P.J. that morning. She could have been thinking about looking wonderful for him instead. She would have let herself be persuaded. Just so as not to be rude.

'It'll be awful,' she grumbled. 'We'll just end up talking about how wonderful cars are, or about our divorces the way I have with every other man I've been out with since Simon.'

'Well, there haven't been many of those,' Thea pointed out reasonably. 'Not enough to form a pattern, anyway.'

'I've been on four blind dates this year,' Nell objected, 'and every single one has been ghastly.'

'That's because they were strangers from the lonely hearts column,' Thea explained patiently. 'It'll be different tonight. Why would I set you up with someone awful? I know this guy tonight, and I think he's great. He's perfect for you.'

'Then why won't you tell me anything about him? Knowing his name is John and that he'll be sitting in Bar Barabbas with a Swahili dictionary tonight isn't much to go on!'

'That's because I don't want you going with any preconceptions,' said Thea. 'You know what you're like. You'll make up your mind about him before you even meet him, and then you'll get nervous and go all prickly on him.'

The way she had with P.J. that morning, thought Nell guiltily as Thea talked on. She wished she hadn't been quite so short. It wasn't his fault that she had felt so flustered, but if only he hadn't been quite so...overwhelming. She could recall everything about him in vivid detail—his hands on the steering wheel, the twitch at the corner of his mouth, the warmth and humour in his eyes as he'd turned to look at her.

And the way she had longed to reach out and touch him. That was what had really made her uneasy. You couldn't go around throwing yourself at ex-boyfriends, especially when they had turned into billionaires overnight...well, over sixteen years, anyway.

Thea broke off, suddenly suspicious. 'Are you listening to me?' she demanded and Nell caught herself up.

'Of course I am,' she lied.

'I've just got a good feeling about today,' said Thea. 'You know how you used to tell me that one day I'd wake up, and not know that that was the day I was going to meet the man who would change my life forever? Well, you were right. One day I had no idea about Rhys's existence, and the next, he was part of my life. All it takes is one day, and your whole life can change.

'I think today is your day,' she finished portentously, 'so all you have to do is go out tonight, relax and be yourself.'

'There's no chance of me relaxing until this meeting is over.' Nell lowered her voice. 'Eve's driving us all nuts about it. I'm so wound up now, I'll be a gibbering wreck by the time we actually get there.'

'Well, you would go for this high-powered job,' said Thea unsympathetically. 'It's more important that you're not a gibbering wreck tonight, so don't be late back. I'll come over early to make sure you don't get those black trousers out.'

P.J.'s assistant opened her mouth to pass on a note-book full of messages but he waved her aside. 'In a minute,' he said. 'Can you get my sister on the line first?'

'P.J.!' Janey was surprised to hear from him. 'You don't usually ring at this time… Nothing's wrong is it?'

'Far from it,' he said cheerfully. 'Guess who I knocked over this morning?'

'You knocked someone over?' Janey was horrified.

'Not really, but it was pretty close.' P.J. put on his best Humphrey Bogart accent. 'But of all the pedestrians on all the pavements in London,' he paraphrased, 'I had to knock over Nell Martindale!'

There was a stunned silence at the other end of the phone. '*Nell?* You're kidding me!'

'No, I'm not.' P.J. grinned. 'And because I know sisters always like to be right, I thought I'd say it

before you had a chance to say, "I told you so."
I've changed my mind and I do want to see her
again. Can you get her number for me from Thea?'

There was another pause. P.J. could practically
hear his sister thinking. 'Why didn't you just ask
Nell out when you saw her?'

'I did, but she turned me down. She said she had
a date tonight.'

'So do you,' said Janey in a dry voice.

The smile was wiped from P.J.'s face. 'Oh, God,
I'd forgotten all about that!' he said, clutching his
hair.

'Don't even *think* about trying to back out of it
now!' Janey warned before he could say any more.

'But, Janey, you're the one who wanted me to get
in touch with Nell!' said P.J., baffled as ever by his
sister's perverted logic. 'I've admitted that you were
right and I was wrong. I do need to get Nell out of
my system. Don't you think it's a bit unfair on
what's-her-name to pretend I'm looking for another
relationship when I'm really only interested in another woman?'

'Her name's Helen,' said Janey coldly, 'and I
don't think it's as unfair as standing her up at such
short notice. She's a lovely person, and she wasn't
that keen on being set up on a blind date with you
either, to be honest. It would be awful for her if you
didn't turn up.'

'I wasn't thinking of leaving her sitting there,' said P.J. defensively. 'I thought you could ring her and explain—'

'Explain what? That my brother is totally perverse? You said you didn't want to see Nell again, P.J. You said you didn't want to rake up the past, and that you were perfectly ready to move on to another relationship. And when I suggested introducing you to Helen, you said you'd like to meet her.'

'I know I did,' said P.J. through gritted teeth, 'but that was before I saw Nell again. Everything's changed now.'

'So you've changed your mind! Who's to say you wouldn't change it again when you meet Helen?' asked Janey. 'Your trouble, P.J., is that you're spoilt. You're too used to getting your own way. You think that because you've got all that money you can snap your fingers and have whatever you want. Well, you can't just dump your date with Helen just because it doesn't suit you to meet her tonight anymore. I'm not one of your flunkies who'll say, ''Yes, sir, no, sir,'' and do your dirty work for you.'

'You know, Janey,' said P.J. thinly, 'if one of my directors spoke to me the way you do, there would be a spare place on the board!'

Janey snorted, unimpressed. 'You go tonight, and you be at your most charming. If you give Helen so much as an *inkling* that you don't really want to be there, you'll be off *my* board!'

'All right.' P.J. swallowed his wrath with some difficulty. 'I'll stick to the arrangement, but will you get Nell's number for me? I really want to see her again.'

'We'll see,' said Janey, enjoying having her brother on the run for once. 'That rather depends on what Helen tells me tomorrow, doesn't it? If she's happy about the way the date went, then I'll give Thea a call.'

'Thank you,' said P.J., his jaw gritted.

If he'd known Janey would carry on like this, he'd have found out Nell's number some other way. He could have asked one of his 'flunkies,' as Janey called them, to track Nell down, but he'd thought she would be delighted to hear about his change of mind. That was sisters for you!

'And who knows?' said Janey, amusement threading her voice. 'Maybe you'll decide that Helen is the right woman for you after all, and you'll ring me tomorrow and tell me you don't need Nell's number anymore!'

P.J. didn't think that was very likely. When Janey had rung off, he sat for a while, staring down at the phone.

He had been so sure that he was over Nell, and, after the years spent dismissing Janey's suggestions that he was simply searching for a substitute for her, it was galling to realise that his sister had been right all along.

Irritably, he swung his chair round and prowled over to the window. Part of him had been overjoyed to see Nell that morning, but there was part of him too that wished she hadn't stepped out in front of him and that he had simply driven past her without knowing that she was there.

No, not that, P.J. corrected himself. He *had* wanted to see her. He just wished that she hadn't been so familiar, that she hadn't still been so easy to talk to, still so beautiful... Now it felt as if everything had changed. Nell wasn't just part of his past, whatever she might say about it. Now she was his present, too. She had been ever since he had looked into her grey eyes that morning and felt his heart squeeze in his chest at the realisation that it was really her, after all this time.

He turned back to his desk, but he didn't sit down again. He felt edgy and restless, almost cross, and it was because of Nell. She had shaken him so easily out of his own sense of certainty. P.J. didn't like the feeling, and he especially didn't like the thought that she had found someone else. Janey had told him that she was divorced, but she hadn't known that Nell already had the oh-so-perfect John to make her happy again. She didn't need P.J., and she had made it plain that she didn't particularly want to see him again.

It had all changed so suddenly, too. He had woken up that morning not knowing that Nell would be part of his life once more before the day was even half-way through. Not knowing that sixteen years of missing her would lead to this moment, and that he would have to face the fact that he still wanted her, and needed her, and that, in the end, nothing had changed at all.

What was it Janey had said about him being too used to having whatever he wanted? P.J. hunched his shoulders uneasily. He didn't think that he was like that, but there was no doubt that realising that he might not be able to have Nell had left him feeling tense and twitchy and exposed. It was a long time since he had felt like this.

Sixteen years, in fact.

But he wasn't twenty two anymore, P.J. reminded himself. He was a grown man, and he didn't have to just accept things anymore. He might not be able to have Nell, but he would do whatever he could to get her back, John or no John. He would go on this date tonight as Janey had insisted, but after that he was going to find Nell, with or without his sister's help. He would have to. He couldn't face the thought of losing her all over again.

CHAPTER SIX

THE meeting was scheduled for three o'clock, by which time Nell was wishing that she had never heard of Sygma or its need for a new director of finance. She knew what electronic meant—sort of, anyway—but that was as far as her awareness of, or interest in, firms at the cutting edge of technology went.

Her boss was much more enthusiastic. 'Sygma are *huge*,' she told Nell, several times. 'They dominate the technology market in North America, and now they're expanding their operations in London to take advantage of the enlarged European community. They're going to have phenomenal influence on the business world here, and if we do a good job for them this time, the possibilities are enormous for us.'

Eve's eyes shone at the prospect. 'We've got to get this meeting right. We're dealing with an American company, remember, so we need to be punchy and assertive. None of this British self-effacement, Nell! We've got a can-do philosophy. We're positive, professional, the best.'

Nell clenched her fist in what she hoped was a suitably gung-ho gesture. 'The best,' she agreed, wishing that Eve would go away and let her get on with her work. 'Absolutely.'

'They've got a reputation as tough negotiators,' Eve went on, 'but we can be tough, too. The important thing is to convince them that we're consummate professionals, and that we can find them *exactly* the right person to be their new director of finance. We don't compromise on quality. Ever.'

Nell suspected that Eve was nervously rehearsing what she would say that afternoon, and after a while she restricted herself to nodding absently. She respected her boss rather than liked her, but she had to admire her when they arrived at Sygma's offices. No sign of Eve's earlier tension showed as she shook hands with Lester Graves, the director of human resources who came to meet them.

Nell was glad that she was wearing her best suit. The Sygma offices were extraordinarily stylish, all glass and steel and unobtrusive quality. She began to see what Eve had meant when she'd talked about the company being a force to be reckoned with, and she tried not to feel intimidated as Lester Graves shook her hand and gestured towards a meeting room on their right.

'Shall we go straight in?'

Punchy, positive, professional, Nell repeated to herself, squaring her shoulders and pulling down her jacket as she followed Eve and Lester across the lobby.

'By the way, our president will be sitting in on the meeting,' Lester said to Eve as he opened the door. 'The director of finance is a key position, and he wants to be sure that you know exactly what we're looking for.'

In other words, the president didn't trust his director of human resources to do his job properly, thought Nell, but Eve didn't miss a beat.

'Naturally,' she said coolly. 'It's essential that we establish clear channels of communication at this stage.'

A man was standing by the window, but he turned at the sound of Lester's voice and came over to greet them. Bringing up the rear and half hidden behind Eve, Nell couldn't see him properly at first.

'Peter, can I introduce Eve Fleming and Nell Shea?' said Lester. 'Ladies, this is our president, Mr Smith.'

Eve shook his hand and said something gracious, and then stepped aside to draw Nell forward.

'My assistant, Nell Shea.'

It was only then that Nell saw who was holding out his hand towards her.

P.J.

The breath seemed to be stuck in P.J.'s throat, and for a moment he could only stare. It wasn't just the surprise at seeing her here, although that was startling enough. It was the way she looked.

He had never seen Nell like this before, poised and elegant in a pale pink suit and high heels, her ash blonde hair twisted up and away from her face. The contrast with the way she had looked that morning, in a faded old sweatshirt and with her face bare and her hair tumbled, could hardly be greater, and P.J. was conscious of an absurd spurt of anger at her for changing, and throwing him once again.

He had only decided to sit in on this meeting because he hadn't been able to concentrate on anything all morning. Lester was more than capable of dealing with recruitment issues, but he had agreed readily when P.J. had suggested that he come along as well.

But then he was hardly going to refuse, was he? P.J. thought, shifting uncomfortably at the memory of Janey's comments about his so-called flunkies who said, 'Yes, sir,' and, 'No, sir,' and jumped whenever he snapped his fingers. 'You think you can have whatever you want,' she had accused him.

Now, P.J. looked at Nell and knew that his sister was right. He couldn't have Nell for a snap of his fingers. The exultance he had felt when he'd seen that fate had put her in his way once more evaporated. She looked so lovely, so cool and professional, that his confidence faltered. This Nell wasn't the girl he remembered. She was a woman, who would have to be wooed and won anew, and she wasn't going to be impressed by his position here, no matter how obsequious his staff were.

Belatedly, P.J. became aware that Lester and Eve were looking at him, evidently waiting for him to finish greeting Nell so that they could get on with their meeting. He glanced back at Nell, and her expression was so appalled that his ready sense of the ridiculous came to his rescue.

If she wanted to pretend that this was a business meeting like any other, so be it.

'Ms Shea,' he said formally as he shook her hand.

Nell pulled her hand out of his as if it were scalded, muttering something in reply. She was totally unprepared to see P.J. here, and her heart, which had lurched into her throat at the sight of him, now seemed to be stuck there, beating so frantically that it was all she could do to stay upright.

How could it be P.J., *here? Again?* Meeting him once had been a bizarre enough coincidence, but twice…!

And he was just behaving as if he had never met her before. Completely thrown, Nell turned and headed blindly after Eve, who was settling down with Lester at the end of a long boardroom table at the other end of the room. So blindly, in fact, that she only just avoided bumping into a massive leather sofa.

Nell was so relieved by her narrow escape that she didn't see the granite coffee-table that some fool had put in front of the sofa, and stubbed her toe so painfully on it that she was only just able to bite back an extremely rude exclamation in time.

'Are you all right?' P.J. asked in concern, and Nell forced back tears of pain.

'I'm fine,' she said grittily, aware that Eve was watching her and clearly wondering what she was doing drawing attention to herself like that.

So much for punchy, positive and professional.

Fixing on a smile, Nell limped on to the table and barely restrained a sigh as she sank down next to Eve, and eased off her shoe so that she could rub her poor foot surreptitiously on her calf. Surely this day would start going right soon?

Although obviously not yet, she sighed inwardly as P.J. sat down opposite her, the one place where it would be impossible for her to avoid noticing him.

He pushed his chair back and turned slightly sideways so that his arm rested on the table. 'Lester's going to take the meeting,' he told Eve pleasantly. 'I'm just here to observe and comment as I think it necessary.'

Yes, and to make things more tense for everybody, thought Nell crossly. Doing her best to ignore the way he sat so lazily relaxed across the table, she put her briefcase on her lap and pulled out a notepad and pen. Placing them neatly in front of her, she put her briefcase down, but as she straightened she made the mistake of catching P.J.'s eye.

He sent her a swift, wicked smile that set her blood tingling in her cheeks and made her poor heart jolt anew. Wrenching her gaze away, Nell straightened her notepad unnecessarily and forced herself to look composed.

Punchy, positive, professional, right?

'Well, if we're all ready...' Lester began.

Nell did her best to look alert and engaged in the discussion between Eve and Lester, but it was very hard with P.J. right *there*. He was listening with apparent interest, and occasionally turning a pen pensively on the table, but something about the way he sat there was incredibly distracting. No matter how hard Nell tried to focus on Lester, every nerve in her body strained to turn her attention back to P.J., so that even when she was almost cross-eyed with the effort of looking at the other two, it was his image that danced in front of her eyes.

He had taken his jacket off, and his tie was loosened, his sleeves rolled up casually, and as her gaze drifted surreptitiously from the hard, exciting line of his cheek to his jaw and the edge of his mouth Nell felt herself submerged beneath another frightening wave of what could only be called lust. She wanted to crawl across the table and into his lap, to run her hands up his arms and over his shoulders, to bury her face into his throat and taste his skin.

She felt hot and feverish, and desperate to get out of the room, and away from him. One part of her was jittery and trembling with the need to touch him, but the other couldn't help resenting P.J. for doing this to her now. Why did he have to turn up and turn over her life today of all days?

This was an important meeting. Eve had intimated that her future with the firm might hinge on it, and she needed to concentrate, but how could she concentrate on career profiles and shortlists when P.J.'s smile was burning behind her eyelids, when his hand and his forearm were within reach and it was all she could do not to stretch out and let fingers slip over the broad male wrist and curl around his, palm against palm?

Stop thinking like that. *Focus.*

Nell dragged her attention back to the meeting. It seemed to be going well, judging by the way Eve was nodding thoughtfully.

'Yes, that's a good point,' she told Lester crisply. 'We'll bear that in mind. Make a note of it, will you, Nell?'

At the sound of her name, Nell started, and fumbled for her pen, glad of something to do at last, and to take her mind off P.J.

The pen wouldn't work.

Nell looked at it in disbelief. It had been working perfectly before. She had checked it deliberately. As discreetly as she could, she scribbled on the pad, but the ink wouldn't flow.

Did she have another pen? Nell wondered desperately. And by the time she had found it, would she remember the point Eve was so anxious for her to note?

Biting her lip, Nell started to bend towards her briefcase very slowly and carefully so that Eve wouldn't notice what she was doing, but before she could feel around for the handle P.J. had leant across the table and was offering her his pen.

'Take mine,' he said.

Of course, at the sound of his voice Eve and Lester paused in mid-conversation and both turned to look disapprovingly at Nell, whose incompetence on the pen front had caused the interruption.

Mortified, Nell had little choice but to take P.J.'s pen with a gritted word of thanks. He couldn't have drawn more attention to her if he had tried. Why didn't he go the whole hog and point out to the other two that she wasn't even professional enough to bring along a pen that worked?

Things weren't improved by Eve repeating the point very slowly and clearly, so that Nell couldn't miss it, although actually this was just as well, as otherwise Nell wouldn't have had a clue what she was supposed to write by that stage. Still, it was humiliating, and it was clear that Eve was not pleased after everything she had had to say about the need to appear the epitome of cool professionalism.

Nell's cheeks were hot as she made the note, and after that she kept her eyes on Eve and Lester, rigidly ignoring P.J. It was an uncomfortable position, though, with her head turned to one side, and it was impossible after a while not to let her eyes slide back to the other side of the table, where P.J. sat, evidently absorbed in the intricacies of board profiles and fee structures. He had found another no doubt perfectly functioning pen from somewhere, and was twisting it absently between his fingers as he listened.

Nell knew what those fingers felt like. She knew how firmly they could grasp her hand, how safe they had made her feel. She knew how warm and strong they were, and how sure they had been as they slid over her skin.

She wished she didn't.

She wished the meeting would end. Nell stole a glance at her watch. They had been in there over an hour, and it felt like a lifetime. Surely there was a limit to how much they could find to talk about? It was only a job, for heaven's sake.

Looking up from her watch, she saw that P.J. was watching her, and their eyes met for another fleeting moment. The corner of his mouth twitched, as if he knew exactly what she had been thinking, and Nell coloured, lifted her chin and turned deliberately away from him.

'I think we've covered pretty much everything by now, don't you?' P.J. said to Eve and Lester, who immediately nodded their agreement. Perversely, Nell wished that they would disagree with him, even if it did mean that she would be late getting home to Clara. At least it would show him that he couldn't always have his own way.

But, no. Of course they were too busy kowtowing to him and sycophantically asking for his comments.

'I thought it was a very interesting discussion,' he said blandly. The blue gaze went back to Nell. 'What do you think, Ms Shea? You've been looking very enigmatic!'

Nell glared at him. What was it she had said that morning? Something about looking enigmatic when she didn't have a clue what was going on. And P.J. had laughed and made a joke out of it. It wasn't fair of him to put her on the spot when he must know quite well how hard she had found it to concentrate.

They were all waiting for her to say something. Nell glanced at Eve, who was telegraphing the need to say exactly the right thing or she could blow it all now, while Lester was waiting courteously enough but obviously wondering why her opinion suddenly mattered so much to his president.

She cleared her throat. 'I hope I've been looking interested rather than enigmatic,' she said with a cool smile. 'I think it's been an extremely useful meeting, that has clarified a number of issues—on both sides,' she added looking directly at P.J.

There. If he wanted to challenge her on exactly what she had found so interesting, or which issues had been clarified, he could. She could always go back to her old job.

But P.J. only smiled his appreciation of the vagueness of her answer, and Eve visibly relaxed.

'We'll be in touch as soon as we've drawn up a list of potential candidates,' she promised as she began to get to her feet.

'Perhaps it might be useful if you both met some of the other senior members of the team?' P.J. suggested, standing as well. 'As you may know, Sygma are sponsoring an exhibition of contemporary British art at the Westruther Gallery, and there's a reception to mark the opening this evening at six-thirty. We'll all be there, and it might be a good opportunity for you to meet them socially and get a feel for the kind of organisation we are. What do you think, Lester?'

'It sounds an excellent idea,' said Lester predictably, and Eve, equally predictably, was delighted.

'We'd love to come, wouldn't we, Nell?'

No, she would not love to come, Nell wanted to shout. She had other things to do this evening, as

P.J. knew, and she hated modern art, which he also knew perfectly well. They had spent a weekend in Paris once arguing heatedly about what they had seen in the Beaubourg, and then made up over coffee and calvados in a tiny little café in Montmartre. He had only issued the invitation to throw out her evening.

But she couldn't say that, could she? Eve's lips were thinning dangerously, and the look she sent Nell was so steely that she might as well have observed in a loud voice that Nell's job was on the line. Nell had no option but to force a smile.

'That sounds lovely,' she said through clenched teeth, and P.J.'s smile broadened at her obvious reluctance.

'Excellent,' he said. 'I'll get your names put on the guest list. You never know, you might even enjoy it!'

'I'm sure we will,' said Eve warmly, with another warning glance at Nell, but by now Nell was too fed up to care. She had had enough of today.

She put her notepad and pen away in her briefcase and pointedly said nothing as Eve turned back to say goodbye to Lester.

'Please, do keep my pen, Ms Shea,' P.J. murmured over Nell's shoulder, and she actually slapped her forehead with an exclamation of frustration.

'I'm sorry,' she said stiffly, making to open her

briefcase. 'I wasn't intending to steal it. I wasn't thinking.'

P.J.'s voice changed. 'Nell, it's only a pen,' he said in an undertone so that Eve and Lester couldn't hear. 'I was just teasing. Of course, it doesn't matter.'

'I think it does.' Nell extracted the pen and handed it back to him, very much on her dignity. 'Thank you so much, *Mr Smith.*'

If she'd hoped to disconcert him, she failed miserably. P.J. only grinned and twirled the pen between his fingers as he stood back to let her past, her briefcase clutched defensively to her chest.

'I'll see you later then, after all,' he said.

CHAPTER SEVEN

'HE MADE me look an absolute fool,' Nell stormed, slamming the lid onto the kettle and banging it back onto its element.

'I don't see how,' said Thea, who was babysitting Clara and had heard all about the meeting over their first cup of tea. 'It wasn't P.J.'s fault that you stubbed your toe, or that your pen ran out, was it?'

It had felt like his fault, Nell thought darkly, but she didn't know how to explain that to Thea.

'*And* he only insisted that we go to that stupid reception tonight because he knew I had a date,' she went on, opting to ignore her sister's reasonable comments.

Thea reached for another biscuit. 'He's obviously keen to see you again,' she said with satisfaction.

'Well, I'm not keen to see him! If Janey asks you for my number, I utterly forbid you to give it to her!'

'He won't need your number,' Thea pointed out through a mouthful of biscuit. 'He knows where you work now.'

That was true. Nell dropped down into a chair with a gusty sigh. 'There'll be fat chance of getting my calls screened either. Eve would make me marry

P.J. if she thought it would get her a long-term contract with Sygma!'

'Well, you could do worse,' her sister said thoughtfully, and Nell glowered at her.

'Make up your mind! I thought I was supposed to be falling for this guy I'm meeting tonight?'

'You know, I really do think you might,' said Thea with a conspiratorial smile. 'Still, there's no harm in having P.J. as a fall-back position, is there?'

'I think you should get back together with P.J.,' said Clara, leaning over Nell's shoulder to pinch another biscuit from the tin. 'I thought he was really nice.'

'You hardly met him,' objected Nell. Why was everyone so determined to push her into P.J.'s arms?

'He had smiley eyes,' Clara said simply.

He *did* have nice eyes. Nell couldn't dispute that. Their warmth and humour was very hard to resist, and she wasn't that surprised that her daughter had fallen for their charm, too.

'I could tell he was pleased to see you, too, Mum,' Clara went on. 'Why were you so unfriendly to him?'

Good question. Nell couldn't explain to Clara that P.J. was much more than a charming smile and an engaging manner. If that was all there was to him, there would be no problem. She would just be able to think of him as an old friend and a nice man, the way everyone else seemed to do.

But old friends didn't make you churn with desire, did they? They didn't set your nerves a-jangle, or make you feel restless and breathless with something that was more fear than pleasure, as if the earth had shifted beneath your feet and sent your life and everything you thought you were, everything you thought you wanted, spinning out of your control?

Steeling herself against the way P.J. made her feel was the only way Nell could keep a grip on reality, but how could she explain *that* to Clara?

'I was just a bit…thrown,' she said after a moment. 'It's an odd feeling coming face to face with your past without warning like that.'

Nell wanted to go back to the way she had been yesterday. Yes, it had been lonely sometimes, but she had Clara, who made everything worthwhile. So life wasn't very exciting? At least it was safe, and she was content. Surely that was better than this twitchy, jittery, scarily *alive* feeling she had had ever since P.J. had crashed back into her life that morning?

'You're supposed to be thinking about the future, not the past,' said Thea, who had been watching her sister's face. Draining her tea, she got to her feet and brushed the biscuit crumbs from her fingers in a determined manner. 'Let's go and make you beautiful for John.'

Between them, Thea and Clara bullied Nell into putting on the dress she had bought in a burst of extravagance to celebrate Thea's wedding the previous Christmas. At first glance it seemed quite plain, just a dress that clung to her figure and whose smoky grey echoed her eyes, but there was a sheen to the material that added a subtle glamour to the subdued colour, and the effect was softened by the chiffon sleeves and overskirt that fluttered and floated as she moved.

Something about the fabric and the cut made Nell feel wonderful whenever she put it on. Even now, when she was churning with anxiety, she was conscious of a frisson of pleasure as the soft material shimmered around her.

Maybe Thea was right. She should be thinking about the future, not the past. Her life was too small at the moment. There seemed no room for anything except Clara and work. No wonder P.J.'s reappearance had had such an effect on her, Nell thought ruefully. He had made her realise just how limited her life had become. If she had been involved in another relationship, she wouldn't be this unsettled by him.

Well, that could change. She would make an effort tonight. This John might be just what she needed, Nell told herself. He might be nice. Thea liked him, which was a good sign, but it was hard to imagine

him at the moment. Whenever she tried to conjure
up a possible picture, all she could see was P.J. smiling at her.

She pushed the image aside once more and concentrated fiercely on imagining a future with a man
she loved. Maybe in years to come, she and John
would look back on this evening as the first night
they met, and they would remember the bar, and how
they had felt and this dress…

'You don't think it's too revealing?' she asked,
regarding herself dubiously in the mirror.

'That's the whole point,' said Thea patiently. 'It's
supposed to be sexy.'

'But I've got to go to this reception first.' And P.J.
would see her wearing it. What if he thought she had
made all this effort for him? 'It's not really appropriate for a work do.'

Thea waved work aside. 'If they want you to turn
up in a suit, they should keep work to office hours,'
she said. 'You've got a heavy date tonight, and it's
more important that you look nice for that. Now,
where are those shoes…? Ah!'

'Thea, I can't possibly walk in those,' Nell protested as her sister pulled a pair of exquisitely delicate sandals from the bottom of her cupboard.

'Who said anything about walking? You can get
taxis this evening,' said Thea. 'I've already ordered
you a cab to get to the gallery. You spent a fortune

on these shoes, Nell, and you never wear them. Anything else will spoil the dress, anyway—unless you were thinking of going in your trainers?' she added sarcastically.

'I could put them in a bag and change when I get there, the way I do for work,' Nell pointed out, but Thea wasn't having any of it.

'You are *not* going to ruin everything by hulking a carrier bag along with you,' she said. Rummaging some more in Nell's wardrobe, she emerged after a few moments with a tiny sequinned bag, which she pushed into her sister's hand. 'Perfect! That is all you're allowed to carry, and I can tell you now the trainers just won't fit.'

She stood back to admire her handiwork. 'You look fabulous!'

'You do,' Clara agreed. She had been sitting cross-legged on the bed, watching Thea take her mother in hand. 'You look beautiful, Mum.'

'Thank you, darling,' said Nell, touched. 'But the truth is that I'd much rather be wearing my dressing gown and staying in for pizza with you and Thea!'

'Instead of which you've got to go out to a glamorous reception and a date with a gorgeous man,' said Thea with spurious sympathy. 'It's a dirty job, I know, but somebody's got to do it, and tonight it's your turn! Don't forget your book,' she added as they went downstairs to wait for the cab.

Resigned, Nell went into the sitting room and ran an eye along the shelves until she found the Swahili phrase book that Thea had apparently arranged for her to carry as a signal.

She wished Thea hadn't chosen this book of all books. Pulling it slowly down from the shelf, she stared at it in her hands and felt the memories wash over her. It was years since she had looked at it. Keeping it hadn't even been a conscious decision, and if anyone had asked her if she had such a phrase book a week ago she would probably have said that she didn't.

'Why did you tell John I would have this with me?'

'Because I've been noticing that book on your shelves ever since I've been babysitting Clara,' said Thea. 'If I'm here on my own and there's nothing on television, I see if I can find something to read, and that Swahili book always seemed to catch my eye. I've often wondered why you had it.'

Nell flicked slowly through the pages. 'P.J. and I used to talk about a trip to East Africa,' she admitted reluctantly. 'It was going to be an extended honeymoon. We planned to spend a few months there and we were both going to learn Swahili...'

Her voice trailed off as she remembered how young and innocent and enthusiastic they had been. She couldn't contemplate a trip like that now without running through all the possible complications and difficulties first. But everything had been simple then. They had loved each other, and the world had been at their feet, and that had been enough.

She remembered going to a cavernous shop in Covent Garden with P.J. and eagerly buying maps and guides and phrase books. That had been just before she'd gone back to university for the last time, and the next time she'd been home, Simon had been there…

'I wish *I* could go to Africa,' sighed Clara. 'I want to go on safari and see the lions and giraffes and elephants.'

Yes, that was what she and P.J. had wanted to do, too.

'What is John going to be carrying, again?' asked Nell, still leafing distractedly through the book.

'A Swahili dictionary,' said Thea. 'He's been to Tanzania, and that's what made me think of saying you'd take your phrase book. I thought it was a brilliant idea,' she added complacently. 'No one else is likely to have one, are they? So you won't be able to mistake each other, and it means you don't need to bother with awkward descriptions.'

'I suppose it'll give us something to talk about, if nothing else,' acknowledged Nell, opening her clutch bag. The phrase book was pocket sized, but the bag was so tiny that she could only just squeeze it in.

The clasp wouldn't close properly, but it was better than carrying the book in her hand. At least this way P.J. wouldn't see it.

It was a slow drive into the centre of London at that time of the evening, and as Nell sat in the back of the minicab and looked out at the bumper-to-bumper traffic she found herself thinking about those old dreams of camping together under a wide African sky.

'We'll lie in our tent and listen to the lions roaring,' P.J. had promised, his face alight. 'We'll watch the sun rise over the Serengeti and we'll be married, and we'll be together, and we'll be the happiest people in the world!'

But they had never made it. She had chosen Simon instead, and that was a choice she had to live with, Nell knew that. On an impulse, she pulled the phrase book out of her bag, and turned it in her hands. For some reason the anger she had felt after that afternoon's meeting had evaporated at the sight of it.

It wasn't really P.J. she was angry with, Nell realised. She was angry with herself for regretting the choices she had made. She was angry because he had come back and made her think about how happy they might have been, might still be, if she had chosen differently. It wasn't P.J.'s fault that he had moved on and made a success of his life without her.

She had Clara. Nell clung to the thought. She

couldn't imagine life without Clara, wouldn't *want* to imagine it. But she could imagine being with someone who loved her and cared for her, someone who would make her laugh and hold her when she was sad, who would celebrate her triumphs with her, and commiserate with her failures. Someone who would share her life instead of shutting her off into a small part of it, the way Simon had done.

P.J. would have been a husband like that. Nell stared unseeing out at the traffic and thought about the mistakes she had made. She had had her chance. She had been lucky enough to meet the right man for her, but she had blown it. She had been too young to appreciate kindness and integrity and strength and humour over good looks and glamour. Now, she could see how lucky she had been to find those qualities in her first love, but now it was too late.

Things might be different if P.J. hadn't been quite so successful, but his immense wealth seemed to Nell to be an insurmountable gulf between them. It changed everything. She didn't want him for his money, but how would he ever believe that now?

She would have to stay on her side of the gulf and make the best of it, Nell decided sadly. She would go and meet John, and make a real effort to start afresh, and maybe after a while she could forget P.J. all over again.

The gallery was already crowded when she got there, the hubbub spilling out into the street. If only she didn't have to face P.J. again! Still, with this crowd, there ought to be a good chance of avoiding him. She would go in, show her face to Eve, talk to a couple of people and then go. She had a previous engagement, after all. She couldn't be expected to rearrange her entire social life around work.

A brief hope that her name might have been missed off the guest list died as she was waved through, so she accepted a glass of champagne and looked cautiously around for Eve.

Of course, the first person she saw was P.J. He wasn't looking her way, but still the sight of him made her heart jolt painfully, and she jerked her glass, sending champagne slopping over the rim and down the front of her dress. Nell brushed herself down with a hand that was shaking slightly, and told herself to get a grip.

She risked another glance. Like many of the other men in the room, P.J. was wearing a dinner jacket, and the severe black and white tailoring made him look powerful and more distinguished than she had ever seen him. He was standing on one side of the gallery, talking to a dark, intense girl who was dressed in such a challenging way that Nell wondered if she was one of the artists.

He seemed absorbed in his conversation, and Nell

let her eyes rest hungrily on him for a moment. It was as if everything about him were in sharp focus, the planes of his face, the set of his shoulders, the white cuff against his brown hand as he gesticulated, and her stomach clenched with longing.

Turning abruptly, she headed off in the opposite direction in search of Eve. There was such a press of people, none of whom seemed to be the slightest bit interested in the pictures and installations that lined the walls, that it was quite hard work pushing through them and when Nell had got as far away from P.J. as she could, she paused. She couldn't see any sign of Eve.

What now?

The whole exercise was pointless anyway, Nell told herself. There was no way they were going to be able to talk properly to anyone in this crush. Perhaps she would just slip away now...

Glancing longingly towards the entrance through a break in the crowd, she found herself staring straight into a pair of familiar warm blue eyes that lit at the sight of her.

P.J. smiled at her, and Nell's bones seemed to dissolve. Appalled, she spun on her heel before she had a chance to think and turned her back pointedly, desperate to break the effect of that glinting blue smile. Her instinct was to bolt for the entrance, but if he saw her leaving now P.J. would know that it was because of him.

Unseeingly, she stared at a picture on the wall instead, pretending to be absorbed in it. Surely P.J. would get the point and leave her alone now?

'What do you think?' His voice came from behind her and Nell jumped. How had he got across the room that fast? Why had he come at all? Couldn't he *see* how hard this was for her?

Her mouth was dry, and she moistened her lips. 'Think?' she repeated stupidly. How could she think when he was standing right beside her, near enough for her to turn and lean into him, to rest against his broad chest and wind her arms around his back and cling to him as if he were her last refuge?

'Of the picture,' P.J. prompted.

'Oh.'

With difficulty, Nell focused on the painting and discovered that she had been apparently absorbed in an extremely explicit male nude study. A wave of colour surged up her cheeks, but somehow she managed to keep her expression composed enough.

'Interesting use of brushwork,' she said stiltedly, and P.J. laughed.

'Don't tell me you've learnt to like contemporary art, Nell!'

'I wouldn't say "like,"' said Nell, 'but maybe

I've learnt to appreciate some of the things I wasn't old enough to appreciate before.'

Their eyes met for a brief moment, and something flared in P.J.'s face, something that made Nell's heart stumble, and she looked away almost fiercely, afraid that she had given too much away.

CHAPTER EIGHT

P.J. LOOKED at Nell's averted face, letting his eyes rest on the pure line of her cheek and the pulse hammering in her throat, and he remembered her as a girl, sitting across a café table in Paris, her expression vivid as she talked and argued and laughed.

Even then he had marvelled that this beautiful creature was really his. That she would love him had seemed too good to be true, and when Simon Shea had swept in and taken her away part of P.J. had told himself that he had always known it couldn't last. Why would a girl like Nell want to be with *him*, with his big nose and lanky frame and utter lack of sophistication?

She was still beautiful, still slender and somehow elusive, and as he watched her P.J.'s earlier confidence drained away. He felt twenty-two all over again, awkward and unsure, dazed by her nearness and gripped by the fear that if he tried to hold on to her, she would slip through his fingers and leave.

As she had.

She had John now. She was happy. Why would she want to start all over again with him? Look at her, sophisticated and desirable in a dress that clung in all the right places. It was a dress that made you think about how soft and warm her body would be beneath the soft, floaty material, how it would slide and slither over her skin, what it would be like to ease down the zip…

P.J. swallowed hard.

'You look stunning,' he said, aware that he sounded abrupt and almost angry, but unable to help himself.

'Thank you,' said Nell a little warily.

'I hope John appreciates that dress.'

John? For a terrible moment, Nell couldn't think who he meant, but then she remembered her blind date, and she clutched at the idea. John represented the future, P.J. the past. Pretending that she had already chosen the future would make it easier in the end to say goodbye to P.J. again.

'John doesn't think clothes are important,' she said. It was the first thing that came into her head, and P.J. wasn't impressed.

'You don't have to think clothes are important to appreciate a beautiful woman in a beautiful dress!' he said. 'He sounds a bit worthy for you, Nell.'

'He's a very nice man,' she said a little defensively.

'Not just a little boring?' P.J. suggested.

'Of course not,' said Nell stiffly.

'It just sounds as if he might be, that's all.'

Nell glared, so irritated by his needling that she almost forgot that she knew absolutely nothing about John. 'He's not like that at all,' she insisted, lifting her chin defiantly. 'He's great. He's...kind and reliable and...clever...*and* he's got a great sense of humour,' she finished as if laying down a challenge.

'I suppose he's incredibly good-looking, too?' said P.J. nastily.

'Not that it matters, but, yes, as a matter of fact, he is!'

In for a penny, in for a pound, thought Nell, wondering what the real John would make of all this. *Would* he have a sense of humour? Would he prove to be kind and clever? Would he be the man who could push P.J. back out of her heart and her mind and her life?

'He sounds perfect.' P.J. glowered down into his glass of champagne. 'So, do you think this is it?' he made himself ask, not wanting to hear the answer but needing to know if he should give up now. 'Are you thinking about getting married?'

'It's too early to think about that,' said Nell, deciding not to get carried away with elaborate wedding plans. 'We haven't known each other that long. Anyway, I've already been married once and engaged twice,' she added, trying to make a joke of it. 'My track record isn't that good, is it?'

'Maybe it'll be third time lucky,' said P.J.

It had been first time lucky, if only she had had the sense to realise it. Nell's heart twisted.

'Maybe,' she agreed, an unconsciously wistful expression in her eyes.

There was a tiny pause. 'What does Clara think of him?'

'Clara?' Nell echoed stupidly.

'She comes with you as part of the package, doesn't she? I presume how she and John get on is important to you?'

'Of course it is,' said Nell, thrown back on the defensive. 'But she doesn't know him very well yet.'

'Clara struck me as the kind of girl who makes up her mind about people straight away,' P.J. observed so accurately that Nell was taken aback. That was *exactly* what Clara did, just as she had done with P.J. that morning. She had looked at him, assessed him, and decided that she liked him, and that was that in Clara's book. Nothing would change her mind now.

'Do you know what I think?' P.J. went on, leaning forward confidentially, and Nell swallowed at his nearness and clutched her glass harder.

'What?'

'I think Clara hasn't got much time for your John,' he said provocatively. 'I think she thinks he's a dull dog, but she doesn't want to tell you, and *that's* why you're hesitant about committing yourself to him.'

'Rubbish!'

'If you loved John and you thought he was the right man, you wouldn't hesitate,' said P.J. 'You're someone who loves completely and unconditionally.'

'Yes, well, maybe I've learnt to look before I leap,' Nell said a little bitterly, thinking of Simon.

The look in her eyes made P.J.'s chest hurt. He was just taking his disappointment out on her, he realised. It wasn't Nell's fault that he was still in love with her. 'I'm sorry,' he apologised in a different voice.

'John's a lucky man,' he went on seriously. 'I was just trying to say that if I was waiting for you, and you walked in wearing that dress, I would be really proud.'

Nell looked at him, and her heart contracted so painfully that she almost winced. If only she *were* going to meet P.J. tonight, instead of the blameless John. The longing to tell him so made it hard to speak, and for a moment she could only stand dumb with wishing that everything could be different.

She didn't want John. He was a friend of Thea's, and he would be nice, and friendly and charming and probably attractive and a perfect date, but he wasn't what she wanted. He couldn't be. She only wanted P.J.

A muscle worked desperately in her jaw to stop her mouth from wobbling, and P.J., understanding that she was upset, but not why, did what he could to lighten the atmosphere.

'That dress is the third outfit I've seen you in today,' he said, 'and it's definitely my favourite. You looked very nice in your track suit and trainers, of *course,* but they don't have quite same the same allure, do they? And to be honest, I didn't think the cool, crisp look you had this afternoon was quite you!'

Grateful to him for changing the subject, Nell made an effort to smile and follow his lead. 'I usually carry off cool and crisp better than I did this afternoon,' she told him. 'My pen always works, and I manage not to walk into the furniture. But then I don't usually walk into a meeting to find that I'm shaking hands with my ex-fiancé! Did you know I was going to be there?'

P.J. shook his head. 'Lester mentioned Eve's name, but not that there would be anyone else with her. I couldn't believe it when I saw you come in. After this morning, it seemed too much of a coincidence.' He smiled crookedly. 'Do you think fate might be trying to tell us something?'

'Only that it's as muddled as the rest of us,' said Nell, as lightly as she could.

A waitress was hovering with a plate of spectacular canapés. Desperate for a distraction, to look at anything other than P.J., Nell took a firm hold of her glass and wedged her sequinned bag under her arm to give herself a free hand. She selected a canapé at random, and was just lifting it to her mouth when someone behind her stepped back into her.

Nell's arm was jolted, and she jerked instinctively to avoid dropping her champagne, but the movement was enough to dislodge the little bag, and, with her other hand full of canapé, there was no way of saving it. If she'd been able to close it properly, no harm would have been done, but the Swahili phrase book burst through the clasp's precarious hold and shot onto the floor, followed by all the other contents.

Had she really had all that stuff in that tiny bag? To Nell, rooted to the spot, it seemed as if the contents had multiplied bizarrely and that she was standing in a scattered sea of keys and lipsticks, mobile phones and credit cards, tissues and perfumes and ten-pound notes, all interspersed with the change from the minicab, which was rolling merrily amongst the shoes in every direction.

'I'm so sorry.' The man who had bumped into her was full of apologies, stooping like P.J. to help gather everything up.

Why was there never anywhere in these places to put a glass down? Nell looked around helplessly. With both hands full, she felt marooned and ridiculous, the two men apparently grovelling at her feet, and she had no choice in the end but to pop the canapé in her mouth.

Still chewing, she bent to retrieve the little bag, and smiled embarrassed thanks as they handed back her scattered belongings. Someone brought over a pound coin that had rolled right into the middle of the room, another person found her comb. Thank goodness she hadn't had anything *really* embarrassing in the bag!

'I think that's everything,' she said, straightening, and turned to thank the man who had bumped into her for his help, and to assure him that there was no harm done, really.

'Except for this.' P.J. stood up with the Swahili phrase book in his hand, a strange expression on his face.

Nell's heart sank at the sight of it. In all the confusion, for a minute there she had forgotten how odd the phrase book would look.

A smile hovered around P.J.'s mouth. 'Don't tell me you're still trying to learn Swahili, Nell?'

'No...I...I'm just lending it to John.'

'Oh?'

'Yes. He's...um...thinking about a holiday in Kenya.' Nell improvised as best she could, but it didn't sound very convincing even to her own ears.

'Really?' P.J. smiled at her, a smile that evaporated the air in her lungs and made her pulse ring in her ears.

'Yes,' she said breathlessly, unable to think of anything else to say.

She wished P.J. would give her the book, but he was flicking through the pages. '*Habarigani*...how are you? Remember that? We used to practise it all the time.'

'Not as often as we practised "two cold beers, please,"' said Nell, trying to make light of it, but her heart was thumping with memories.

P.J. screwed up his face and held up his hand. 'Hold on...*nataka beer mbili, baridi sana,*' he said triumphantly after a moment. 'You see, I remember!'

'I'm impressed,' she said. 'I would never have been able to remember that.'

'I remember everything.' His voice changed. 'I remember how to say "I love you," too. *Nakupenda sana.* I would have said that to you every day.'

Treacherous tears pricked at Nell's eyes, and she bent her head, pretending to check that the bag was properly closed this time. 'It's all a long time ago,' she managed after a moment.

'Sixteen years,' said P.J. 'Remember what plans we had? We were going to do all the game parks, and climb Kilimanjaro and swim in the Indian Ocean...and then there was Zanzibar... Didn't we talk about driving across the Sahara at one time, when getting on a plane seemed too tame?'

'We must have been mad,' said Nell, resisting the lure of the memories with a physical effort. 'When you think about it now, it seems totally unrealistic.'

'We were young,' said P.J. gently. 'Don't you ever wish you could still be that unrealistic?'

Nell nodded sadly. She had had enough reality over the last few years. 'You can't recapture that feeling though. You're never that young again.'

'It doesn't mean you have to give up on dreams,' he said.

'No, but it's easier to be realistic in the long run.' Nell bit her lip. 'It's less disappointing that way.'

P.J. closed the phrase book and handed it back to her. 'Did you ever go to Africa?'

'No.' Nell shook her head.

Simon wouldn't even consider an adventure holiday. They had always gone to expensive resorts where the rooms were air-conditioned and the plumbing always worked and the pool was carefully filtered. Nell had used to suggest going out to see something of the country they were in, but Simon had never been interested. 'We're here to relax, Nell,' he would say exasperatedly. 'It's all right for you, but I've been working flat out for months.'

Nell pushed the memory aside. 'What about you?'

'I went to Tanzania once a few years ago.'

'Was it as wonderful?' she asked, trying to keep the envy out of her voice.

'It was beautiful,' P.J. said slowly. 'Even more so than we imagined.'

But he hadn't really enjoyed it being there without her. He had found himself watching the sunset and thinking about Nell and what it would have been like if they'd come together as they'd planned.

He had never asked for two cold beers in Swahili. Marian was strictly a champagne and cocktails girl, who wouldn't touch beer and who complained about the heat and the insects and the lack of any decent shops. The whole holiday had been disastrous. It had certainly spelt the end of *that* relationship.

'I'm glad,' said Nell. 'We spent so much time dreaming about that trip, it would have been a shame if neither of us had gone.'

'Yes, a shame,' P.J. agreed, and their eyes met for a brief moment before Nell's slid awkwardly away.

She was having trouble breathing again, and the silence lengthened as she tried desperately to think of something to say. She had the strangest sensation of being trapped in a bubble, isolated somehow from the chatter and the crowds that surrounded them, so that there was only P.J. and the silence and the memories that clamoured and jangled between them.

She had to break out, to get away from the bitter-sweet knowledge of what might have been.

'I…I haven't met any of the other members of your team yet,' she said at last with an edge of desperation. 'Perhaps you could introduce me?'

P.J. didn't move. 'Eve's busy chatting them all up.'

'I should go and join her, then.' Nell could hear the tell-tale huskiness in her voice and cleared her throat. 'That's what I'm here for, after all.'

'I think Eve would prefer you to stay right where you are,' he said with a lazy smile. 'She'll think you're doing a good job of sucking up to the boss.'

In a strange way, Nell was grateful to him for making her cross. 'I wasn't aware that I had been sucking up,' she said tightly.

'You haven't—but there's no need for Eve to know that, is there?'

'Then what was the point of making me come here tonight?'

P.J. feigned surprise. 'I didn't *make* you do anything, did I? I merely invited you for a glass of free champagne.'

'Yes, knowing perfectly well that I was in no position to refuse,' said Nell, deliberately feeding her anger, which was so much easier to deal with than the memories. 'Never mind that I've got a date tonight, which you also knew perfectly well!' She looked at her watch. 'And now I'm going to be late!'

CHAPTER NINE

'I'M SURE John will understand,' said P.J. 'Why don't you give him a call and tell him you'll be a little late?'

Nell bit her lip. There was no way she was going to admit now that John was a blind date and that the only way she could contact him was to depend on him recognising her Swahili phrase book.

P.J. had picked up her mobile from the floor, so she could hardly claim that she had no way of getting in touch. And even if she did, he would probably just offer her his phone.

'He doesn't have a mobile,' she said, driven into a corner.

P.J. looked surprised. 'He doesn't? Why not?'

'He thinks they're an intrusion,' Nell improvised and then was vexed with herself for making the blameless John sound so boring. For all she knew, John had the latest technology coming out of his ears. 'Anyway, I'm sure he'll wait, but I'd better get going...'

'Where are you meeting him?'

'At Covent Garden.'

'In a restaurant?'

'No, in a bar—not that it's any business of yours!'

'Which one?'

'Look, what's with the interrogation?' demanded Nell, ruffled.

P.J. held up his hands. 'No interrogation. It's just that I'm on my way to Covent Garden myself. I could give you a lift.'

'There's really no need,' she began, but P.J. interrupted her.

'I insist,' he said. 'As you've just pointed out, it's my fault that you're late, so it's the least I can do.'

'I'll take the tube,' said Nell stiffly, distrusting his motives. 'It will be easier.'

'In those shoes?' P.J. nodded down at her feet. You didn't need to be an aficionado of footwear to realise that those delicate straps and elegant heels weren't meant for walking. 'You know how far you have to walk along the tunnels underground, and I didn't see a spare pair of shoes in that bag. It wouldn't do that ankle of yours any good.'

That was unanswerable. This was Thea's fault, Nell thought vengefully.

'I wouldn't have had to walk at all if you hadn't made me come here,' she grumbled, falling back on accusation. 'I haven't met a single one of your precious team and I'm just as much in the dark about your famous company culture as I was this afternoon! It's been a complete waste of time.'

'I wouldn't say that,' said P.J., and the undercurrent of amusement in his voice made Nell look at him sharply.

'What on earth was the point of inviting me, then?'

'I wanted to see you again,' he said simply. 'You wouldn't have dinner with me, and getting you to come along this evening was the best I could think of on the spur of the moment.'

'P.J...' Nell wrenched her gaze away from the dancing blue depths. Couldn't he *see* how impossible it would be? 'I...I'd better go,' she stammered, looking around for somewhere to put down her glass.

'Yes, you mustn't keep John waiting any longer,' P.J. agreed affably. 'Here, let me take that glass.' As if by magic, a waiter materialised at his side and he put the glasses on the tray with a nod of thanks before turning back to Nell. 'Ready?'

'Really, I'll be fine...'

'Nell, I'm just an old friend offering you a lift,' said P.J. patiently. 'What's the harm in that?'

None, if she could think of him as just an old friend. But he could never be that to her now. The current of awareness still ran between them too strongly for that.

'What about everyone here?' She hung back, gesturing around the crowded room.

'What about them?'

'I thought you were sponsoring this event. Won't they miss you?'

'It's nothing to do with me,' said P.J., unconcerned. 'I don't even get to sign the cheques anymore. It's a corporate affair, and I'm just invited along with everyone else. Anyway, I've got a date myself.'

'Oh.' Nell was horrified at the wave of sickening jealousy that engulfed her.

'That's why I'm on my way to Covent Garden,' he explained, flipping open a tiny mobile phone and pressing a button. 'I'm meeting her there.'

'Oh,' said Nell again in a hollow voice.

'Come on, let's go.'

There was no point in arguing any further. One warm hand on her elbow, P.J. propelled her firmly through the crowd, nodding and smiling at various people, but stopping for no one.

By the time they made it to the entrance, his car was already waiting. The driver got out, and handed the keys to P.J. before vanishing discreetly.

'Very convenient,' said Nell, trying to recover some of her earlier combative spirit.

'Isn't it?' said P.J. cheerfully as he opened the door for her. 'I just buzz him when I'm ready to leave, and he has the car waiting for me outside.'

'It must be nice never to have to worry about parking tickets.'

'One of the bonuses of being a billionaire,' he agreed with a sidelong grin, and got in beside her.

Something had changed, Nell thought suspiciously, eyeing him under her lashes as he slotted the key into the ignition. He had been unusually prickly earlier, almost unpleasant when he was needling her about John, and it had crossed her mind that he might even have been jealous, but there was no sign of that tension now. His normal good humour was completely restored. She could see it in the curve of his mouth and in the glint of his eyes, hear it in the undercurrent of teasing laughter in his voice. He seemed almost...*elated* was the only word that sprang to mind.

He was obviously looking forward to his evening, and why not? There was no reason for P.J. to dread his date the way she was dreading hers.

The news that P.J. was dating someone had left Nell with a sick feeling in the pit of her stomach. She felt ridiculous. All that fuss she had made about the need to resist him! She had been so sure that he too was conscious of the surge and crackle of awareness between them, and she had been afraid that he would try and resurrect their relationship. Now it turned out that she could have spared herself the effort of worrying about it all!

P.J. hadn't mentioned anyone, so she had just assumed that he didn't have a girlfriend, but she should have known better. Of *course* a man like P.J. would have someone special in his life.

He had said that he wanted to see her, though, Nell reminded herself. But then, what did that mean? He might simply want to catch up on old times. It didn't mean that he wanted to pick up where they had left off sixteen years ago, did it?

And now he had a date. P.J. was strictly a one-woman man, so obviously she really was just an old friend as far as P.J. was concerned. She ought to be pleased, Nell thought mournfully. Wasn't it exactly what she had decided herself? She had been determined not to let him back into her life, and now it looked as if she wouldn't have to. Everything was perfect.

Everything being perfect should have made things easier, but instead Nell felt even more awkward than before.

'So…are you meeting someone nice?' she managed at last.

'Oh, yes,' said P.J. and turned to smile his heart-stopping smile. 'She's the nicest person I know. And the most beautiful,' he added.

'She sounds lovely.' Nell fixed on an answering smile so bright it made her jaw ache. 'Lucky you.'

'I hope so.'

She turned slightly in her seat to look at him in surprise. 'What do you mean?'

'I'm not sure how she feels about me,' said P.J. carefully.

She was probably head over heels in love with him, thought Nell. How could she not be?

'You should ask her,' she said. That was the kind of advice one old friend gave to another, wasn't it?

P.J. seemed very interested in her opinion. 'Do you really think so?'

'Of course.' Nell managed a careless shrug, as if it didn't make any difference to her one way or another. 'At least then you'll know where you are.'

'But what if she tells me she doesn't love me?'

Inside Nell, it felt as if a cold hand were clamped around her heart, squeezing it so painfully that it was hard to breathe. 'It's better if you're both honest about how you feel, isn't it?' she managed.

'That's the thing,' said P.J. 'I don't think she *has* been entirely honest with me so far.'

'Why not?'

'She's been hurt,' he said slowly. 'She doesn't trust me.'

'Perhaps she doesn't trust herself,' said Nell, concentrating on breathing in and out and on not thinking about the pain in her heart at the knowledge of how deeply P.J. loved the new woman in his life.

P.J. glanced at her thoughtfully. 'I think you might be right, Nell,' he said. 'How can I make her trust me, though?'

Nell's throat hurt with the effort of not crying. 'You need to be patient, that's all.'

'It's hard being patient,' he said.

'I know, but if you really love her, she's worth it, isn't she?' Her voice cracked slightly at the end, and she looked fiercely out of the passenger window.

'Oh, yes,' said P.J. 'She's worth everything.'

Nell couldn't see his expression, but she could hear the warmth and the tenderness in his voice, and the cruel grip on her heart tightened, but she made herself swallow and take a deep breath.

'I'm so glad you've found someone you can love like that, P.J.,' she said, proud of how steady her voice sounded. 'I hope it works out for you.'

'I hope so, too,' he said. He glanced at her. 'And thanks for your advice, Nell. That's helped me a lot.'

'Good.' Nell's smile wavered a little, but she forced it back into place. 'I'm really happy for you.'

But she didn't feel happy. She felt desolate at the thought of him loving someone else.

Why had he come back? She had been fine on her own, Nell thought bitterly. She had been bumbling along with Clara, missing having someone to hold sometimes, wishing there were someone to hold her when times were hard, but on the whole…she was OK. More than OK. She had been happy. Happyish, anyway.

And now P.J. had spoilt that. He had made her

think about how empty her life was beyond Clara. He had made the future seem bleak and lonely, where before it had simply been more of the same. It had taken her years to bury her memories of him, but a single day to bring them all back. It was like waking up to find a dream being dangled tantalisingly in front of her, only to vanish the moment she thought about reaching for it and making it real, and now she felt sick with disappointment and yearning.

And these might be the last few minutes she would have with him, Nell realised with a spurt of panic. He had a new woman in his life, and there would be no reason for them to meet again.

She longed to touch P.J. one more time. She wanted to reach over and put her hand on his thigh, to lean across and press her lips to his throat. She wanted to make him stop and pull the car over and kiss her. She wanted to roll back time, to go back sixteen years and have her chance again, and this time she wouldn't blow it. She would make the right choice.

But there was no going back, was there? Time only went one way.

The silence was excruciating. Nell was afraid that P.J. would hear her heart thumping, and the pounding of her pulse as she clutched her hands around the little bag to keep them from crawling across to him. The traffic was very heavy, and the journey seemed to take forever.

By the time they got to Trafalgar Square, Nell could stand it no longer.

'I think it'll be quicker for me if I walk from here,' she said as the traffic light turned red once more.

'But what about your feet?' P.J. asked in concern. 'It's still quite a walk from here in those shoes.'

'They'll be fine,' Nell insisted. 'It's not that far now, and I don't want to keep John waiting any longer.'

'Well, if you're sure…'

Nell didn't know whether to be relieved or sorry when P.J. made no further protest. His mind was obviously on the evening to come and the woman he loved.

'I'm sure.' She undid her seat belt with hands that trembled slightly and reached for the door handle. 'I hope you won't be late for your own date.'

P.J. glanced at his watch. 'I think she'll understand if I'm a few minutes late,' he said, and a smile touched the corners of his mouth in a way that made Nell's heart clench. 'Anyone can see what the traffic is like tonight. You might even find that you get to your bar before John,' he added. 'But I'm sure that won't be a problem. He sounds like a guy worth waiting for.'

'Oh, yes,' said Nell, wishing she had never embarked on the whole John fantasy. Still, it was too late to put P.J. right now. 'Yes, he is.'

She opened the door. 'Well, good luck with everything,' she said, as casually as she could.

'You, too.'

The lights would change if she didn't get on with it. It was all Nell could do to get out of the car and fix on a bright smile as she closed the door and bent to say goodbye through the open window. 'Thanks again for the lift.'

P.J. smiled. 'Goodbye, Nell,' he said softly.

At the last moment, Nell's brave smile slipped. 'Goodbye,' she said, a treacherous wobble in her voice, and she turned quickly and made herself walk away before he could see the tears in her eyes.

She was limping badly by the time she made it to the bar where she was to meet John, but in a strange way it was almost a comfort to concentrate on the pain in her feet rather than on the pain in her heart.

Never had she felt less like a blind date! The thought of sitting and trying to be friendly and interested in a man who, however nice he was, wasn't P.J. made Nell feel more miserable than ever, but she was here now, and it wouldn't be fair to John to just leave him sitting there.

The fairest thing would be to tell him straight that she was in love with somebody else, she realised.

There was no point in pretending anything else. Thea would be cross with her, but if John was as nice as her sister had said, he would understand. He would probably rather be told the truth. Hadn't she told P.J. that it was better to be honest about how you felt?

Nell looked at her watch. After all of that, she wasn't as late as she had thought. Pushing open the door, she went in and hesitated just inside, looking around for anyone who looked as if he might be called John. The bar wasn't too busy, and there were only two men there on their own, neither of whom looked old enough to be John. Nell tried not to look as if she was staring as she walked past the tables where they were sitting, but there was no sign of a Swahili dictionary, and, anyway, neither of them appeared to be looking for her.

The traffic *was* bad, though, as P.J. had pointed out. Maybe John was stuck somewhere. She had better give him a chance to turn up, anyway.

Choosing a seat where she could be seen from the door, Nell ordered herself a glass of wine and carefully put the Swahili phrase book in full view on the table in front of her. She would give John half an hour, and then she would go.

Normally Nell would have felt very conspicuous at being so obviously waiting for a blind date, but right then she didn't care about anything other than the fact that she had just said goodbye to P.J. again. How was she going to bear it?

For something to do, she picked up the phrase book and studied it dully, but it was too full of the memories that P.J. had brought back so vividly. She thought about the good times they had had, the dreams they had dreamed together, and just for a moment she let herself imagine what it would have been like if she hadn't chosen Simon.

But she had, and she had to take responsibility for that. Nobody had made her choose him, she had done that herself. She had made a mistake, and she had to live with it. In so many ways she was lucky, Nell reminded herself. Clara was healthy and happy. She had loving family and friends, a place to live, and a good job.

She just didn't have P.J.

Well, she had managed without him before and she would manage without him again...but, oh, it was going to be so much harder now. In spite of her determination to keep up a good face, a tear trickled down Nell's nose and she brushed it angrily away just as a Swahili dictionary was laid quietly on the table in front of her.

CHAPTER TEN

'I'M SORRY I'm late.'

Nell stared at the hand on the dictionary, riveted by the whiteness of the cuff against brown skin, by the gleam of gold cufflinks and the fine dark hairs at the broad male wrist. Very, very slowly, her stunned grey gaze travelled up the sleeve of the dinner jacket, along the shoulder and up at last to the face that went with the voice.

P.J.

Still in thrall to utter disbelief, she dropped her eyes down to the dictionary as if to confirm it was what she thought it was, and then lifted them back to his face.

'You?' she whispered.

'Peter John,' P.J. reminded her. He pulled out a chair and sat down opposite her. 'Janey and Thea decided you wouldn't come if you knew it was me, so they used my second name instead.'

Nell sat mouse-still, staring at him like an owl, hardly daring to believe what was happening, and too stunned to understand anything beyond the fact that suddenly, miraculously, he was there. She felt almost frightened, as if she had conjured him up by the power of her longing and he weren't quite real.

'*I* thought I was coming to meet someone called Helen,' P.J. went on, more unnerved by her silence than he wanted to admit. 'Why didn't I know that about you? I didn't realise Nell was an abbreviation of Helen, although I know that's not why you're called Nell…'

He could hear himself burbling nervously and made himself stop. 'I'm talking too much,' he acknowledged, and looked straight into Nell's beautiful grey eyes. 'Do you mind?' he asked simply.

'Mind?' echoed Nell, although the word came out as barely more than a croak.

'That it's me, instead of another John?'

The uncertainty in his expression broke the spell that held Nell motionless. This wasn't a dream. This was a real man, unsure of himself after all, and she gave something between a laugh and a sob, and shook her head.

'No,' she said, smiling through the tears that brimmed her eyes, 'I don't mind.'

P.J. reached out and took her hands in his, holding them tightly across the table in a warm, firm grasp. 'I'm glad,' he said. 'Part of me was afraid that you would be angry.'

'I should be,' said Nell, but fingers were twining

round his. 'But not with you. I presume this is Thea and Janey's doing?'

'They set it up between them, apparently. After they got in touch on that internet site, Janey couldn't wait to tell Thea her favourite theory about me.'

'What theory is that?'

'The one that says that I'd never got over you,' said P.J. with a rueful smile. 'Ever since I came back to London, and she discovered from Thea that you were divorced, Janey's been going on and on at me to get in touch with you, but I was afraid of raking up the past. I thought it would be better to leave things as they were…and then I saw you this morning, and I realised that Janey had been right all along, which of course she's absolutely delighted about!'

Nell couldn't help laughing at his expression. 'Thea will be unbearable, too. She's been doing the same thing. Why didn't I contact you? Why didn't I give you a ring and just say hello? You can imagine! And the more she talked about you, the more I refused to see you.'

'Were you anxious about the past, too?' asked P.J., and she thought about it a while.

'That was part of it, of course, but mainly I was really intimidated because I'd heard that you were so rich and successful. It just seemed like we had different lives now and that it would be better to keep them that way.'

'I know what you mean,' he said thoughtfully. 'It's as if we've been on separate paths, that have gone off in different directions, and twisted and turned, but still somehow been meant to bring us back together today. We'll let our sisters think it was down to them, but, really, I think we'd have met anyway. I think that was the way it was meant to be.'

'I wonder,' said Nell, thinking about what he had said. 'Certainly the first two meetings today had nothing to do with Thea or Janey, did they?'

'No, and the third time was me deciding to take a hand in my own affairs,' said P.J. with a grin. 'I thought fate had done enough and it was up to me to get you back—although, as it turned out, I could have left it to my sister!'

Nell smiled, and he released her hands at last. She took a sip of her wine, conscious of the tension slowly trickling away from her spine and her shoulders. 'When did you know that it was me you were meeting tonight?'

'Not until you dropped your bag. All Janey would tell me about the blind date she'd set me up on was that I was to meet a divorced friend of hers called— she said—Helen, who was very nice and I'd know her because she'd have a Swahili phrase book with her. When I saw that it had fallen out of your bag, I felt...'

P.J. trailed off, trying to find the right words to explain how everything had suddenly fallen into place, and the world had lifted from his shoulders. 'I can't describe how I felt.' He gave up at last. 'When I dropped you at Trafalgar Square, I rang Janey and asked her straight out if it was you I was supposed to be meeting, and she confessed.'

'Why on earth didn't they just tell us?' grumbled Nell.

'I think they thought that we would bottle out if we knew what they were planning.'

'I probably would have done,' she conceded reluctantly, 'but at least it might have saved me making a colossal fool of myself! I'm going to kill Thea when I see her! You must have thought I was an idiot, pretending that I'd found the perfect man in John!'

'I'm just relieved that he's turned out to be me, to be honest,' said P.J. with a crooked smile. 'The thought of him gave me some bad moments! I was pretty jealous of him.'

Nell put down her glass in surprise. 'Surely you guessed that he wasn't real?'

'Only after I saw the phrase book. He sounded so perfect, so exactly what you wanted. I had no reason to believe that he wasn't real.'

She flushed, remembering the fibs she had told. 'I don't know why I made up all that about him,' she said, twisting the stem of the glass between her fingers. 'I suppose I didn't want you to think that I was just a sad divorcee.'

It was P.J.'s turn to look surprised. 'There was no chance of that, Nell! Why on earth would I think that? There you were, with a lovely daughter, a good job and—it seemed—a great man. It looked to me as if you had your life under perfect control.'

'Whereas in fact I'm chaotic and clumsy, with daughter who bosses me around and an imaginary lover,' said Nell, amused at the very idea of her having her life under control. If only!

'I know better now,' P.J. agreed solemnly. 'I'll admit it was a relief to discover that you weren't *quite* as perfect as you seemed at first.' Smiling, he lifted his hand to trace the line of her cheek with infinite tenderness. 'Although you'll always be pretty perfect to me,' he said softly.

'Oh, P.J...' Sudden tears trembled on Nell's lashes. 'How can you say that when I hurt you so much? I was so stupid about Simon,' she told him. 'I'm so sorry.'

'I hurt you, too,' he pointed out gently. 'I should have paid you more attention when you needed it. I was too busy thinking about the future when I should have been listening to you and what you wanted in the present.'

Reaching for her hand, he closed his fingers

around hers firmly. 'That's the thing about relationships. It takes two to make it, two to break it. It wasn't just you, Nell. At least you were honest with me. You told me as soon as you realised that you were attracted to Simon, and that must have taken guts. It didn't help that I went off the deep end. If I'd been older, I might have stuck it out, and given you some space to think about things instead of ending it all there and then.'

'I was such a fool. I had no idea how lucky I was.' A single tear wobbled over Nell's lashes and trickled down the side of her nose until P.J. wiped it away tenderly with his thumb.

'Nell, it was a long time ago.'

'I just wish I could do it all again better.'

'But then you wouldn't have Clara, and I wouldn't have my company. The last sixteen years haven't been *all* bad, have they?'

'No,' Nell had to agree, thinking of her daughter.

'I have missed you, though,' P.J. confessed.

'For sixteen years?' She smiled, still a little tearfully. 'I don't believe you've been pining all that time!'

'I wouldn't say I'd been pining exactly,' he admitted. 'I haven't been unhappy, and there have been women, yes. But none of them were you, Nell. Another of Janey's theories is that all my girlfriends looked like you, and that I spent my time trying to find a substitute for you. She thinks that's why my relationships never came to anything. I wanted them to, but subconsciously maybe I *was* comparing them to you.'

He smiled and shook his head. 'The crazy thing is that if you'd told me yesterday that that was what I felt—as Janey always did—I would have insisted that it wasn't true, but all I had to do was look at you this morning, in your old jogging suit and trainers, and I knew that I had loved you all along.

'I went straight into work and rang Janey and tried to get out of the date she'd set me up on tonight, but she wouldn't let me. I should have guessed what she was up to, but I didn't. I thought I was going to have to spend the evening making polite small talk with a divorcee when all I wanted was to be with you.

'Janey was right.' Still holding her hand, P.J. looked deep into Nell's grey eyes. 'It's only ever been you, Nell. You're my one and only, just like they used to say. Being near you again was like coming home for me. I was so desperate to see you again, and it was a real blow when you said you didn't want to see me.'

Nell tightened her fingers around his. 'I was afraid,' she said honestly, and his brows drew together slightly.

'Of me?'

'Of the way you made me feel,' she said. 'I'm like

you. I've spent sixteen years telling myself I'd forgotten you, and then a couple of weeks ago Thea mentioned your name... Since then I've been remembering, and regretting, and just wanting something I knew couldn't have.' Her smile twisted. 'I'm not sure what it was. I think probably I just wanted to be that confident and certain again. I wanted to be loved the way you used to love me.'

'Then why not have dinner with me when I asked you this morning?'

Nell sighed. 'I don't know... It all just seemed too difficult somehow. We were different people, and I thought everything had changed, but the more I saw of you today, the more it seemed that nothing had changed at all, and that made it even worse!

'I told myself that it would be easier if I didn't get involved, that it would be better to draw a line under the past again, all of that. I did my best to resist,' she told him as if he had accused her of not making enough of an effort to forget him. 'It didn't do any good, but I couldn't admit that deep down I wanted to see you again desperately. I was afraid you would think that I only loved you for your money now.'

'*Do* you?' asked P.J. urgently.

'Of course not!'

His grip on her hands tightened. 'No...I mean, do you love me?'

Nell let her eyes rest on the familiar, exciting lines of his face, seeing there the boy who had loved her, the man who loved her still, and her heart swelled with happiness.

'Yes, I do.' It was such a relief to be able to say it at last. 'I know it's crazy when we've only been back together a day, but there's nothing I can do about it. Not loving you, letting myself forget you… It was like losing part of me, and, this morning, it seemed as if I had found it again.'

'That's how I feel, too.' The smile that had started in P.J.'s eyes when she'd told him that she loved him spread over his face, and the strength of his feeling seemed to reverberate through the touch of his hands all the way up Nell's arm. 'I love you, too, Nell. I've always loved you. There's been a bit missing from me, ever since we've been apart, and you're the only person who can put it back.'

'P.J…' At the look in his eyes, the air evaporated from Nell's lungs.

'Come here,' he said softly, leaning forward and pulling her towards him so that he could kiss her across the table.

The touch of his lips unlocked a torrent of emotion in Nell. It cascaded through her, a joyous blend of relief and release, of pleasure and promise, of excitement and the sheer exhilaration of loving and being loved. She had forgotten what a wonderful feeling that was, and she kissed him back with a kind of desperation, needing to show him how he made her feel.

'Let's go.' P.J.'s voice was ragged as they broke the kiss at last. 'I can't kiss you properly here.'

Nell's bones were liquid with desire, but somehow she got to her feet, belatedly remembering her bag and the phrase book. 'My wine…' she said, groping for some money.

'Here.' Too impatient to bother about change, P.J. tucked a ten-pound note under her glass. Picking up his dictionary, he took a firm hold of Nell with his other hand and they practically ran for the door.

They could hardly wait until they were outside. P.J. pulled her into the nearest doorway and they kissed hungrily.

This time there was no table between them, and it felt so good to be able to put her arms round him at last, to cling to the glorious granite strength of his body, to hold him and touch him and smell the deliciously clean male scent of his skin. Nell couldn't kiss him long enough, hold him close enough, and it was only the need to breathe that made her break away at last and rest her face against his throat with a long, shuddering sigh of contentment.

P.J. smiled into her hair as he held her. 'We could do without all these bags and books,' he pretended to grumble. 'They're hampering my style!'

'It would be nice to have two hands,' Nell agreed, laughing. 'Let's find somewhere to sit.'

They wandered round the busy piazza in search of a bench, but ended up sitting on some stone steps. At least they could put down the books, and hold each other properly.

'It feels like being teenagers again, doesn't it?' said P.J. as Nell nestled into the circle of his arm. 'Trying to find somewhere to kiss where no one would walk in on us—particularly your mother!'

Nell smiled, but then sobered at the realisation that they weren't in fact teenagers anymore. 'I wish things could be as simple as they were then,' she said wistfully.

'I love you and you love me,' he said. 'It seems simple enough to me.'

'But it isn't, is it? There's Clara to think about.'

'Of course.' P.J. turned to look down into Nell's face, and he frowned at her worried expression. 'You don't think it will be a problem for her, do you?'

Nell thought about what Clara had said about P.J. 'To be honest, I think she'll be delighted. She worries about me being on my own, and she liked you. She thought you had smiley eyes.'

She shook her head. 'No, Clara won't mind…but will you? I don't exactly come unencumbered. I'm not the same person I was before, P.J. I've got all the emotional baggage of a nasty divorce, and a child who takes up a lot of my attention. Clara's fantastic, but it's not always easy.'

She sighed. 'I wish we could just pick up where we left off, but I don't see how we can do that.'

'We can't, but we can start again, can't we?' P.J. took her hand and turned it over, running his finger over the veins and the faint beginnings of fine lines. 'I did love you in the past, Nell, and it's true that I carried a dream of you all these years, but I'm not in love with a memory. Clara is part of who you are now, and that's the you I love. I don't want you the way you were, because I'm not the way I was then either.'

Gently, he touched the edges of her eyes. 'I want the Nell who's older and wiser and has laughter lines around her eyes and wears sensible shoes to walk to work.'

And he drew her close and kissed her again, and Nell felt her last doubts dissolve. 'Marry me, Nell,' he said. 'Marry me, and we'll take Clara to Africa with us on our honeymoon. Let's do all the things we always dreamed of doing, but let's do them together this time.'

Nell drew back slightly, her eyes intent as she looked at him. Like her, he was older, a little bit battered around the edges, but he was still P.J. She loved the boy he had been, and she loved the man he had become, and it was hard to believe how lucky she was. Against all the odds, she had been given a second chance, and she had to grasp it with both hands.

'Yes,' she said, 'let's do that,' and she smiled back at him as he pulled her towards him to seal their promise with a long, sweet kiss.

It was much later when a yawn caught Nell by surprise, and P.J. hauled her to her feet. 'It's time I took you home,' he said as they laughed ruefully at the stiffness of their definitely non-adolescent bones after sitting still on the stone steps for so long. 'It's been a long day.'

'It's been an incredible day,' said Nell, rubbing her bottom, weary but ballooning with happiness. 'I can't believe how much has happened,' she marvelled. 'Twenty-four hours ago, I couldn't have imagined meeting you again, loving you again, actually agreeing to *marry* you again, and yet, here we are, just a day later, and my life has changed utterly and completely.'

P.J. smiled and put his arm around her to lead her back to the car and take her home. 'Sometimes a day is all it takes,' he said.

WIN a romantic weekend in PARíS

To celebrate Valentine's Day we are offering you the chance to WIN one of 3 romantic weekend breaks to Paris.

Imagine you're in Paris; strolling down the Champs Elysées, pottering through the Latin Quarter or taking an evening cruise down the Seine. Whatever your mood, Paris has something to offer everyone.

For your chance to make this dream a reality simply enter this prize draw by filling in the entry form below:

Name _____

Address _____

_____Tel no: _____

Closing date for entries is 30th June 2005

Please send your entry to:

Valentine's Day Prize Draw
PO Box 676, Richmond, Surrey, TW9 1WU

MILLS & BOON®

Live the emotion

Virgin Brides

**In March 2005 By Request brings
back three favourite novels by our
bestselling Mills & Boon authors:**

The Virgin Bride *by Miranda Lee*
One Bridegroom Required!
by Sharon Kendrick
No Holding Back *by Kate Walker*

**These brides have kept their
innocence for their perfect
husbands-to-be...**

On sale 4th March 2005

0205/05 V2